H40 830 389 3

WILSON
FICTION

-9 JAN 1999   2 6 OCT 2000

-5 FEB 2001

-8 JUN 2001

3 0 JAN 1999   25 JUN 2001

1 8 MAR 1999

2 8 OCT 1999   2 1 FEB 2002

-7 JAN 2003

1 1 AUG 2000   1 8 OCT 2003

1st Sep 2000

Please renew/return this item by the last date shown.

So that your telephone call is charged at local rate,
please call the numbers as set out below:

	From Area codes 01923 or 0208:	From the rest of Herts:
Renewals:	01923 471373	01438 737373
Enquiries:	01923 471333	01438 737333
Minicom:	01923	

L32b

Do White Whales Sing at the Edge of the World?

Paul Wilson was born in 1960. He is married and has two sons. He is also the author of *The Fall from Grace of Harry Angel*, and *Days of Good Hope*. *Do White Whales Sing at the Edge of the World?* is his third novel. He lives in Blackburn, Lancashire.

Also by Paul Wilson

The Fall from Grace of Harry Angel
Days of Good Hope

Do White Whales Sing at the Edge of the World?

PAUL WILSON

Granta Books
London

First published in Great Britain by Granta Books 1997
This edition published by Granta Books 1998

Copyright © 1997 by Paul Wilson

Paul Wilson has asserted his moral right under the
Copyright, Designs and Patents Act, 1988, to be
identified as the author of this work.

A CIP catalogue record for this book is available from
the British Library.

1 3 5 7 9 10 8 6 4 2

Typeset in Janson by M Rules
Printed and bound in Great Britain by
Mackays of Chatham PLC

Contents

In memory of Bill Lang,
my grandfather

If a god must shatter me upon the wine-dark sea, so be it.

– Odysseus

I

Two tricks

What they see is Gabriel, sitting on the floor, slow to move. Perhaps he doesn't understand what is being asked of him? He sits, arms and legs tucked all about him. The others, on chairs, Athol, Ingerman, Peary, the rest of us – men shy of each other after forty years – look on.

Gabriel is so still.

Henry Kyle, who founded the colony, always thought of it as a voltage problem. That there wasn't enough. Henry Kyle's principal discovery in travelling through the continent that was Gabriel was that this voltage was never enough to drive the whole of him. Henry Kyle is dead now, and the colony is closing down.

Gabriel has been placed in the middle of the room. Rose has told him to lie down, his arms not across or guarding him but down by his side. Gabriel's predicament is this: he was disturbed yesterday while he was masturbating in the boiler room. It isn't his first offence. The picture in his head as he pumped slowly back and forth was of Rose. Gabriel was saying her name in his flat dull voice like a man who recites a number on his way to the telephone to remember it, remember it, remember it.

I have always tried to keep an eye on Gabriel. Long ago, it became a vocation. It was a kind of debt I owed to him, because once it was Gabriel who had saved me. I try to keep him, as Rose might say, out of harm's way. Sometimes harm gets by me, sometimes not. When I do get there first I tidy him up. I move him on. I set him on his way. But this time it was suppertime and I was busy. It was Rose who found him. Rose is more easily shocked than she likes to admit. Rose calls us all 'her little charges'. She sees it as an affront to her that we don't always respond to her cajoling, to her willingness to see us improve.

'Was he doing it again, Lukic?' she will ask me each time it happens.

'No,' I will say, 'he was only sitting there. He must have been daydreaming again.'

She is a little slovenly, I think, not that I know so much about women. Her hair seems darker at the roots than at the tips. She has a square, heavy face, a heavy body, lovely doe eyes, a runny Irish nose and she carries a torch for Sallis who is our director. In her home town they probably thought of fat Rose with the crew cut as a big boy of a girl, which is probably why she fled to England one day on the Holyhead ferry to search for bright lights and the kind of love that sparkles. I don't think Sallis sees her. Not as a woman. Not with the torch she carries. And so she deals in other commodities.

Finally, Gabriel lies, according to Rose's instruction, staring at the ceiling pattern – Gabriel who believes in angels, Gabriel with the sweet smile when it comes, with the dull face, the jarred haircut, the two tricks that make him special, keep him from falling off the edge of the world. Sometimes it's like he never grew up at all, stayed inside himself, maybe with insufficient voltage.

Gabriel's two tricks are these. First, he can feel the pain that others feel, give expression to it eerily and accurately, no matter how bleak or silent that pain in someone's head might be. I believe this. I have seen it happen. Henry Kyle always put Gabriel's ability down to superstition on the part of the other residents that they believed it, or flukes. It didn't fit, you see, into Henry Kyle's scheme of things. But it's true. It still happens sometimes. He can tune into people's heads like he was tuning into radio stations. There's no control over it. It will just happen, sometimes in a quiet moment, sometimes surrounded by a hundred people, tuning into some old maid's grief. I asked Rose if she believed it. Rose is not a real doctor. She has no letters after her name. Rose is, in Athol's phrase, an extra pair of hands, though she would be irked to hear that being said of her. I asked her once if she was qualified (since, after all, she had first started with us in physical therapy).

'I am invaluable to Dr Sallis,' she said. 'Let us leave it there.' And she clapped her hands, as I recall, and moved us swiftly on. Rose protests that Gabriel's phenomenon isn't in the books. She says I am just causing mischief. I know I am a disappointment to Rose.

'You have failed me, Lukic,' she says sadly. She thought I was her star pupil, but in the end, like Sallis, like love, like life itself, I am in danger of becoming a disappointment to her.

And second. What's second? Second is that sometimes, when the timing's right, Gabriel can dream himself away from here.

All along, Gabriel did what he supposed was being asked of him. That is, he helped out as instructed by the attendants and murdered no one and offered gratifying evidence now and then of his degeneracy. So minutes passed, and years. But now Gabriel is more easily distracted. Now it seems, there is a need to go in search of things; there is a need to see what's out there. After all, every man is a story and has an end to fashion, and sometimes the smallest leaning into the light can be enough.

The colony is built on thirty acres. It sits high up on the fells of northern England. Below the colony, five hundred feet below and connected by the single road which runs between the high ground and the coastal plain, is a village of three hundred people. Mostly the people who lived in the village worked up at Henry Kyle's colony. Now the colony is closing down and the staff, like the residents, are being reduced to a recalcitrant and unpromising rump.

From the village, the colony rises abruptly from its shoulder of land. At night it has the look of a castle – it is all dark stone and narrow lights and seems set to repel invaders. In daylight, it seems more like a small medieval village, the kind you might stumble unexpectedly across in the Pyrenees of Spain: ugly and unashamed and wedded to simple routines which have lasted centuries and which have no recourse to the outside world.

The road into the colony has gates of wrought iron, though these days the gates are seldom closed. The gateposts are each carved with figures from the Bible – Jonah, Lazarus, Abraham. The centre of the colony, past the administration block of offices and ancillary services, consists of a ring of black stone dormitories. Each dormitory, at one time, had beds for seventy residents. Further back are the former blocks for the acutes and the suicidals and the epileptics. They are all empty

4

now. So is the infirmary. The dormitories were for the main body of quiet and working residents. One of the dormitories (the only one still inhabited) has an annexe attached to it with lino on the floor and an old TV installed. The annexe was known to the attendants as the Bear Pit.

Some of the residents took to gathering in the Bear Pit as opposed to sitting out the unstructured hours of their lives in the dormitories or the corridors or lying on their beds, passing each long afternoon. They still gather there, the few who are left: Athol, Roland, Peary, Ingerman, Gabriel. Still squabble. Still breathe in and out. In and out. I am a more solitary animal, myself. I've had enough of crowds. At one time I would have done anything for a crowd, but no longer. Now I am happiest alone, I think. There are so few members of the club left to gather in the Bear Pit. Men disappear. Something is happening. Roland hasn't been seen lately. Something is happening.

Rose tells us that she herself dreams of redemption. She believes in Jesus. She goes to Mass on Sundays at St Bees. She prays for us. She believes that, with effort and a little prayer, everyone can be a little Jesus. This is her approach to the therapy she offers us. From the start, Rose looked upon us as blank tablets, as lives gone awry and necessarily scrubbed clean. She believed that she was teaching us things, she kept believing that she was making progress – writing us out anew. She kept reporting this progress back to Sallis, the director who has been charged with winding the colony down. But so many of us keep forgetting. Gabriel for one keeps forgetting. Rose is struggling and she takes it personally. She is struggling in her battle to turn each of us into a little Jesus. She is struggling even to get the director to notice her. The need for love does not sparkle.

Rose is a good Catholic girl. When I was a boy I admired the Catholic girls we had in our town. They had more money than we Lutheran Protestants. The Catholics had good houses. They were all handsome people it seemed to me. They believed in Hell and seemed to know that they themselves would have no dealings with it. This town I grew up in wasn't like any of the English towns I've seen. There were no fells. The land I knew as a boy was a land of flat fields spawning cabbages and potatoes and mud. It left people dissatisfied. It didn't cradle or contain them. There was nothing to break the contour of the land like the land in England. People had to dream. My father dreamed of accruing more fields of potatoes at the expense of the Catholic Poles. My mother dreamed of the day she could afford to throw my father out of the house. Most of my father's friends in the village, like him, dreamed of being German, even though our town was under Polish rule. They dreamed of regaining Danzig. They dreamed of relinquishing the Polishness that the Treaty of Versailles had thrust upon them. As for me, I used to watch people sometimes pass through the village on the way to Gdynia – travellers, merchants, government officials. Once when I was seven a circus rode past, and even though it didn't stop in our village to perform, it was the finest thing I'd ever seen. And this seemed the stuff of better dreams than potatoes, or exile, or sending men to the Reichstag.

Gabriel can hear Rose's voice pressing at the edge of his space, but he will not let it enter. The distance he engineers from the world, his still eyes seem unchanged from when he first arrived. I had already been here some time when Gabriel came. I remember it well. I have good reason to.

6

'Gabriel.'

There is the voice again. It's a still and unambitious voice. Gabriel's eyes are closed but he knows we're all out here – all these watching faces. He won't look at people. Not even at Athol and Peary and Ingerman. And not at me. It wouldn't matter if he looked across this way, anyhow. He wouldn't see me, that's for sure. He would look right through me, although I am every bit as much flesh and blood as he is. He would look but he wouldn't see *me*. But he isn't looking across at any of us. He isn't looking at anything.

Athol, next to Gabriel, has his hands pressed together. He seems deep in concentration. He could be praying, or thinking about anything. His eyes are narrowed. He's probably thinking about sex. Rose says he is a dirty old goat.

'He isn't trying,' she will say. 'He should *try* harder.' Her pale-moon face will frown in disappointment as she says it.

I tell Rose, 'He's just a man.'

'He should know better,' she says, '– at his age. He should *try*.'

It's hard to say what Peary's eyes are doing, or what he is thinking. Peary's head, as ever, is hidden by the long funnel of the hood of his coat. Peary, out from under his hood, would seem as naked and bizarre as a turtle spliced from its shell. Peary used to work as a butcher's assistant in the Icehouse where the meat for the colony was stored and kept cool. The smell of the meat has stayed with him. It has stayed *on* him. Down inside the hood he wears I imagine is a certain peace, a certain privacy which suits him. The Parish Priest told Peary's parents that the boy's skin disease was religious in origin. I suppose it's no wonder that after everything that was done to cure him, he preferred a little privacy down there in the

7

hollow of his big coat. Peary write scraps of notes to himself all day down there when he has free moments. Lord knows what he does with them.

'What are they for?' Roland would ask him, irritated by not knowing what it was that Peary wrote. 'Is it about us? What?' Roland used to ask. But Peary wouldn't say. Peary never said. Not to Roland. Not to anyone. Even men kept together for forty years have fields in which only they may walk.

As for Ingerman, his hands are busy. This is his way of escaping from the room. If I lean forward I can see that Ingerman has one of those three-dimensional picture cards that is engrossing him. They are multi-coloured rows of zigzags. They don't seem to be pictures of anything at first. They come in the cereal packets – you have to fish for them buried two-thirds down in the mound of cereal inside the cellophane. The idea is that you hold the card away from you – in Ingerman's case down on his lap – and look at the picture. You are supposed to look *through* the picture. And, after a while, if your eyes are relaxed enough, they will draw out a different picture which is coded within the first – a three-dimensional image which rises out at you, an image which was there all the time but which you hadn't been able to see until then – which your eyes hadn't interpreted. They remind me of how men at home in the village, when I was small, looked out at the fields of potatoes and mud and some saw nationality and some saw prestige and some saw only a harvest, or a road to the horizon where a circus may have passed. They fascinate Ingerman. He has a collection of them from the cornflakes packets. He can spend hours, engrossed, looking at them, falling into them, seeing what didn't seem at first to be there. I remember when it used to be a set of rosary beads he played with in his hands. Some time after that it was an ancient miniature abacus. Then later it was a Rubik cube which he'd somehow managed to get hold of. Ingerman would spend all day twisting the Rubik cube this way and that, working to match up all the small squares which made up the six sides of the cube into the necessary order of colours. All of these items in turn – the beads, the abacus, the Rubik cube – he kept safe in a brown cotton sack tied at the neck with a cord, along with other things we never saw which he always carried around with him over his shoulder. The sack was lost some time ago. Like other things – like Athol's lamp, and the photographs Peary had of his sisters who were beautiful and nothing like Peary, and so on – the sack got lost. Rose put it down to our carelessness. And perhaps it's true that we have become more careless, more distracted, as the years have passed.

'How will you cope outside,' she says, 'if you cannot even be trusted to look after your own few belongings in this place?' Oh, we are such a disappointment to Rose.

Ingerman raids the food store each week for three-dimensional picture cards in the cereals. When Rose asks about the decimated cereal packets, I tell her that we must have mice. She doesn't believe me. She sighs. The sigh tells us that we are no more use than book-ends. Of course I know that in reality it's Ingerman who will have been in the cereal. It's my job to know. I am the food orderly.

Ever since Henry Kyle established the colony, all the residents have had jobs – to help make the colony as self-sufficient as possible. That was part of Henry Kyle's ethos. It's my job as food orderly, for example, to ring the bell before each meal to summon the residents past the whitewashed walls, the tiled corridor, to eat. It's a handbell, like the ones that were formerly used in schools and in kindergartens. There is a push-button bell which I could use, but I prefer the old handbell. It's more reliable. It's more substantial. There is much more skill involved in giving half a dozen solid, clean, intermittent rings on the handbell to summon the residents than in simply pushing a buzzer three times a day. And best of all, my job makes allowance for the fact that I have one useless arm.

Gabriel has his eyes closed, his hands down by his side, his legs out as instructed, and swims in the darkness. The only sound in the big room that he can hear, above the tell-tale pull of his breathing, is the scrabbling of two gerbils which we have been allowed to keep over by the window. The gerbils are biting at the bars of their cage, rhythmically searching for escape.

'I want you to move now from that position to one in which, as best you can, surrounded by the staff and your fellow residents, you are at ease. One that mirrors how you feel in front of us – how you see yourself in the group.'

And, first sitting and drawing himself together, testing, he folds, slow piece by piece, making himself small, smaller; folds into a foetal cradle, his head buried in his chest and the wrap of limbs, which encloses him in the high room in the madhouse, and in his head, I know, is the sound of the weather and a big sky and a tormenting wind and a man pulling, pulling, through the snow and the ash-coloured sky – a man whose face he can barely discern but whose labours he can feel, striving for the peace that surely lies on the far side of his struggle and of dreams.

I know what sounds are in his head.

Gabriel rocks gently. His eyes are closed. He is sustained by a journey in a singing sea of ice, deep in the undiscovered interior of him which Henry Kyle and the colony never chanced upon.

2

Still remains

They thought at first it was an apparition, brought on by the extremes of the landscape. This was a place where men could meet their fears and be overwhelmed by them. But it was not an apparition. It was real.

The men of the *California* watched as it slipped past them. The pinnace was iced up in her entirety. Her spars, her decks, were all petrified. Her sails and rigging had long since perished. She was silent.

A party boarded her later that day when the *California* herself had pushed free of the frazil ice which had been obstructing her. Despite her Arctic resting place, the small vessel's wooden hull had been lead-plated against the shipworms of the warm southern ocean. There was no sign of life, but there were the remnants of some rations, and some instruments which had been left about the place and preserved in the organized positions in which they had been abandoned. There was a quantity of amphibolite – mineral rock – bagged here and there around the sleeping quarters.

The master's cabin, like the rest of the ship, was empty of human remains. The design of the pinnace suggested to the whalers who found her that she must have set sail well before 1700. There was no quadrant or sextant on board. The ship did have an astrolabe, though, which would have allowed the crew to establish a rough latitude, and a nocturnal to reckon the hour of the night.

They discovered the slowly decaying ship to be named *Endeavour*. It would turn out that she was English registered, sailing from the north-country port of Laing. The captain had been one Gabriel Emerson. Emerson's log entries on the *Endeavour* scrupulously set out her position for each day of the voyage. However, the log gave no indication as to why such a small pinnace was where she was. There was no obvious reason for her to be here. They could only guess as to why she had sailed into the Arctic, into a land where there was seldom night and day as men understood it, and why she had been deserted.

It's this that Gabriel dreams of. It's hard for him to return. Sometimes I have to repeat the bell for lunch before he hears it, before I eventually see him coming down the corridor. Typically, he arrives last and takes his place at the end of the long table when prayers have already begun.

There are less than a hundred residents left in the colony and so we no longer use the Great Hall for meals. The Great Hall used to hold six hundred people at a time to eat, and back in the colony's heyday there were two sittings, even with the specialist dormitories eating separately. The noise of so many quiet men eating, the banging of plates and the heaviness of all those men's thoughts used to rise like smoke and hang under the high ceiling and weigh upon us all and make us breathless and uneasy. A hundred residents fit easily into the smaller canteen which was once the staff's and now, near to the end, is used for those few of us who are left. Meals are less formal than they were. Some traditions, though, like prayers before all meals, stay with us.

Communal prayers were always said, of course, at the insistence of our founder, Henry Kyle. Most of us are getting on in years now. We know the prayers by heart, although there are many other thing we have forgotten.

The prayers seldom rise above a mumble, even though everyone knows them. The tone of the words rises and falls as we join in here and there out of a lifetime's habit until we reach the final 'Amen'. When Sallis first arrived and suggested that the practice of communal prayers before meals be ended, he found himself faced with a hallful of residents still reciting the words. We couldn't help ourselves. We had said them for so many years that we couldn't stop. It embarrassed Sallis so much to hear so many men mumbling helplessly to themselves that he reintroduced the formality of prayers before each meal and, against his better judgement, nominated someone to lead them. That way, Sallis was at least able to coordinate the mumbled thanks to God.

Henry Kyle had always eaten with the residents. He ate at his own small table raised on the stage of the Great Hall. Each day he led the prayers from up on the stage himself. He expected each resident to join in with prayers, and all of them did, with only one exception – Athol. Athol had always been a big man. Though he is old now, he is still a big man. Athol still has appetites, sexual and otherwise.

Athol and his brother were twins. They slept in the same bed in the orphanage. They had been born thirty minutes apart, and the matron said they seemed intent on spending the rest of their lives making up for this separation. The nuns in Accrington guessed that the twins' mother was one of the mill girls. Maybe she'd got herself into trouble. Maybe she couldn't face the prospect, or the expense, of two sons. Athol and Artemis had no memory of their mother. From birth they slept in the same bed, limbs interlocked as if only together they made a single whole. They were so alike that Athol had a red ribbon tied to his arm and Artemis a blue one so that the nuns could tell the difference, and it helped till the boys grew old enough for devilment and took delight in swapping the ribbons and playing at being each other.

Time and again the matron announced that it was necessary for them to begin sleeping in separate beds. When they were separated at night, though, the two boys' appetites diminished and Athol, the sturdier of the two – Artemis was the one prone to chills and fevers – would creep into the dormitory where Artemis lay awake under the sheets, and Artemis would make room for him. When the matron took to locking the dormitory that Artemis had been put in, Athol would sleep badly, would wake constantly and sometimes go to sit through the night on the landing, waiting for the door to be opened in the morning for his brother. Their learning suffered, and in precisely equal measures. In the end, the matron gave up and left them to sleep together, each of them wrapped in the embrace and the rough scent of the other, and together they prospered.

Athol grew stronger and the more heavily built. Artemis was always the more sickly. But as they grew it was Artemis who became the public face of the pair. Artemis was the one who read more, the one to whom words came more easily. Although Athol was the dominant one within the partnership, it was Artemis who spoke *for* them in public – that is, with anyone outside the close world of the two of them in which spoken words were unnecessary. Everyone knew that Athol's brother had died, though no one knew for sure how.

In the colony, the attendants left Athol alone more than the others. Maybe it was his size, or the way he carried himself, or the knowledge that his brother had died and that a half of Athol had seemed to die with him. But Henry Kyle would not leave him alone. Henry Kyle *needed* Athol to say prayers. Henry Kyle believed it was his duty to force compliance, and that over a number of years any man could be broken. Now Athol is, perhaps, not as brave, nor as much a man, as he once was when his brother was with him. But no matter what Henry Kyle did to him, Athol never said prayers.

Henry Kyle saw the practice of the public recitation of prayers as a rehearsal for the annual pageant of the residents when we were marched in pairs to the church in the village two miles down in the valley. In the Church of the Redeemer we said prayers in front of the invited trustees of the colony. It was a chance for Henry Kyle to demonstrate to the trustees who had supported the colony how things were moving in the right direction.

From the pulpit of the packed church, Henry Kyle would read the lesson and then the bidding prayers. We were all well rehearsed. We were all expected to respond to each of the bidding prayers he read out. Usually (except for Athol, of course) we managed it, and delighted the trustees with this sign of our satisfactory spiritual progress.

'I knoweth that my Redeemer saves me,' Henry Kyle would read from his pulpit whilst the colony's trustees looked on from their seats in the side altar. We knew he meant himself.

We knew that he didn't mean any of us gathered in the rows of pews beneath him. We knew, for sure, that he didn't mean Athol who would not pray with him. We knew that for all of us there was to be no saving from Henry Kyle's redeemer.

The crew of the *California* left the silent *Endeavour* afloat in Lancaster Sound at latitude seventy-three degrees north, a thousand miles from anything that might be thought of as safety for a vessel of her kind.

The *California* herself was a Greenland whaler, sailing at what was then, in 1822, the height of the Arctic whalehunting boom. She carried a full cargo from her three months of duty and was bound back through the Davis Strait for Nantucket before the Arctic winter closed in again on anything left behind. There was some scorn, I am sure, over the ship named *Endeavour* and over the undiscovered Emerson still out there with his torments and his dreams. The men of the *California* called him crazy. They said it was obvious he lacked the technical and navigational skills needed to survive, if the *Endeavour* was anything to go by. What kind of men would sail past a harvest of whales which, when killed and stripped and reassembled into blubber butts and sperm oil and fins, would fetch £2,000 a carcass. What larger prize could drive men on past riches like this?

When the *California* returned to port, the only guess anyone could hazard about the *Endeavour* was that Emerson, all those years ago, had been searching for a North-West Passage. Someone calculated that the *Endeavour* had been preserved, held still and frozen in the ghosted Arctic for six generations. Only the especially mild summer of 1822 had thrown her free into the path of a crew of sour-faced whalers for one brief flicker of freedom before the winter took her in again.

In 1984, the stilled remains of Emerson's expedition to find the North-West Passage came to light. What was left of three men and small items of equipment were discovered by accident by an American scientific crew who were studying beluga whales for the American Scientific Institute in Victoria Strait, two hundred miles south west of the position in which the *Endeavour* had once been sighted and then boarded by whalers. The find made news for a little while because the bodies found by the scientists on King William Island had been so well preserved in the frozen tundra. It was clear that one of the bodies found was Emerson's since the remnants of his journal were beside him. The journal that Emerson had kept was still legible in places. It had survived wrapped in sealskin – an old eskimo trick. The cold which brought death had preserved the moment of life's passing.

Some newspapers ran the story. They printed pictures of the bodies. There were several photographs of the faces of the dead men. I have seen them – the faces of men looking out on to this different world from their own long gone one. The photographs were certainly striking. I know that they had an impact on Gabriel because he cut the pictures out and stuck them on his locker in the dormitory. Everyone believed that it was this which started Gabriel's obsession. Everyone except for me. I knew it had started long before the pictures appeared. I knew it had started before Gabriel arrived at the colony. I was there.

I think it is the stillness in the tale of the *Endeavour* (and its rediscovery) which compels Gabriel. I think the photographs (which he came across in an old magazine in the colony's infirmary) provided the jolt to set a kind of motion in him. It made him anxious. It made him need to know more about Emerson. That, and the knowledge that the *Endeavour* had originally sailed from the Cumberland port of Laing one dawn in the spring of 1620 – the same year in which the *Mayflower* had sailed from Plymouth for New England. It is the stillness which fills him, and the vastness of the white canvas on which the tale is painted.

It puzzles Gabriel that they have spent all those years watching him and yet have not discovered him.

Gabriel's visitor has gone.

He had grown used to having no one come. There is a rhythm to being alone for so long, a kind of comfort. Suddenly to have a regular visitor is something to grow accustomed to, slowly – though this is no ordinary visitor. She comes so silently. No one ever sees her enter the Bear Pit (I have asked them), though it is true that the television and its noise is so distracting to them. She comes in the afternoons and leaves before the early winter tea-time dusk. She sits patiently, waiting for Gabriel one day to acknowledge her (which he has not done yet). She comes, and then she goes. She's gone now. She prefers, as I say, the light to darkness.

Gabriel hurries across the colony. It has been a clean winter's day. The afternoon presses down a purple light that softens the lines of the black-brick dormitories. Builders' signs around the grounds welcome visitors to this doomed community, advertising 'The Village of the Future'. The signs spell out the names of the project architects – Cumersome Stent – for the Brantwood Executive Housing Village. The strapline underneath says there will be twenty-four-hour security and an exclusive village leisure complex. I follow Gabriel at a careful distance.

The number of residents still remaining in the colony is falling week by week. Gabriel worries that they're taking them out at night and shooting them. Bodies float down the river and into the Irish Sea before dawn breaks. No one has caught them. Now there are just a hundred left to dispose of.

Gabriel walks on, past the main drive, past the car park for staff and for visitors to the colony. Sometimes people would come to visit residents, especially in the early days. It wasn't particularly encouraged, that link with the outside world, but sometimes it happened. Gabriel would watch people arrive, not knowing where they came from, but knowing how they felt at being here, their hearts going boom-de-boom. Gabriel could tell. Could feel it like radio being broadcast in his head. It was the silence and the sudden noises across the colony, the bang of doors, keys, a shout sometimes that couldn't be traced, the hush of powerless men. It was that which made their hearts run fast. It was the stillness and the sense of quiet violence; the way those with authority talked of sex and of the residents loudly, without the need for caution or convention. No wonder Gabriel felt men's hearts quicken. Well hidden, he would watch them. As for Gabriel himself, no one came to visit him. As though he had no past, as though there was no one left to remember him.

When he first arrived at the colony it was recorded by Henry Kyle – who recorded everything, that was his way – that Gabriel was dumb, except for the recitation of names; fictional characters, Henry Kyle wrote, that Gabriel must have read about. Henry Kyle's records of Gabriel and of the rest of us are still kept in the colony. (An American university is buying the archive. Solicitors have negotiated the sale on behalf of the Kyle estate. The archive is being catalogued by Sallis, the director, in readiness for their transportation. It needed cataloguing. Henry Kyle's notes go all the way back to 1922.)

For many years, the staff at the colony believed that Gabriel was caught in a fixation to become the fictional characters he once chuntered about, but it didn't get them anywhere. It turned out he had an excellent random memory. He had a fondness at one time for long Germanic novels which I supplied him with. He was a slow, methodical reader. Time has not been an enemy, at least not until recently, until the colony's looming closure, until other events began to cast shadows, until the days began to run out.

Over the years he was taught hesitantly to speak. Henry Kyle took credit for the breakthrough when it came. I heard Gabriel when he first began to speak in the colony. It seemed to me as though his words had been translated from a different language; as though the distance travelled by the speaker was too great for all of him and so a messenger had been sent.

'Friegang, Kasperl, Jacob Brolin.'

That was how it went, on and on. Poor Gabriel. His surname wasn't recorded when he was first admitted. He had a tendency to breathe through his open mouth. He held himself still, cold to the touch. He was easily startled.

I follow Gabriel gradually across the former lawn where Ingerman feeds the birds each day (as he has always done), then past the limes and beeches. And now we are swallowed by the early dusk to anyone looking out from the administration block. We move past the allotments (derelict now), finally to the Icehouse, nestled in a paddock against the far boundary of the grounds between older trees, unused, forgotten – and he has not seen me. Nor will he. Would it surprise you if I said that Gabriel would not see me – not recognize me for who I am – even if I were to walk out from where I am and stand in front of him. That's all right. Sometimes I have lost sight of myself in the same way. That's how it feels. It's a foolish, old man's perspective, but then life is sometimes best explained by how it *feels*.

Sometimes, when I am ringing my handbell for meals, the residents walking past look round at me as if they had not noticed me before. They see one thing, and Gabriel sees another. Like Ingerman, peering at his three-dimensional puzzle picture from the cereal packets, I have learned that reality can be more than one single thing at once, depending on where the focus is.

The Icehouse is built of concrete. It has not been used for fifteen years, not since they last had a thousand residents on the site, enough to make its operation for cold storage of meats viable. This is where the lorries came to deliver supplies of meat, sometimes jointed, sometimes carcassed to be hung in rows. The colony once had its own butcher to cater for a community of two thousand in its heyday. The nearest village, after all, is half an hour's walk away down the valley.

The colony is excluded from all other life. That's why the arrival of Gabriel's visitor, when she first appeared, was so remarkable – some would say miraculous – after all these years. Gabriel believes these visitations to be those of the angel he has been waiting for. He will tell you that it is an angel. He will tell you that he remembers.

He presses his face to the hair's breadth gap between the two steel doors that slide on rails. He can't see much from the outside. He is looking to see that nothing has been disturbed. That no one has broken the old lock which still holds the doors of the Icehouse fast. The gap between the steel doors offers a glimpse inside. It is a cold, dark place; part aircraft hangar, part mausoleum. But Gabriel sees something other. He imagines stepping inside, breathing fast, the doors ringing shut behind him, the Icehouse swallowing him.

The men from the American Scientific Institute survey retrieved some of the notes from Emerson's log decomposing inside the sealskin and some of the expedition remains in order to take them back after their tour of duty. They took photographs of the remarkably preserved bodies of the three men they had found before re-burying them and setting down new wooden crosses to mark the site of the burial. The skin had still been retained on the bone. For all the world these men could have been dead just a few days. There had been a bluish tinge on the flesh of one man's jaw, but that was only from the dye of the blanket which had lain over him, partly covering his face. The eyes of the men dead for almost four centuries had looked into the lenses of the camera, looked through the photographs that would make news for a week around the world and beyond into a different space.

The scientists who found them, Gabriel knows, had never heard of Emerson the mariner. They were marine biologists. They were patiently uncovering what remained unknown about beluga whales. They did not see themselves as sailing to the edge of the earth and then beyond, as the early sailors did. The scientists who stumbled upon the bodies thought of the environment in which they worked not as the end of the earth but as a playground and a resource and a retreat made in the image of a beneficent but distant God. It fed their souls to work up there and they were paid for this steady, solemn work. They had spoken on their radio transmitters to their families. They would soon be home.

In one of the entries which could still be read, Emerson claimed to have discovered the North-West Passage. The fragments of notes found with him said that he had found what he'd been looking for. He described the Anian Strait – the still, blue Pacific waters beyond the neck of the passage: Marco Polo's frozen northern Asia on the far bank, the American Arctic lands to the near. He described white whales swimming alongside the ship which seemed intent on guiding them. The scraps of journal indicated that Emerson and his men had died on the return leg of the walk across the ice, trying to make it back to their ship which still lay trapped in the early-year ice to the north of their final position.

Emerson had written that his life seemed sufficient now. The last entry in his journal was New Year's Day, 1622. It was in the form of a letter to his son. The writing was uncertain. The man was near to death. Emerson and his two last crew lay undisturbed at the bleak edge of the world in a natural cave in the landscape that some time after their death had become sealed in an avalanche below the level of the permafrost, until their bodies were unearthed by men counting whales three hundred and fifty years later.

Emerson's claims had quickly been dismissed by the scientific establishment. The wretch had obviously fabricated the records and positional readings kept in his diary. The journey that he described was seen to be an impossibility. Most of the notes anyhow had been lost or had disintegrated over time, worn by the weather or the wind, or meant nothing and were confused and inconsistent. And anyhow, didn't he know that the Anian Strait was a fiction? Didn't he know that McClintock Sound, the furthest such a ship could sail without being frozen in the winter ice, was two thousand miles from the Bering Strait? He was shown to be a fraud. He became a peculiar footnote to a particular obsession.

3

The symmetry that knits men's dreams together

Scraps of memory – rags flapping at the wind. Empty beaches of black rock and black sand. The smell of coal and potash everywhere about the place. It was the first thing a man arriving in Laing down off the fells would notice. It is the thing I think of first, remembering my detention there in the war. It is the smell that takes me back.

The houses are made of dull green slate. The miners of Laing live in rows of these houses pitched on terraces rising from the harbour, surrounded by fields of wet roots. Geese from the estuary fly over the houses. The heavy roofs shine from the sea's damp and from the mist lying on the sea early in the mornings. The smell of coal and potash gets into women's washing and into men's lungs but there is nothing to be done about it. The mines run out to sea underground. Water sometimes leaks down into the shafts, but the water that drips in is fresh, not salty.

In Laing, men are miners. Daniel Defoe called it the pre-eminent port in England for the shipping of coals on his tour of the British Isles. He compared it to industrial ports on the continent of Europe – to Amsterdam and Bremerhaven and Mauther. He called Laing the Mauther of England. He recalled that every man in Laing knew the story of how the town had been founded.

Laing men had come to Cumberland, like Israelites, across the parted sea of Morecambe Bay. They were followers of the teachings of John Calvin – Lancashire Puritans of a particular hue led by the widower Erland Kyle and his sons. Erland Kyle was a lobsterman – red-faced and free of the compromise that women bring to men's lives – in the village of Heysham perched on the edge of Morecambe Bay. He raised five boys alone and made a decent living out of a hard life, and his sons, all of them by now apprenticed, respected and feared him more than loved him. That is probably how he wished it. That is probably how he thought it was meant to be.

Erland Kyle came to find his calling in preaching a spartan brand of puritanism that came from his own cold-roomed heart as much as from the passion of Calvin or the intellect of Voetius. He set up his church in a Meeting House which was little more than a lobster shed with a high, rough, wooden cross planted into the ground beside it – the Sheriff of Lancaster called it a wretched band of servants and sinners – and yet he seemed to be so much a people's champion that his small congregation slowly grew to two hundred members. Mostly they were poor men, happy to hear that it was *they* who were chosen and that wealthy landowners were not. Erland Kyle baptized men in the sea as they stood up to their waists and when he brought them out above the water, gasping, it seemed he had given them the very gift of life itself. These were men who had not reckoned up the world but who were persuaded by Kyle's oratory and his soup. Erland Kyle fed his flock where the Bishops would welcome a little starvation to keep the numbers down and general discipline intact. Fifty years before Cromwell, Erland Kyle dreamed of founding a commonwealth of men, and his church's growing numbers began to excite the authorities.

When the daughter of the Lancaster sheriff was found to have taken up with Kyle's church herself, the sheriff felt compelled to act. He tried to exert control over the preacher by threatening the positions of his sons. But Erland Kyle continued all the more, since this seemed proof to him of the corruption he was opposing. And when his sons did lose their apprenticeships as the sheriff had threatened, Erland Kyle recruited them as his lieutenants and they lived on donations from the poor and prospered all the more. Finally, grounds were found under the Recusancy Laws to have Erland Kyle and his sons arrested. Instructions were sent by the sheriff for the Lancaster garrison to deal with the matter. When the sheriff's troops were in place the following day, they were to arrest Erland Kyle for sedition and the assets of Kyle's followers were to be seized under ecclesiastical law as bounty.

The only road out of the town was blocked off overnight. Erland Kyle heard about the plan. He had his two hundred and seventy men, women and children gather on the cold December sands at dawn with their meagre belongings.

'God will protect us,' he said, even though they were trapped between the sea and the sheriff's men. And there they prayed. Then God told Erland Kyle to lead his flock across the sea – to *walk* across the sea. He led them across the fourteen miles of treacherous quicksands that covered the Bay at low tide. His followers carried their few belongings with them. As for Erland Kyle, he led them taking no belongings of his own but carrying the rough wooden cross which had stood eight feet high beside his lobster shed in Heysham. As they walked, Erland Kyle's flesh where the cross had lain on his shoulder was torn away to the bone and he bled copiously. It was said that some of the Sheriff of Lancaster's men, realizing what was happening, realizing they were losing their prey, pursued Erland Kyle's fleeing church across the sands on horseback and drowned – as everyone else who had ever ventured out into the full extent of the Bay had done. As for Erland Kyle, he led his community of men across the Irish Sea of the Bay into Cumberland, then north up the coast to a natural virgin harbour, sheltered by the fells behind it and with sea-coal on the beach outcrops as if God had placed it there with them – his people – in mind all along.

Within ten years, production of coal from bell pits dug close to the grey beach was the staple industry of Erland Kyle's new Jerusalem, which he called Laing, taking his mother's maiden name to christen the place. The work was honest toil which pleased Erland Kyle. Their houses were built on the terraces of land above the harbour and these terraces, below the woods where the slate and the stone was mined for the houses, they called the Heights of Abraham. Kyle's community led lives framed by the need for coal. They became, out of necessity, miners. They built a small town, and a Meeting House in which they prayed together to the God who'd brought them safely here for a purpose – to build a community of like-minded men, not yearning, it seemed, for other men's fields of potatoes or their ports or parliaments.

Coal money built a town for them. When Erland Kyle had brought his followers across the parted Irish Sea, there had been only disparate settlements in the land around what would be Laing. They were tinkers mostly, descended from an earlier Celtic settlement of Cumberland, men who had hacked coal from the beach outcrops for fuel with spades. These original settlers, unpersuaded by Erland Kyle's evangelism, were easily displaced to Salem Turn up the coast, leaving the Lancashire men free to build Jerusalem on their harbour land. They were free to see the world just as they chose, though over the years Erland Kyle began to seem less the man he'd once appeared now that there was no one to fight against for his beliefs. It was as though this lack of a tide to swim against weakened his resolve and increased his nervousness and his suspicion of those around him who claimed to be loyal. While Erland Kyle spent more and more of his time pursuing plots against his authority which he imagined were being hatched, it was his sons who negotiated deals for Laing's coal. It was they who made the money. It was the Kyles who kept it to save the miners' souls. And so Laing grew and filled out the valley and celebrated the founding of the town each midwinter with a fair down on the beach. Men chipped at the hard, small, narrow stuff of life confronting them. Fortunes made elsewhere – the glitz of cities – were all well and good, but they lacked substance. They were less honourable. They were houses of cards. The reputations of Laing men were of more permanent stuff; these were *earned*. They were surely written on stone tablets and kept safe somewhere by the Kyles who arched like a glass dome across the sky above such steady and necessary lives.

The Kyles now are mystical creatures, dreaming up the coal, holding up the sky, living on their own estates away from Laing. It is the men of Laing who still dig coal – though from vast tracts under the sea and not from simple bell pits – who are themselves the government of the town. But the authority men hold seems benign and unselfconscious because everyone in the town knows everything there is to be known from the scaled-down pattern of their own lives, and its leaders simply speak for that experience. Without agonizing over it (and working men have no time and little energy to agonize), Laing men are given assurance that their lives are good, that they are relevant and necessary – part of a larger system, part of a balanced universe with Heaven above and Hell below and Henry Kyle's colony far out on the wet fells. It is a necessary orderliness of lives lived close together. Figures everywhere, and movement, but so still at its centre, so breathtakingly silent, such a sense of place, a gravity. A tension holding men's notions of the world together. Maybe that's why strangers are a source of suspicion in Laing. Maybe outsiders threaten such an undemanding faith, such a simple contract with the world. The fear of the stranger is the fear of the chaos that might follow if the brittle equilibrium is ever to fall apart and men are forced to see the world, and themselves, differently.

Walt Emerson has lived all his life in Laing. He doesn't remember his father. Someone told Walt that his father sometimes wore a uniform, that he left town before Walt was born. Walt just shrugged when he heard this.

'He wasn't worth the bother with,' his mother tells him when Walt asks about him. 'Don't think of him – he never thought of us, of you. We're better off without him.'

As a result of developing childhood bronchial pneumonia Walt is sent to the Open Air School for slow learners and fever convalescents at Salem Turn. Each week he catches the stopping train that the pupils board one by one at consecutive stations. They will stay there for the week and travel back home on Friday. The pupils of the Open Air School have the last carriage saved for them. Walt is one of the first into the carriage as they ride to Salem Turn. Each week when he gets on, there is just one pale girl sitting in the carriage. She never says where she got on. She looks hard at things through fat brown spectacles. She won't speak much to Walt. She doesn't speak much at all. After Walt, the train stops for Brock Spivey who sits with Walt and then one by one the rest of them board at stations down the line till finally all of them alight at Salem Turn and are walked up together to the Open Air School for the week. Brock Spivey will sometimes try to start a conversation in his ponderous way with the girl wearing the brown spectacles sitting at the back of the carriage. He has no more luck with her than Walt, except for the one time when she speaks the only complete sentence Walt will ever be able to recall her saying any time.

'I am learning to play the violin, but it must stay at home,' she says to Brock Spivey when he asks her about the sheet music that she stares intently at throughout the journey on the train each week.

In all the time they know her at the Open Air School, neither Walt nor Brock Spivey ever sees her with a violin, though she is often to be found reading sheet music and hearing the notes, they suppose, in her head.

Walt's own schooling somehow seems to fall away. He never masters reading and writing; the letters of the words have minds of their own – they won't sit still in place for him. It doesn't seem so important to the authorities at the school who are content that Walt has turned out placid, that he can remember the catechism of how Laing was founded and, as he gets older, that he can deputize for the teacher's absences here and there and keep a good-humoured order in class amongst the little ones.

As with all the scholars of Salem Turn, he is discouraged from physical activity. He grows tall and pale, a forced plant that stays scrawny and slight and expends all its energy reaching upwards for the light. He is distinct from the other boys his age around Laing. He is distinct from the four Filbin brothers who surround him in age and live on the next street, and the other miners' sons. These other boys follow football and attend the Parish School in Laing and worship at the Meeting House and run wild at the annual Laing Fair on the beach and wonder amongst themselves why they call Laing the Mother of England. Even as they continue to grow and fill out and emerge clean-limbed and bright-faced from childhood and take a fancy to various of the red-haired Tillotson girls, they still play their own brutal form of football out on the rec and wrestle cumbersomely on the ground with each other like dogs whenever the mood takes them – confirmed in their size and the safety of their small world. All the while, Walt watches.

Walt doesn't develop the tight, triangular upper body shape of these other young men in Laing who will go to work in the pits, and on the small fleets of fishing boats. At the Open Air School the boys are runtish or gangly, and the girls insipid, as if somehow all of them are plants struggling to grow in poorer soil than the Parish School's – as if Laing, by comparison, is truly the Mother of England, nurturing her offspring as she feeds England with the coal it craves for warmth and industry.

The only exception to this rule at the Open Air School is Brock Spivey from the Spivey smallholding on the top road above the woods whose size seems earned at the expense of other parts of him. Brock is big and sullen and follows Walt around the Open Air School. The reasoning around Laing for the slowness that afflicts Brock Spivey is that he's *touched*. Their explanations for this are sometimes that he was less loved by God; or that he was born in calfing season and somehow inherited a bull's size and a bull's temperament; or that Laing, like any mother, will throw up one slower runt as the price for a healthy litter of a dozen; or that his father was Old Nick himself. Because who else would choose to visit the Spiveys' smallholding up there below Beacon Fell near the snowline? Who else would go up there? Who else would fuck with Mrs Spivey? That's the story the Filbin boys in Laing and the freckled Tillotson girls will tell, and their mothers will hint at conspiratorially coming out of church, and their fathers will roar when they are drunk down in the harbour pubs.

Away from school, Brock Spivey is taunted by the Filbin boys and teased by the Tillotson girls in Laing. He is used by all of them as men might sometimes use a dog – for sport, for amusement. Sometimes Brock Spivey is filled with rages: against himself as much as others; against his not fitting in; against his exile at the Open Air School; against his size, his predicament – against his *uselessness*. Only Walt and his patience with the world seems able to placate Brock, to coax the boy out of his black moods.

On speech day at the Open Air School, one of the Kyles comes from somewhere beyond Laing to speak. Walt can't remember which one of them it is who comes. The school is funded by the Needs Committee and donations to the Committee come somehow from the Kyles who watch over Laing. Walt can't remember what they say, only that they say it without much thought or passion. The pupils should try hard for Laing, the Kyles say: they should fear God; they should keep out of trouble; they should be useful. They should fit in. The mountainous Brock shuffles on his seat next to Walt. Brock Spivey will afterwards go to work on his mother's smallholding. At night, he'll go down into Laing and drink at the Harbour Inn or the Seven Stars. He'll chase after the conversations that other men – back from the Kyles' pits – have around him in the pub. To the regulars in the Harbour Inn and the Seven Stars he'll become a kind of performing bear: they'll have him arm-wrestling three men at once, or balancing glasses of beer on his head, or dancing with a dog on the tables, or leaping into the harbour water fully clothed. When he has the money, Brock will get properly drunk and this will ease the discomfort he feels amongst other men. Brock Spivey's favourite pastime is shooting geese out in the wet fields by the estuary. The geese gather there each season's end on their way to or from their breeding grounds. Brock Spivey takes his dogs, and the dogs slaver and spit, crouched with tension as Brock Spivey himself grins and shoots, grins and bangs shots at the geese for sport.

Brock Spivey will live with, though never marry, one of the insipid girls he knew at the Open Air School – the girl with fat brown spectacles who was always first to board the carriage on the train to Salem Turn each week and wouldn't speak to them. They'll have a kind of life. No one taught them how to love – only how to survive, how to fight for space. He'll love her sober, and he'll storm about the place breaking things when he's drunk, and when his mother dies the smallholding will become Brock Spivey's place and Walt will never see it, only imagine what kind of place it is.

'Who would *want* to see the Spivey place?' the Filbin boys and the Tillotson girls and the drinkers at the Harbour Inn and the Seven Stars will say, always out of earshot of the man himself, and all the while they'll have him performing like some Laing bear.

When he leaves school, as a former pupil of the Open Air School, as a former Salem Turn boy, they will not take Walt at the pits or the Miners' Social or the offices, even though many young men are off to war against the Kaiser. It's not Walt's place; that seems evident enough. Salem Turn boys are not taken on at the pit. Laing has always had a need since the days of Erland Kyle to look after its own. Laing has always wanted to believe that what lay beyond its boundaries was less true, was not to be included, was susceptible to decay, was foreign – not just to Laing but to God. Walt shops, he tends the house, he nurses his mother who's been sick and forgetful with developing Parkinson's symptoms since Walt was nine or ten. He helps out sometimes back at the Open Air School. Sometimes he stays over and gets paid an allowance for acting as sitter-up through the night for boys who sleep there during the week. He learns to pace his life, not to strain needlessly against god-given constraints. Already his life has a different tone and texture than those of the filled-out Filbin boys shaped by the steady accrual of coal and the Tillotson girls with their come-hither looks. Already, without knowing it or understanding why, he has been left behind.

The three small, white feathers slip from the envelope. Walt takes them to his room. He holds them to the light. He brushes them against his lips, smooths down the quills where the threads of down have pulled apart.

The feathers have been sent by an organization of women in Laing called the Women's Protection League. The League had been founded with the aim of safeguarding the standard of public morals in Laing which they saw as being constantly under threat. The League looked to the town's founder, Erland Kyle, for inspiration. They saw the kind of town he had fought to create. They saw what he had stood for. And they believed that his inheritance had been betrayed, or at least obscured, and so they took up his cross and walked. They wished for the women of Laing to act together for the well-being of the town: to raise issues, to petition, to do what must be done. Its members, wives of those men sitting on the Needs Committee and on the Council of Laing, had compelled the magistrate's office to act against a tinker woman in Salem Turn who carried out abortions on Laing girls for money; they had compelled the Parish School to keep the one Jew out of morning assemblies at which acts of Christian worship were undertaken; they had raised money, by subscription, for a new roof for the Meeting House.

As for the war, it had not seemed very much to be the League's business until, in the summer of 1915, a German U-boat fired two shots on the town from the Irish Sea beyond the harbour before scuttling away. The shots did no damage, except for moving the women of Laing to action – to knitting clothing for soldiers, to holding raffles at the weekly public dance in Laing, to making sure that everyone was pulling his weight in working to win the war – Laing's war now.

Walt has just turned sixteen when the envelope containing the three feathers is sent to him. They come in the post.

Perhaps the Women's Protection League believes he is old enough to serve in the army because he is so tall for his age (all that absence of exercise and the forced growing it seemed to compel in him); perhaps they have lost count, as he did not attend the Parish School with their own children, or have not the time to check; perhaps it is because Walt's prominence in town – his always being seen running daily errands for his mother and being so obliging and apparently content – reminds people over and over that real men, real sons, are fighting at the front for Laing whilst former pupils of the Open Air School wander dilatorily around the town. Walt knows, of course, what the feathers are for. He knows they are telling him to do what must be done.

He lies about his age when he goes to the conscripting centre in the Meeting House in Laing. He joins the Cumberland and Westmorlands. He becomes a rifleman. He becomes one of the Cumberland Pals. He remembers not to mention the bronchial pneumonia he suffered as a child or his schooling at the Open Air School to the recruiting sergeant writing down his details. He puts on his uniform for his mother the night before he goes away. He hopes the sight of it will make her happy, will bring her round a little from the vagueness which afflicts her more and more these days. He hopes it will give her something to remember while he is away. The effect when he puts on the uniform is different, though. The effect when he tries on the uniform in front of her is that, somehow, his mother becomes convinced that the figure here in the front room is not her son at all but is her childhood sweetheart, the one who was briefly married to her and left her pregnant, the one who fathered Walt but never saw him.

'I knew you'd be back, Josh,' she says, clutching his hand. 'I always knew. I prayed every night all my life that you'd be back. You'll come back, Josh, won't you, after you've fought. I prayed, Josh, truly I did. It's all I wanted.'

Walt watches her. 'I'll be back,' is all he can think to say to her. 'I'm glad you prayed.'

And the war?

In the war Walt is a kind of hero, the kind ordinary men can be in the chaos that passes for victory and defeat. He helps a man back behind the lines. He gets a small medal for it. Later he loses his foot as a result of a bullet lodged there. The surgeon leaves him with a stump like a rounded baseball bat two inches above the ankle. The surgeon tells him that he is lucky and Walt believes him. He gets an allowance which goes towards helping out at home.

When eventually, some years later, his mother dies, the Needs Committee in Laing helps Walt to bury her. Stent, the Secretary of the Needs Committee, assures Walt that Laing does not forget her debts. Stent in particular hasn't forgotten. He remembers Walt Emerson from the war. Stent had been a lieutenant in the same company. He remembers how Walt had rescued a man. Stent, like Walt, is a Laing man. Stent is a local boy made good. He'd been born in one of the miners' terraces on the Heights of Abraham. He'd been a clever boy, sent to the Grammar School in Broughton on a bursary provided by the same Needs Committee in Laing which Stent, as a notable solicitor, now presides over.

Stent organizes a job for Walt in one of the town's hotels. There are three hotels in Laing: the elegant half-moon Crescent set on the bend of the seafront; a sturdy, family-run place set further down the coast which is thought of as a guest house; a third-class hotel with no obvious name to it which is hardly a hotel at all – it is much more a boarding house. The third-class hotel had been established with those passing through Laing on trade in mind – salesmen and the like. It is seldom full. It has need of a night porter. It is the smallest of the three hotels in Laing and it is run by a woman named Joannie Kilner, whose husband had worked with Stent before the man had died of a heart condition. Stent says that the woman needs some help and can pay, though not much. There are rooms to be taken as part of the job – and Walt, willing and undemonstrative, takes it.

'You might make something of it,' Stent says to Walt. 'A man like you might have prospered elsewhere instead of coming to this.'

Walt doesn't understand why Stent might feel pity for him. He works alone, as night porter, in the third-class hotel which is really a boarding house. It's fine. It suits Walt. He likes the time and the space it gives him to think. People come in and out of the hotel now and then through the evening and the early hours. Walt directs them. He watches over the place. The residents of the hotel, and Joannie Kilner (who has her own rooms high up at the back), get used to the tap tap of Walt's one good leg and one fitted shoe moving about the hotel through the night. Once, he calls the police when a man is drunk. Once, he breaks up a fight. He likes being up through the night – the small death and then the dawn and the ending of his shift, and walking to the seafront to wash the night out of him and then returning to the hotel and going upstairs after that in the very early morning to sleep in his rooms under the attic with the view out to sea above the other houses of the town.

*

Evelyn is married to a mining engineer. He is older than her. Twice he leaves her, but he comes back. They arrive in Laing in 1935 with their small boy when her husband is employed to work for the Kyles' mining company. It is a new start for them. He dies when a pit prop in a shaft he is helping to sink collapses. It is believed that he was at fault. As an outsider, there is no compensation, no money – no compulsion for Laing's Needs Committee to intercede, although the Kyles send a message of regret through Stent who acts for them in such matters. Evelyn elects to stay in Laing, though there is a distance between herself and the world that even William, her boy, cannot always break. She doesn't come to worship at the Meeting House. She has few friends. She has upset people, upset the Women's Protection League, by declining to sign a petition organized by them deploring the actions of the national miners' union in supporting the Republican move-ment in the Civil War in Spain.

'You believe that Guernica is forgivable?' she had asked them.

'We believe socialism to be a blasphemy against God,' she was told. 'We believe we know what is best. We believe we know what should be done.'

The boy is moody, fractious, missing his father whose absence she cannot explain except in terms of resentment and abandonment which wash over him. She has no one to explain this to, these two worlds of hers and William's entwined in one life together. Apart from the need to nurture him, she has no destiny left, no sense of direction. She is perfunctory, polite, goes through the motions of a life.

She resorts to earning money by teaching, by private tuition of English, of speech, of elocution; she was a teacher for a little while before her marriage. That's how she meets Walt Emerson. He turns up at her door one day, asking if the lady will teach him to read books. She sees a tall, reedy man with a fine shock of blond hair and sharp brown eyes that react to everything. Something about him says he's still really a boy – comfortable with his own small world but cautious beyond it, anxious not to infringe on her space, on her life. (She will only notice his leg, she reports in her diary, when he walks down the steps to the street afterwards. It will be twelve months before he will tell her about it. He will not show her the medal until their wedding night.)

Walt comes to her with only a rudimentary knowledge of the alphabet. He is embarrassed to find that he has inter-rupted her whilst she is calming a child who has been crying. He is protective with her, says perhaps he should come back another time.

'Motherhood does not impede my ability to teach,' she says. He blushes, laughs at his stupidity. He is frightened of her, the way a child is frightened of the night – not knowing its meaning or its depth.

He wants to learn to read properly. He mouths the words. He struggles patiently through the work she sets for him, working hard on the sounds and missing the thoughts lying quietly behind them. He works and works. He learns to read. Each week he turns up on time. He is courteous, respectful, sometimes funny. Each week he takes away the work she has set him and does it with the utmost care, at first for him (so that he will learn), later (he thinks) for her.

After a year she begins to give him passages from novels to read to bring him on. Hardy, Dickens, George Eliot. They are her own worn-through copies of the books. He reads the passages she has set him through the still night while he is on duty in the third-class hotel, his finger following the line of words. Their big themes puzzle him and contrast with his own passive faith in things. Hardy's fatalism, Dickens' passionate indignation, sound bells in hollow parts of him.

'*Whether I shall turn out to be the hero of my own life,*' Walt reads to her, '*or whether that station will be held by anybody else, these pages must show.*'

He struggles to find words to surround and capture what he feels, about the books, about her. He reports back to her whilst she rocks William or prepares the child's bed, or whilst the child sits on her lap and watches Walt, and Walt makes shapes with his fingers and claps to make sounds and the child laughs. He accepts Evelyn's chastising when he misses or misunderstands things. He is a conscientious student. He makes her laugh at herself. He expects nothing that he cannot uncover himself by patience. He brings her back to life. She falls in love with him.

Walt Emerson is a virgin when he marries Evelyn. Knowing nothing. Sailing on a raft of faith.

'Are you sure?' Evelyn asks, wondering about his taking on another man's child. But Walt is so settled about the new life ahead of them that she is reassured. He regards his own sexual feelings, his ability to be aroused, to take and more particularly to give pleasure within sex, with a sense of astonishment and unceasing wonder.

Evelyn is twenty-five when she marries Walt Emerson. She is his junior but feels herself to be older. Walt somehow has a simple, shining faith in things that Evelyn's wariness, her sense of being a stranger in the town, will not allow in her. He is sustained by a belief that, in the end, the world must be weighted and measured in favour of good men. She makes him giddy with contentment. Her willingness to have a second child after the father of her first has been crushed underground is a testament to Walt Emerson's belief that things will work out. He takes her to the Laing Fair that midwinter. They hold one of the torches between them out on the cold beach and watch the masked procession go by and the children whooping and hollering, and see the bonfire being lit and the prayers being said for Laing.

'I'll never leave you,' he tells her, 'because things will always be grand for us.'

'I know you won't leave,' she says, 'but don't say it. It's unlucky to say it.' She knows what happens to men when their view of the world is diluted or is wrenched apart by lust or by the kind of egotism men call curiosity.

And so he stops saying it, but he still believes it, because it is easy to believe it. Because, like his faith (which says that good things happen to good people – and Evelyn is proof of that to him) the thought has a certain symmetry that knits all his dreams together.

Evelyn becomes pregnant. From early on in her pregnancy she begins to say that the child she is carrying – Walt Emerson's child – is different. She says that he talks to her in the womb. Not in words, of course, but in ways that let his thoughts drift into her. He can see things, make things possible, make small wishes for her happen as if he, or she, or they, had willed them into being. She is ashamed of this. She is an educated woman, a former kindergarten teacher before her first marriage had uprooted her – not one of the sleepwalking men of Laing she sees around her. But she feels these things for the child, nonetheless. She writes them down in a note-book that she keeps.

Evelyn likes to write. Walt encourages her. She writes about the dreams she has for the golden child that she carries inside her; for Gabriel – that's what she calls him. She makes sketches in the margins of her book. She draws the angels bringing him to her. She has a talent for sketching that she has never developed. Her drawings are hesitant and rudimentary. Other women (Filbins, Tillotsons, members of the Women's Protection League who meet monthly and stand guardians to the moral life of Laing) tell her: every woman thinks each child of hers will be special. They think she is a young woman with fanciful notions, an outsider. She doesn't protest. She feels she knows the truth of it. She calls the rising weight of her pregnancy her golden child and it pleases her to say it.

If Evelyn has any doubts, she does not share them aloud with Walt. Perhaps she buries her doubts somewhere in fields under earth on days when he isn't there.

4

Gabriel's angel

The lulling television on the far side of the room in the colony plays loudly. The contrast is turned up too high. The characters on the screen carry vague purple auras ghosted around them. The maid has gone to bed and left Tom in charge of the kitchen. Tom falls into a barrel of cider chasing Jerry. Peary clutches the remote control resting on his lap, keeping up a steady commentary on the action on the TV down the length of his parka hood. Ingerman sits cross-legged and very still apart from the flapping of one heavy foot. There are two or three others closer to the TV. They could be dead, they sit so still. Like me they are outsiders – part of the rump of residents still in the colony and clinging together. Tom staggers out of the barrel, drunk. He starts handing out food from the fridge to the surprised mouse.

'Look, he's got his arm stuck through the chicken. He can't get it off.' Tom is sobering up. He starts to chase Jerry again, but he collides with the drinks cabinet. The brandy bottle falls open into his mouth. Glug, glug, glug.

'He's got the brandy now!' Peary says. Gabriel leans a little forward, the arch of his spine not resting against the chair's back. Perhaps there's something through the window where his attention seems to be focused. But it's difficult to see what's there. The light throws reflections back into the lit November room. All that seems to be there is Gabriel's shape and that of the others, cast on the window's insubstantial glass. Until, that is, you notice that there *is* someone, sitting very still. Gabriel knows that the angel is with him. The angel sits in the high-backed chair across from him in the alcove created by the bay window where only Gabriel of the four of them has a clear view of the visitor. Gabriel knows it is an angel. He has been waiting, after all, for an angel, or for Death, to collect him. He understands that he is going to die soon, that his time is nearly over. He knows that the angel's visiting him like this is preparation for his being taken, though whether to Heaven or to Hell he is not so sure. He is unclear of the difference. He imagines that everyone sees Death or an angel at the conclusion of their life. This is the purpose of the angel's coming; this is its warning – that time is short.

Each time it appears, the angel sits quietly close by him for a while in the Bear Pit. Watching over him. He imagines it is undetected by the others. They sit dulled around the television and seem to see and hear nothing as a rule until I ring each mealtime bell. Usually the angel is happy to sit in silence with him, as if to say, 'There is time yet.' The dimming sun on fine winter days like this adds to the sense of glow and the vagueness of the apparition. Sometimes, Gabriel's angel seems to make an effort to reassure him, to tell him 'Its all right – everyone in the end has an angel who comes to collect him, to say that time is almost up.' Gabriel watches, and wonders. The two gerbils in the cage are scratching at their bars in unison, unhurried. Jerry mouse is in full flight away from the cat again. The floozy background jazz chords speed up. Jerry propels a saucepan back through the air. The music stops abruptly as it hits Tom flush between the eyes. When it drops, the cat is stationary, Tom's face now flat where the saucepan has struck. He falls, hits the ground with a clang, rocks like a fallen dish until he is still.

When Gabriel realizes that the angel has gone (sometimes it's hard to know, sometimes he has to guess), he walks the grounds to clear his head, to think things through. The wall enclosing the colony runs for two miles around its perimeter. As part of one of the occasional working parties which were assigned to the chore, Gabriel once helped repair this wall with clean stone which residents before him had built when Henry Kyle had first established the colony. I was excused from this particular chore. A one-armed labourer is of little help. I was always given lighter duties. It added to the further sense of isolation from the world which has so cradled and comforted me here, and sent me for consolation to my books and my wanderings at night, bringing me full circle. The child who dreamed of all the kinds of life that lay beyond the village's potato fields, who as a young man during the war was interned and excluded from life and dreamed of rescue, is now the old man wrapped in daydreamed worlds of imagination to escape the present once again.

Now, all this time later, the stone is irrevocably scarred by Cumberland soot and by wind off the fells, and its masonry has cracked. Now everyone left in the colony is old. These days the gates to the colony where the wall begins and ends are open, but nobody flees.

To visitors, the place must always have seemed sluggish, ornate – a decorous liner from another age too grand for us left-over residents who shuffle by on our way to somewhere in carpet slippers or the wood-soled clogs that Henry Kyle had made for us. Our predecessors, they believe, must surely have been more exotic than us small grey men. And as for the liner, in Henry Kyle's scheme of things it was meant to always be in transit – never destined to reach a port, forever sailing, the only way to leave by leaping into the thrilling sea beyond the rails of the deck and drowning for sure. Henry Kyle, of course, could never imagine that we could want to leap. The very act of leaping – the thought of it – he came to see as something to be treated, as an impulse that needed correcting in his charges. He imagined that, since he had worked out the world, what he wanted others would want. Thus he was distanced from any pain that was not his own. Henry Kyle could never hear the echo of any possible scream.

Each day now, Gabriel walks the perimeter of the wall. He always walks the same way round, the same pace, marking out the edges of the known world, dreaming his dream of Emerson the mariner and sharing it with Athol and Ingerman and Peary. That's how he came across the Icehouse.

Once, men fell off the edge of the world.

Others tried. They drowned.

It happened. Those who stayed behind will tell you. Gabriel will tell you. He read it – he knows it to be true.

Somehow, men lost their certainty. The innocence, the sense of tranquillity which had sustained them, bled away. In the restlessness and longing of the Renaissance, life for its own sake became more precious and more immediate. So did the world all about.

There had already been singular travellers alive to the world with their own private desires. There was Brendon and his dozen Irish monks who, in the sixth century, sailed as far as Iceland in their open wicker curraghs. There were Norsemen under Eric the Red who went sailing for lands in northern waters beyond Iceland and never came back. But while the rest of the world was slowly being uncovered, the northern world stayed a mystery. While Columbus fell by accident upon America, and men rounded the Cape of Good Hope to India and to Marco Polo's China, and spied Brazil, the land at the top of the world stayed something to be dreamed, and feared.

It was the last magical quest set before men – a North-West Passage. A short cut to the riches of the Orient over the top of the remaining unknown world. There was no footmark preceding them here. No breath. No imagination. The only imprint on the land was from the original hand of God. The man to find this passage, to sail through, would advance the causes of the world a thousand years in wealth and knowledge, would unlock the last supposed mystery of geography set by the Creator, would see in passing through this first land, this original earth, into the mind of God.

And now it seems, of the men who sailed for it in their three-masted wooden-hulled ships, Gabriel Emerson was the last, certainly the least remembered, perhaps the greatest.

Clocks stop.

There is no sense of distance. The run of air and the vague radar that is sometimes called fear has them tipping into a night that falls away before them.

The locks snapped off. It seemed so necessary to do it. It was Athol, I saw, who did it, as if locks were an affront to him. Once, Athol, like all of us, spent time isolated in the sideroom as punishment. Unlike the others, he coped less well in enclosed spaces. He is a big man. The more he protested, the more time he spent in the sideroom, having food pushed under the door.

As they approached the Icehouse, a line of birds took flight from the flat roof. Ingerman feeds the birds each day. Henry Kyle used to punish him for it – the birds ate the seeded grass and shat on the cars – but Ingerman would not desist. The birds circled the building, then flew overhead, close enough for the *clap clap* of their wings to be felt like percussion over the men's heads. Then the birds were gone. The four of them were alone – they could not see me hidden – and it was silent all around them.

The heavy doors on runners fought against being pushed back. Athol, who was the strongest, stopped at one point and nursed his hands in his armpits to thaw the sting of the cold steel and the pressure welts in his palms. When they were inside and easing off the pressure they had kept up, the doors rolled back together behind them on the tension of springs. The impact rang low like a bell around the interior of the Icehouse, like a call to order or to silence for the four of them.

Across the colony, the resocialization class is running. Fat Rose is welding her little men into rough-hewn shapes for Sallis and a radio is playing in the background. All the others who are left will be there, except for Roland. There is no sign of Roland.

Athol leads them in. Athol worked in the infirmary as an auxiliary until it was closed down. He was gentle for his large size. He was patient with those who were sick. He was happy with the human contact it involved, though it should also be said that his size made him capable of violence. Once, Athol broke the neck of one of Henry Kyle's attendants who had deserved it.

In the past, it is believed, Athol has extracted sexual favours from some of the residents; for certain from Ingerman, perhaps from Gabriel. It's hard to say. But certainly, men locked away and given food and warmth will then hunt for sexual relief. Henry Kyle knew this. There used to be a women's dormitory in the colony. Kyle spent all his life patiently keeping the sexes apart in accordance with his plan of things. All his life, Athol fought for sexual gratification, or was it love, within the colony. It's hard to say who won. Whoever did, Henry Kyle is now dead and Athol, who once had a brother and who grew up as half of a whole in an orphanage in Accrington, is sixty-four years old, with a face and hands worn to leather.

When they had been conscripted to work in the mines as Bevan boys, it was Athol who took more easily to it because of the refuge of his natural strength and his ability to lose himself in the work. Artemis, more studious, more thoughtful, found the work difficult, and Athol had to compensate for him.

At first they worked together, though the others on the shift were suspicious of their closeness. It was said they slept together in the room they'd been allotted in the schoolteacher's house. And when the gallery foreman noticed that Athol was consistently working harder to cover Artemis's shortcomings, he made the assumption that it would be more efficient to split them up. After that, he made them work separately. In the end, they gave up trying to get a decent day's work out of Artemis who hacked and coughed his way through every shift because of the coal dust that lay on his lungs, and they put him in charge of the pit ponies on the bottom gallery. He liked that. It was better than shovelling coal into the conveyor buckets all day until his arms seized up, although it was scant consolation for being separated from his brother.

In the first moments their sight betrays them, stays stubbornly unaccustomed to the dark. It forms a blackness painted on their eyes. The smell of animal urine and of damp hangs on them. Gabriel rests a minute, catches his breath with hands on knees, still recovering from the effort of prizing apart the doors. They go further in, slowly. Their eyes begin adjusting to the dark.

'This is it,' Peary says.

Gabriel nods at him. 'This is it,' he says.

From my position now, peering in through the crack between the heavy doors, I hear Athol say, 'There used to be a light.'

Peary worked in the Icehouse. A long time ago. Everybody worked. They remember Peary hacking at slabs of meat, his arms full of blood and grease, cracking through bone, clean through to the chopping slab beneath, and coming back to the dormitory smelling of blood. Even after bathing, Peary smelled of blood. Peary feels his way along the side wall and grasps for the switch that he remembers used to be there. A bulb blinks twice, then steadies itself. A pool of light is thrown thirty feet across the arena of the floor before it tails off into darkness beyond that. He throws a second switch. The same thing happens further down the hall.

'It still has electric here.'

Echoes of the words shimmy back off the far wall.

'Hallo-woah.'

Peary shouts again. 'Hallohallohallowowoah.'

The shout, held inside the building, ricochets helplessly, overlapping all about him. In the great days of the colony, the building had doubled as a slaughterhouse for produce which sometimes was bought live from nearby hill farmers. The sounds of the animals arriving for slaughter unsettled some of the residents. Henry Kyle had the building soundproofed by local craftsmen as best they could with asbestos and straw thatch.

Through my crack in the door I see Gabriel wander off on his own. Athol stays near to the doors, picking things up and examining them. Athol has no love of enclosed spaces. Peary pokes around in the litter of the steel racks. The canvas sacks, the hooks and poles have been left on the broken floor from the old days when the Icehouse had provided the colony's food for two thousand souls. Ingerman watches. His big loose feet tap rhythms on the concrete floor of the Icehouse because he is nervous. Ingerman is nervous without the comforting weight of the sack that he carried for years and which like other things – like Athol's lamp, like Peary's photograph of his sisters, like hope – got lost. Peary shouts, waiting for the echoes. Minutes pass. Then a slow hum sets up inside the building and finds a pitch and gets a little louder.

'Christ,' Peary says. 'The refrigeration. It still works. Gabriel? Where are you?'

His words bounce again like rubber balls.

'Here.'

A moment later Gabriel emerges from the small plant room

at the far end. Now Gabriel is as happy with the world as a child. He can hear the noise that the other three can, and can hear what Peary is shouting. He stands alone, looking back at the three of them. He sits down on the concrete floor. Closes his eyes. Dreams a little.

'It's still here, after all.'

'It's here,' Gabriel says. 'Are you ready?'

Athol nods.

'Will you come?'

'We've nothing left here.'

'They'll let you out soon. They'll find you places to live like the others.'

'A dosshouse like Roland was sent to? A bedsit, alone? After forty years? Boys peeing through the letter box? Finding us dead and cold in front of the television in a year? Pah! This is the end we should write together. You think so, Peary? A little glory. A little living. A little *life*.'

Then Gabriel makes a sound. The others cannot say what kind of sound it is. They've never heard the sound before, and never will again. It's like the vibration set up when a wet finger is run around the rim of a half-empty glass. It's low and wide and unwavering, and seems as if it could travel half a day and ring in the bellies of men two counties away. No, they've never heard anything like it, but the men of the *Endeavour* if they were here would know it. They've heard it, I am sure. Wondered. Thought it to be ghosts, or mermaids. It sounds for half a minute, then fades as Gabriel loses breath and lets the sound fall from low in his diaphragm till there is silence again around them.

Damp lips down under the ceiling of their dormitory. When

it rains it takes ten minutes for the moisture to appear in small pearls that now and then slide off. The paint on the far wall is pock-marked with rain sores. The skirting has crusted white in one spot, black in others. It's only in one small area, but the dripping keeps men awake some nights. Rose says there is no money to make repairs, and what's the point as the colony edges towards closure. Roland used to say that the attendants were stealing money from the place. That's why there was none left, Roland said. That's why only a few of the colonists got decent flats when they were moved out. That's why Roland said he wanted to make sure he was at the head of the queue.

Sometimes at night there's a noise, a shout, from down the corridor, from the sideroom. Sometimes it's the wind that shouts. Sometimes it's memory. Memory can be so sudden. There's no one in the sideroom any more. Only the wind shouts now. I used to hear Gabriel singing out loud the distress in the head of whichever imprisoned man was in the sideroom for punishment. I watched him echoing the distress that Athol or Peary or Roland or Ingerman felt each time they were interned in there. Of course each time he misbehaved in this way, they were forced to put Gabriel away as well, but it didn't make him stop. It was as if he was tuned in to their distress. It was as if he couldn't help it. In the end, especially in Henry Kyle's later years, it wore Kyle down, I think, to know that Gabriel would do this for any of the residents in the Bear Pit. In the end, Henry Kyle stuck more and more to simply restricting the privileges of the others and to siderooming Gabriel himself on the slightest pretext. It was an unspoken debt but a real one. It seemed inevitable that Gabriel, by virtue of the suffering he had embraced for all of them, would assume a sort of leadership. In the end he seemed ready for it. After so many years of Henry Kyle, it seemed that Gabriel might offer those who were left in the Bear Pit an ending they could fashion for themselves.

The door to the dormitory in which we sleep is locked until six-thirty when an attendant opens up for the day. It's an old routine. Some of the old ones still survive. In Henry Kyle's day everyone knew where they stood. Everyone knew the rules. The whys and wherefores. Which helped the attendants who were at the sharp end. Who were exposed to what went on. What might go on. The attendants were happier then.

We are all restless sleepers at night. Ingerman is worst of all, flinging his sheets off, hollering in his sleep; those incoherent, slack-jawed syllables of his, like the incantation of prayer in an unfamiliar church. Once, Ingerman was put in the sideroom for twenty-two days. It was the longest continuous spell I remember anyone being given. Even Athol when he broke the neck of an attendant didn't get as long as that. It's hard now to remember what he'd done. Perhaps he'd been feeding the birds again. I don't know. No one can remember any more – neither the residents, nor the attendants. I expect the records would show why Ingerman was put in the sideroom for twenty-two days. Now, people say to forget. Rose says to forget. To make it go away.

Ingerman's name is Nathan. Ingerman's name went away. Ingerman is tall and thin. He has a light-blue v-necked pullover that he found in the spare box and wears all the time, and big brown shoes. Huge shoes. He wears glasses which he is always breaking. Physically, he is not a good speaker. He drops things.

Ingerman's mother used to come and see him. She came every week for years. We used to watch her come each Sunday. She seemed old for a mother. She stroked his hair and called him Nathan, and he lay his head down in her lap. No one else knew her. I don't think Gabriel knew her. I was the only one who recognized her as the woman who lived with, but never married, Brock Spivey – the one who had travelled on the train each week to the Open Air School in Salem Turn with Walt Emerson when he'd been a boy, the one who wouldn't speak to Walt or to anyone else but who finished up living with Brock Spivey and who seemed to love her son. She came each week for years and then she stopped. No one knows why. Ingerman doesn't know why. He was twenty-four when she stopped. Ingerman is fifty-seven now, so Henry Kyle's records say.

Ingerman's limbs only thrash about at night when he is dreaming. When he is conscious he is just slow. Under the resocialization programme which Rose runs for us, Ingerman has been given an exercise in which the component parts of a particular action – making a cup of tea or going to the toilet – have been broken down, and Ingerman must repeat these component parts ten or twenty times in a session. Stand up, Ingerman. Walk to the toilet door, Ingerman. Open the door, Ingerman. And so on. It is to promote his independence. An attendant instructs, cajoles, goes away, comes back, in the meantime having perhaps despatched another corpse down the Duddon where it washes towards the sea.

Sometimes, when Ingerman was carrying a cup of tea across to the kettle for the eighth time in a sequence pre-scribed for him, Roland would appear and would yell 'Drop' from the doorway as he was passing. And Ingerman would drop the cup, and Roland would roll away laughing, and Ingerman would wait to see what should happen next. The attendant assigned to the job would curse and go looking for a brush and shovel while Ingerman waited, and the attendant would make some score-times up to save the bother and would cuss his luck because things were more straightforward in Henry Kyle's day. And now even Roland has gone. Something is happening.

Everyone in the dormitory fights their way through sleep to a tetchy peace. To a truce with the day gone from them. Finding a pause before the door is unlocked on the next day. Only Gabriel, who sometimes gets lost in himself, will be laying awake, turning again on his pillow. Men around him will scratch and toss and turn. Out in the darkness, the refrigeration unit in the Icehouse hums steadily. Soon, the first tacky glaze will appear on metal surfaces. Ice is forming.

5

Setting sail

The canvas sheets, knotted together, make a kind of wide sail
hung from a hook which has been left hanging from the ceiling. They have reached it by positioning a metal stacking
trolley on a line of planks which themselves are laid on packing boxes. The sides of the canvas sail are loosely tied to two
other stacking trolleys positioned to stretch the canvas wide.
From two wider hooks, they manufacture the lines of two
other masts, making lines of smaller sails by weighting squares
of canvas with hand-size pieces of concrete from the broken
floor of the hall. There are small changes in temperatures
between the lowest and highest parts of the building as the
refrigeration generator hums on and off to keep a mean temperature and as the warmer air rises to the ceiling, and this
makes the sails shimmer on their moorings as if the wind were
catching them. Sometimes one of them tugs sharply and the
noise causes Gabriel to look up from where he stands and to
scour the high ceiling as if he were looking for the weather
coming in over a far line of sight.

My own vantage point is high above them in the Icehouse,
in the small loft space above the refrigeration unit where the
ventilation shaft is situated. The only way up to it is by using

the metal fire-ladder on the outside of the building. From the inside it looks as though the high space under the eaves is out of reach, and the boatbuilders – the voyagers to be – have no idea that they are being spied upon. From here, I can look down on the men building the boat in total anonymity. It will be a lonely vigil, but one for which I am well rehearsed. Besides, I am better off up here than down there as part of the performance. I am no use as a builder of ships or as a voyager with only one good arm. I am *made* for this.

They build the shape of the boat from the floor upwards, first using packing boxes and then planks laid across them. They build a kind of helmsman's hut. Athol robs the abandoned infirmary across the colony of mattresses and blankets. They hang a hundred wires up from hooks for rigging. Gabriel fixes a shelf under the deck planks for books and charts just as Emerson took books and charts. This is where he plans to sleep and to chart his course. He carries the details of Gabriel Emerson's voyage, and nails to the side of his bunk a reproduction of the Zeno map of the northern world showing the coasts of Europe and of the Americas, and Greenland and the edges of what would be Hudson Bay and where the Arctic gold was imagined by the cartographer to lie like Laing's beach coal – outcropped in the basalt, and how beyond seventy-nine degrees north and how west of what would later be called Baffin Island the map becomes pristine white (imagine – nothing), and the images men might hold of life and geography fade and disappear and men can still imagine falling off the edge, or encountering God, or whatever else can haunt or inspire them because nothing is there before their imagining it.

All this takes time. And after that they set sail together. It took Emerson eight weeks for the sea journey, until land was sighted at Julianehaab. Without leaving Henry Kyle's colony, these men too will sail the same journey, sleep below deck, will get back to the dormitory before lights on at six-thirty in the morning. In this way, Gabriel will retrace Emerson's steps, will make the voyage he needs to make. And the year? The year, I believe, inside the Icehouse as I look down on it from my solitary height, inside the head of Gabriel who would be a sailor, is 1620.

The mariner Gabriel Emerson was thirty-four when he sailed from Laing to search for the North-West Passage. He had been the first child born in Laing – the first born to parents who had made the walk across the Morecambe Bay from Lancashire with Erland Kyle. He had returned to the town after an absence of twenty years to persuade Laing men to build him the boat he needed to make his voyage. But is he a tall man? A brave one? A good leader of men? What drives him on? What makes him what he is? This man, who was apprenticed on a coal boat out of Laing for Liverpool, who sailed with Baffin, studied at the university in Padua, did a deal back in Laing for ships, and kept a journal of his walk across the ice.

Perhaps less is known about Emerson than any of the other voyagers before him who had been part of this Elizabethan obsession – Frobisher and Hudson and John Davis – because his base was the north-country port of Laing and not, as theirs was, the hub of exploration, the Devon ports. Because his lowly birth prevented him from winning backing for the voyage from the Crown. Because courtiers, anxious to please the monarch, anxious to explain the world, anxious to simplify the map on which it was represented, were wary of the failures (as they saw it) which had preceded Emerson's expedition. Because they had found Baffin's tales of northern Greenland as far-fetched and bizarre – as unhelpful – as men once found Pytheas' frozen sea. Because Emerson didn't come back. Because the men of Laing would disown him; betrayed, they would tear his monument down in the dark of night.

I know it takes so much effort from Gabriel to will this other Emerson into life again. To find him. To retrieve what is left. To breathe life into old, lost bones. For days and days he tries, hovering between two worlds, made anxious and forgetful by the effort. Gabriel must find names. You see, at some point Emerson must discuss the voyage with the men who'll be his officers on board, must sit with them, these two men who will be Athol and Peary – one thick-set, one slight and calculating – discussing the matter, debating how to raise the capital for the voyage, the route, the hopes, the need to journey, the idea of returning to Laing to ask his kinsmen to build him a boat to take him there. It's a need that lies insistently on Gabriel like dull sleep, makes him drowsy to the larger world about him, makes him distracted, forgetful of the angel which sometimes hovers by him, makes him angry, subdued, possessed, beatified as he struggles through the fog of thought. But what is it that drives Emerson on? What thing? How can any man be sure after almost four centuries? How can any man know what drives any other?

Gabriel spends hours, nights, with faces drifting past him, men he's seen, an identity parade, and slowly, slyly, I believe, Gabriel discovers he can almost picture how it goes. Can picture, just, Emerson, still vague, still a shadowy figure obscured by almost four centuries, talking to two men who will be

Peary and Athol. They are discussing the ships they'll need. Later, Emerson will write it up in his journal. So too does Gabriel. This is the gist of the ship's log Gabriel keeps on board his homemade *Endeavour*. Each dawn, when they have gone back to the dormitory, I come down and pick over the bones of the night's preparation for the voyage in the Icehouse, reading what's passed through Gabriel's head. (Poor Lukic, you may say; poor man – reduced at the end of his own inexacting performance of a life to sniffing around the embers of other men's bonfires. Poor Lukic indeed.)

Gabriel writes that he has viewed the wood in the Forest of Grizedale from where they are to make choices for their frame. He writes that they have chosen the best and fittest trees for the task, which have been marked accordingly. These trees have been felled and drawn down to Laing by horse and pulley, to be squared and sawed there, and so the frame is made ready.

What of the plans for the ship?

There is no plan beyond that for one midship section, as the practice of the day demands. Every plank used in the construction helps unfold the curving of the sides, plank after plank from the keel, trusting for the contour of the boat to a practised eye and the blend of clean-grained wood.

The keel of the *Endeavour* is laid in place in the dockside of the Laing estuary with all the town watching. The keel is the first and lowest timber in the ship to which all the rest is fastened. It is a huge tree, taken and then cut to the proportion of her burden, laid by a right angle in the bottom of the dock. The day the keel is laid, a drink is taken to the voyage and its success by the three friends. The taverner serves them. A boy sits there too, close beside Emerson, with Peary and Athol across the table. Athol has a dog which sits by his feet under the table, a shabby, loyal thing. The dog will sail with them as companion for the men on the *Endeavour*.

'So the great voyager returns, eh?' the taverner says.

Emerson shakes his head. 'Just a man, like you.'

The taverner laughs. 'But without my debts, eh? And my wife?'

The boy seems nine or ten years old. He is Emerson's son. The taverner asks if the boy will sail with his father, the great sailor. The boy looks up at his father, at Emerson whose face Gabriel, watching, cannot see; says yes, of course.

The taverner asks the boy if he's afraid.

The boys says he is afraid of nothing.

'Not even of what you might find there?'

'No,' the boy says.

'What about the mermaids who sing to men from the rocks and drive them mad? What about the sea-whales who swallow ships whole? And the unicorn whales who spear sailors clean with horns eight feet long? What about the men in the Book of Wonders who live at the top of the world, savages with seven heads and three legs who can run faster than a lion? And the fires in the sky that can burn a man to salt if he looks straight at them?'

'Everything has a reason, my father says,' the boy tells him. 'Everything has an explanation.'

'Is that so, Emerson?' the taverner says. 'And aren't you afraid of what's out there?'

Emerson ponders the question. 'Sometimes,' he says. 'Sometimes the thought of the voyage makes me afraid.'

'Then you're stupid to go. Stay at home. Find a woman.'

'I'd be stupid to stay by the fireside all my life for the sake of keeping a handful of fears at bay.' And Emerson leans across and kisses the boy, his son, on the forehead. The boy's mother is dead. The child is his father's responsibility alone. The boy knows he'll sail with his father. He knows they'll journey together.

Gabriel's written version of all this is so immediate, so vivid as I read it, that I think he must almost feel it for real even though it was all so long ago. I believe he *sees* it there, projected all about him, the way concentration and a little willpower allows Ingerman to see three-dimensional shapes rise out of flat sheets from zigzag patterned cards he steals each week from cereal packets. I think he *sees* the huge timber, scarfed into one end of the ship, and the butt ends of the forward planks fixed to it, rising upwards. The stem, Gabriel's log says, takes six horses half a day to drag it into position for the men to work on. The stern post is let into the keel at the other end, somewhat sloping, and from it rise the two fashion pieces like the horns of a dragon. All of the planks that run to the aft end of the ship are fastened to these. And in watching the vessel created before them, Gabriel writes that planking a ship in this way is like the adding of tissue and skin and sinew and heart to an animal newly created, and Gabriel knows that a carpenter and a shipwright are truer alchemists than any bookish man pouring over manuscripts and potions. When it is finished, this animal will weigh ninety tons. It will run twenty-eight strides from bow to stern. It will sail through the North-West Passage.

They purchase another ship to be fitted out for its own particular purpose as Emerson's second vessel. This second ship will accompany the *Endeavour* as far as the Zeno map and then Baffin's sketches will take the voyagers as far as John

Davis's Strait up the west coast of Greenland. After that, in agreement with the Council of Laing, the second ship will sail back home with the gold they will have dug, which they are persuaded from the Zeno map is there along the Arctic route. Then Laing's investment, Laing's faith – the Kyles' faith – in Emerson will have been repaid.

Finally, the *Endeavour* is lined with lead on its hull. The purpose of the lead is to guard the living wood against the shipworms that threaten to infect an unprepared vessel in the southern oceans, for after the *Endeavour* has passed through the Strait they seek, when she's sailing south to Cathay.

I watch over Gabriel, like he once watched over me. I see him sleep. Dream. Stir. Sometimes I wonder what he thought of me when he stood guard over my rough, broken sleep in Laing all that time ago and watched me rising and falling into and out of the world. The weight of sleep in him rises like dough until, filled with muddied dreams, still dripping and unformed, he is spilled across from a land too far to cross in a single night, and so he is returned. But to what?

In his first moment he seems unsure what's him and what isn't. He is raw and unfinished, his panic submerged in the rhythm of the journey's end. He opens his eyes. In spite of everything – instinct and will – he's drawn together, condensed. The cold shrinks him by degrees to the size of a sudden man, a man with a back grown sore in the night. And the betrayal of his mortality strikes him and he howls for home and wishes death on the otherness of the world, but silently as good men do. There is, it seems, a birth of recognition on his face. An edge of air drags at the sail. The boat bobs. Surely he feels it.

The Icehouse registers at minus four. The feelings in his body's parts open out from being drenched in sleep. He breathes in cold air, appearing conscious of pulling it in and of releasing warmer breaths, slowly. He rises from the low-roofed cabin where his books and maps are stored around his sleeping space, and stares all around the Icehouse – his sea. He's slept under two blankets (brought by Athol). Gazing out now, he's still wrapped in one of them, his eyes level with the deck rail as he looks.

It's been the first night of the voyage. He will have counted seven hours of sailing. Slept for some of that. It's surely easier now they're underway to start getting under Emerson's skin, to feel what Emerson might be feeling in these early days. I know that Gabriel still can't see him. He says so in the log he's keeping. It doesn't matter. There are almost four hundred years between them. Days on the voyage will heal the distance. Below him, Athol stirs hugely from sleep. He nods. The two gerbils that Ingerman has stolen in their cage from the Bear Pit are awake. Rose is annoyed about their disappearance. She calls it a breach of trust. She has begun an investigation. No one is talking.

It was the place of greatest dignity on earth. That's what men said, those few who had seen this unknown continent of ice and dreams. Henry VIII had sent two ships, persuaded by merchants that Cathay could be reached through a passage north of the Americas. One ship sank. The other made a run for the West Indies after losing heart part way up the Labrador coast. Men calculated where the passage lay, measured how it might be traversed. A monk named Antonio Urdaneta claimed to have sailed through it in the 1550s.

Martin Chacque, a Portuguese, said he'd passed through west to east in 1556.

Poppycock. Gabriel and I, like other scholars, know. Mariners continued to sail for it, though – Frobisher and John Davis and Henry Hudson, men in tiny, wooden-hulled pinnaces, men who seem to me (reading about them) to be like astronauts in capsules adrift in a mapless universe.

In the end it was William Baffin who guessed for certain from the tides that any possible passage must lie still further north through Davis Strait and not the channels around Hudson Bay. He sailed with a young lieutenant named Gabriel Emerson on board to seventy-nine degrees north on the Greenland coast, eight hundred miles inside the Arctic Circle, further north than any western sailor would go for two hundred years. Baffin, with his lieutenant, mapped everywhere that he went. And like Pytheas, on his return he was disbelieved.

Emerson must have been a most remarkable man. His own small library on board ship included Pomponazzi and Bacon and Aristotle. He had them shelved by his bunk on board the ship. Men who would find him almost four centuries later whilst logging the migration patterns of beluga whales would find pages torn from such books in the sealskin pouch pressed to his frozen corpse. He built on the calculation that the Passage ran through Davis Strait and reckoned, from what he and Baffin had learned, that it ran west over what would become Baffin Island.

But Emerson was a commoner from Laing. He was like Columbus, with ideas, with dreams, beyond his station. And so Emerson was forced, at a price, to return home to ask for backing from his kinsmen in Laing who themselves were finally lured not by Baffin's remarkable findings, or science, or the dreams that must have possessed Emerson himself, but by the theories of earlier maps about gold formed in the pure Arctic air close to the pole star.

At this stage it surely seems to Emerson's men to be a practised route. Hard, yes. At the extremities of the world, of what is sailable, bearable. But still sailed before. Sailed by Norsemen and by fishermen, and by a handful of previous crews whose route took them all at least as far as the Newfoundland banks. And Julianehaab and the southern ridge of Greenland is barely further north than the Hebrides for all its sense of otherness.

So in these first days there is trepidation and newness, high swells, big raw days, (the team of miners they have brought from Laing being sick over the side of the boat and fearing every swell), but no white fear, no ache, no abyss. There is a confidence that things are fathomable, that this crew of men are still within the world that can be imagined, conjured up by people who sit back in the Old World wondering about them, that the crews aboard will prosper finally through science and, failing that, the magic of belief. And the dominant theme of these men's days above all, now that they have set out – the reality, the truest thing – is that there is no turning back, and this motion breeds a certain content.

There is mention in the journal that survived Emerson's voyage of the *Endeavour* being blessed against witchcraft before she left Laing. Emerson, in writing about it, days out into the sway of the Atlantic, is dismissive, uncomfortable with the charade but tolerating the ceremony for the sake of the voyage – for the sake of the Laing men who had laboured to build the vessel over the previous year.

There is a report about this same ceremony in the Register of the Council of Laing. The tone of the reporting here is different to Emerson's. The Register's report sees the blessing as being as much of a necessity for the safety of the ship and the success of the voyage as the securing of the masts or the accuracy of the ship's charts. Those writing in the Register knew that good and evil were as tangible in the world, and as easily separated, as bread and bricks.

They knew when they had come to Cumberland that this was witch country. They knew that vigilance was necessary. It was the energy required to see their vision through which surprised them. It was the way that evil swam around their small community of Laing hid out in the large fells; it was the way evil looked to take every opportunity to undermine Erland Kyle's vision.

In the forty-two years between the founding of Laing and the sailing of Emerson's *Endeavour* in the spring of 1620, the books about Cumberland that I've read here in my captivity say that seven witches were put to death in Laing for setting demons against the town. At first, it seems, the Kyles were too trusting. At first they had thought it necessary (to keep evil at bay) only to ensure that *good* men prevailed in positions of authority. It was simple enough to rule that only those who worshipped at the Meeting House could be eligible for positions of office – for magistrate, for councilman. At first it seemed necessary simply to outlaw unchristian acts (had not the young Emerson himself been beaten as a boy and made to wear a Jew's hat for a day for drawing suspect mathematical calculations on the stone flags in the town square?). Later, they needed to move on to expelling those of the original

Celtic settlers who wouldn't conform to Henry Kyle's vision, and so a small exodus was begun to Salem Turn. But the authorities in Laing came to realize that the evil they faced was too powerful to be discouraged by such simple and naive precautions. They saw incidents of dissent and dissatisfaction against Laing's administration, against Erland Kyle's sons, begin to grow, and they realized that this was the witches' doing and said so. The witches seemed to watch over the town on the fells disguised as wolves, and infiltrated the life of Laing in a dozen other guises and subterfuges.

In the end, just seven witches in total were burned for acting against Laing, though the community, frightened by the discovery, knew it couldn't afford to be complacent any more. It is known what Emerson said in his parting speech on the harbour-side of Laing before his two ships sailed, because he made reference to it in his log. It's known that he thanked the good men of Laing for building him the fine boat that they had in the *Endeavour*. It's known that he thanked Laing for the chance he'd had to teach the children of the town a little mathematics and science at the Parish School throughout that winter and spring of 1619 whilst his ship was under construction down in the harbour. He hoped that they'd remember what he'd taught and that this would prove the foundation of a new academy based on one he'd seen in Padua which taught the classical sciences and humanities to commoners' children and which he envisaged being built with some of the gold to be sent back to Laing as a way of repaying the town. It's known that Emerson thanked the Council of Laing for their faith in him – a faith so great that the Kyles had even borrowed money from Manchester lenders in order to finance a proportion of the construction costs of the ship as an investment in the wealth Emerson's voyage promised to bring back. Emerson said he hoped to repay the faith that Laing had shown in him, its first-born son. He hoped to find the North-West Passage. He hoped to advance the cause of science, and of the geography of the world. He hoped the children of Laing would have a chance one day to learn as fact what he hoped to discover. And he said one more thing. He said he knew that the ship on which he stood had been so skilfully constructed by Laing's fine men that there was truly no need to bless the *Endeavour* against witchcraft or any other kind of sorcery; it was the ship itself – so well crafted – and the men on board he had gathered and formed into a crew – so skilled in seamanship – who would ensure the success of the voyage. And he quoted Pomponazzi, his old teacher in Padua, telling them not to fear, telling them that in the true universe there was no room for unnatural demons – telling them that knowledge would see the voyage through.

Emerson's final piece of business in Laing before his departure had been to agree the collateral demanded by the Council of Laing. He had, after all, left Laing once before, as a young man and had not returned. They were glad that their first-born son had returned to them, a man of the world, a scholar, a successful sailor. But he was no longer one of them. He was not *of Laing*. He was not entirely to be trusted since he had taken up with the outside world. He would need to provide some collateral if the Kyles were to allow him to sail out of the harbour in Laing in two fine ships and with thirty of the town's miners on board. What guarantee could Laing be given of Emerson's good offices?

The second ship, it was agreed, was to return to Laing within eight months, stocked with the Arctic gold which would serve to repay Laing's investment in the voyage whilst Emerson sailed on for the Passage. Emerson, or news of him, should surely reach Laing within a year and a half – or the collateral would be forfeit – although they said they knew he'd be back. They said they knew he'd make Laing wealthy; they said in jest they'd make him King of Laing when he returned – king of their commonwealth.

They raised a monument to the journey in Laing before the sailing, its supporting plinth positioned on the harbour wall, facing out to sea, waiting for the sailors' return.

And the collateral?

Emerson's son. Emerson would sail for the North-West Passage searching out the Anian Strait but his son would stay behind in Laing, held as surety that Emerson would return – must return. So it was that the monument on the harbour wall faced out to sea, waiting with Laing men for Emerson's return, waiting for him to return to claim his son and bring them gold. They still wait.

They have sailed the first night. They make their way back in time for the breakfast bell at seven which I, having slept as best I can in my cramped position in the loft of the Icehouse, having hurried back after them, will ring; Athol, squinting at the new day, looking all around him, Gabriel preoccupied, Peary breathing heavily down the funnel of his hood, Ingerman legs flapping – making their way. There is a promise of light in the half-formed sky. It catches and defines the four figures. They move across the compound, filled with light, with life.

6

Hunting the terragot

Under a milk-white Laing sun, a raft of marsh geese, resting, float on the winter estuary. Now and then a single goose takes off. Another paddles, settles. They drift with the morning. In the distance a small boy appears. The noise he's making sounds as if it's coming down a long tunnel, far away. He's running, down the hill, arms helter-skeltering, shouting, getting closer, closer, down and down. It's Evelyn's child. It's Gabriel; five years old and with all his life before him. He claps his hands, running towards them, beseeching them. They turn, unsure for a moment on the water, then rise before him in a percussion of noise. The panic of their wings flapping churns the water. A thousand geese rise like columns of smoke into the air about him, white and crying. Brock Spivey, gun over his shoulder and dogs slavering at the barking geese, watches them fly out of his reach and just grins and shouts down to Gabriel above the frantic noise not to worry, that they'll all be back for him and for his gun next year, they'll all be coming back and then he'll have them. And down in the wet estuary fields below him, the boy, arms flapping, barking, wet to the knees, is left behind, watching the geese rise and rise and go.

Bundled in his blanket each night at ten, Gabriel is lifted up from the couch where he is lying, wrapped in the consolation of sleep. The boyish smell of him fills Walt with the weight of love and fear. The air on the landing is dark, and tense with cold. Gabriel is carried out to the flat high up at the back of the hotel where Joannie Kilner will, in her grave and disarming way, watch over him and William (William who is walking down beside his father with his jacket over his buttoned pyjamas) whilst Walt works through the night. She will wake them in the morning in the double bed they share whilst Walt still works, (Joannie Kilner with her solitary outlook has no need of double beds). She will see them off to school while the sky is lighting and Walt is already asleep after his ten-hour shift as night porter in the third-class hotel in Laing, the boarding house, by which time the morning shift of miners – the cutting shift – will be two miles out to sea, still dry and digging coal, the sleep still there and dull in their faces.

There is a something that enters Joannie Kilner's room at night. It comes for Gabriel, hunting him. To speak of it is to invite a kind of death, to have the angels come and take him back. He lies awake, waiting for it. William – dull William – is asleep beside him in the bed. This is between Gabriel and the something. He can tell when it is near because he feels it. The something is preceded by the rumble of its energy, of the tread of floorboards it is running over to get to his own particular room. Then there's a pause that has Gabriel breathless, tense like a cat and waiting. Suddenly, without a noise (its clumsy approach up to the room is over now and stealth is everything if it's to take Gabriel unawares), it's in the room, diving frantically beneath the door, pelting across the wall that separates the room they have from Joannie Kilner's box room where she sleeps, soundly. It moves furtively, flat against the wall in a practised route to the foot of the big bed. It can bend. It arches its supple back and leaps across spaces in the room, searching for Gabriel who, if he's found, will be taken by the something, by the terragot – his mother's name for unnamed fears she used in her private thoughts, the ones she buried on a hill under earth and which somehow in her absence, in the denial of her life, grew. The something, the terragot grown in the earth, circles the room, slyly, searching in its blind and organized way for life, and Gabriel freezes, imagining nothing lest the terragot hears his thought and is upon him. It stays until it has searched and sniffed enough all around the room and is satisfied that Gabriel, who it hunts nightly, isn't there and then speeds through the solid window, gone for another night, picking up speed as it flies across the rooftops back to its secret lair. I will find the terragot, Gabriel thinks. I will find its lair and strike it dead before it strikes me one night in my sleep. And so Gabriel Emerson, afraid of nothing but stalked by his mother's doubts – the terragots – plans how to hunt it down.

A child new to school will often wander on the edge of things. He arrives in the class once the hubbub has formed and before the formality and tide of register, and prayers, and learning have taken hold. He will move – swim – from space to space, pausing on the edge of groups. He will place a hand on the side of a table here and there. His uniform is unfamiliar. His collar is chafing him. His older brother's gone to class else-where. He is unsure how, tethered, his vague notions can be traded for friendship and for rescue. He is unsure of the dance. He feels the bulk of him when he is cramped up like this to be a useless currency. This is Gabriel Emerson, motherless, looked out for by all the women of Laing as he flies through the town, a brilliant shining life inside him but so unsure of the dance. His mother is a line of energy, a fixed point, a notion, a hill fortress, a mood, a sound like water. His father is a quiet man. Gabriel has lived his small years in their rooms on the top floor of the third-class hotel in which Walt works as the night porter. He lives with a father who doesn't fit in. He pulls at the collar of his small uniform. Feels the world fronted by the classroom tugging at him. Then, like a fish held for a moment on a line lying over the water, he slips away, free, back out into that sea in which he is part of the living breathing world (not set against it), diving, forgetful that he was ever momentarily hooked. As he settles at his small desk and finds moments less pressing and immediate on him, he begins to weave a singular world about himself, renders himself safe, makes some small part of himself relevant to the world. Somewhere a bell rings. Things move on.

They learn how Laing is the Mother of England. They learn that Laing boys will be miners, that cleanliness is next to godliness, that Jesus watches out for them all and makes them safe. As part of their introduction to the life of the Parish School in Laing, the Parish School reception teacher, Mrs Ingol, tells each child to draw a picture of how they'd like to be. They hand in the pictures at the end of class – of boys, as men, being miners and footballers, and girls as brides on wedding days. Gabriel hands in a blank sheet of paper.

'Why didn't you do it?' Mrs Ingol asks Gabriel. There is some stifled laughing from somewhere in the class.

'I didn't know where to end,' Gabriel says. 'I left it empty so everything could be in, so nothing was left out.'

She makes him stay in class at break to redo the work. Gabriel Emerson draws fields in a bowl of sky, a globe, makes the signature of land a kind of face. The running estuary that he fills in smiles in the way it bends into the sea. Birds fly through his hair. His picture says that the world dreams of him, that the season of doubt hasn't broken yet, that all terragots can be defeated in the world he's authored.

Beyond the canopy of Laing, Gabriel runs free. He believes himself, unfettered, to be a magical beast as his mother said he'd be. He's read his mother's words. Walt gave him what she wrote to him and already, driven by the need to know, he's read them, coached clumsily by Walt himself till Gabriel's knowledge outstripped his father's. He wanders. He peers in through windows from the street, unseen, watching tableaux of still, unsatisfactory life, then vanishes. He gets lost. He's not worried. He makes incomplete maps of his world which somehow suffice and get him home.

When Brock Spivey comes into town from his smallholding with his snarling, snapping dogs on long leashes, Gabriel is the only one they'll yield to. He stands in front of them and they quieten.

I would like to believe that all men are magical when they set out in their relationships with the world – their two lives, inner and outer, blurred as if there were an indecision between the land and the sea. Gabriel thinks he'll stay like this all his life, thanks to the distracting noises of passing days and a mother who died in the frantic effort of bringing him safe and alive to the world. And his Dada is vague after long nights alone and days asleep and an inability to judge the world. He says only 'Sure, Gabriel, sure – you're magic all right, just as your Mama promised.' And he smiles for his boy, and then afterwards for William.

Gabriel's reading, to Mrs Ingol's grim satisfaction, is ahead of every other child in school, even the ten- and eleven-year-olds. He tells stories. He dreams. Dada encourages him, marvels at him, at Evelyn's prophecy unfolding close by him.

Some days Gabriel skips school. His curiosity is too huge. He's had fights with boys at school. Bigger boys. Sometimes with William's friends: Rolf Stent, who is the son of the Needs Committee Secretary and who'll be going to a small public school in Carnforth when he's old enough, and Morton Filbin, and Joseph Tillotson and his brother Billy who is older than them all. He's fought William once. Violence, when it comes in him, doesn't well up and explode in pieces but comes naturally; it is casual and immediate and is gone just as soon, and the boy he's fought, whoever it is, often bigger than him, is beaten in a fury of fists and knees.

Gabriel's favourite places become further and further out, where he can have a sense of the open land around the old mineworkings in the woods above Laing; the drenched fields where the geese in their gracious 'V's come in each autumn from the north. William is less sure but follows him in all of this as Gabriel's reluctant guardian appointed by Walt, looking over his shoulder, back at the town, concern like a shadow on his face. William has Gabriel's features but set in a minor key, with a longer, narrower face, a sense of reserve about him; more moon than sun, Evelyn had said. Where Gabriel seems barely to eat, William is bound to the earth by his appetite, by his need for steady and regular intakes of comfort food. He carries biscuits in his pockets. He hides cake around the hotel. How hard it is for him to be filled up.

One of the slate caves is carved into the rock like a high cathedral arch. The children in Mrs Ingol's class know that this was carved by Jesus – that Jesus lives there in the winter when there's no one else about so that he can keep a close eye on how things are being run in Laing. If you pray in Cathedral Gill, Morton Filbin's brother says, you get double your money.

William and Gabriel often lie in the grass that runs below Cathedral Gill where the road snakes up to the fells. William's pockets are full of biscuits. Gabriel's head is full of dreams.

'You lie down, Bubba,' Gabriel will say, 'Lie down, Bubba.' And then Gabriel teaches dull William how to fly, how to set himself free and go flying with the birds high over the land, eyes closed, heart thrilling, over Laing, right over Laing. Believing in yourself at five, sure of your marriage to the world – the contract of faith – you may slip from yourself, become invisible, enter into animals and trees and feel their exultation and their pain. You are the cause of things and their reason. Even *I* remember that of childhood. And as for Gabriel, he has read his Mama's diary. He knows about the golden child, the angels. Out near to the sea, clear of the sea wall by a quarter mile, Gabriel makes a habit of walking the grey sandbanks before the tide comes in. He is unclear why he does it. He doesn't think, 'This is a challenge; this is a dice with death.' One day he gets stranded on the banks as the tide finally beats him back to the harbour. He stands looking back at the town, a rush of water spreads between himself and the safety of the shoreline, not panicking but wondering. The angels will watch over him. The world will save him. The time to die's not yet.

Men from the town set out in row boats to rescue him. They row and row but can't reach him against the swell of the incoming tide. Then, it seems to them, he walks back across the water to dry land. They ask him. He looks curiously at them. He doesn't understand. He is thrashed by an embarrassed Walt. But he doesn't care. He is happy, because nothing before has required so much of him. He has never felt so real.

The first time, after his rescue from the sandbank, that he is left to play alone unescorted by William or by his Dada, he fixes the point of a far fell beyond the town and sets off for it. He reaches the woods beneath it and can see the town below. After a while he cannot see the town any more. Later, he cannot see the fell either but he carries on. He knows he is the first person ever to see this far. He finds his way back. Each day he presses on further through the woods. One day he surfaces on the other side, and finds? The Spiveys' smallholding – less ramshackle than Walt, or the Filbins and the Tillotsons will imagine it, more ordinary, more lived in. Brock Spivey has three barns, four fields, land bordering the open fells. The world stretches further. Over the snowline and on to Salem Turn. Gabriel's map grows, back to the fell and forward to the sea and to the line of the horizon. He goes further. He loves this thing, this movement that requires him to be alive and brave, unlike the slack-jawed boys that William is drawn to who stay together and mock the world and throw stones at the geese along the estuary and toss honeyed sarcasm at Joannie Kilner's women.

Joannie Kilner finds him one night half a mile away, beyond the Heights of Abraham, at the head of the Wellington Pit which is sunk above the houses of the town. Something disturbs her sleep and she wakes and looks in to check on them.

Only William lies asleep in the bed. She dresses and goes down to tell Walt who is on duty at the front of the hotel. She tells him that Gabriel is gone. They put their coats on and begin a search of the surrounding streets. They separate. An hour later she finds him above the town, curled asleep in his pyjamas and coat and shoes, close by the winding gear of the pit which is sunk a mile deep and then runs out beyond the town under the sea. She wakes him gently. He sits up, not surprised at where he is or that he has been found – defiantly five years old and confident and so tired. He is not upset or anxious.

'I killed the terragot,' is all he says quietly. 'We can go home now.'

The following night, Joannie Kilner sits with Gabriel, listening out, waiting. It is dark now. They grow sleepy. They sit resting against each other in the big wicker chair across from the window. There is a sound beyond the window.

'Is that another one of them coming?' she asks him.

Gabriel nods. Gabriel had asked her not to tell his Dada about the terragot. He doesn't know why. Instinct. The way his Mama kept them from Walt by burying her doubts on a hill. He fears Walt is not strong enough for doubt. Walt would, he knew, somehow come to believe that the terragots were *his fault* – that he had not imagined the world clearly enough for Gabriel. Joannie Kilner agreed reluctantly not to tell Walt why Gabriel had gone out on to the hill alone the previous night. But, in return, she wanted to know about them herself, to know how it felt to be Gabriel waiting for the terragot each night and doing battle with his five-year-old's fear alone.

'What did you do?' Joannie Kilner asks him. She means in

the silence, in the pause each night before the terragot appeared and began to stalk him.

'I prayed to Mama's angels,' Gabriel says. He means the ones who brought him. The ones who took his Mama back at the same time. The ones who helped to carve a cathedral from the rock above Laing. The ones who'll take him back when it's time.

The vibration increases slightly, then suddenly it is in the room – the terragot – circling them, as it has done each night, hunting for Gabriel – his predator. It is the light from the winding house up the hill as the winding gear brings out the second shift of miners in the cage, then sends down the night shift. The light, as it spills out men in the dark and takes in more and is fractured by the moving winder, can be seen from the window of Joannie Kilner's room high up at the back of the hotel where Gabriel and William sleep when Walt is working. The winding gear moving the cage rotates the light, sending it spinning and diving across the room in sudden, juddering bursts, first one way as the gear winds up, then the other as it unwinds to send men back down underground in several trips for the night's blasting.

'It's just the lights on the mine,' Gabriel says. 'The terragot is just the lights on the mine.'

That was all it was – all along. All that summer – that continent of a boy's childhood. The vibration that precedes and follows each nightly terragot is the winding gear bringing the cage up before it reaches the surfaces and then stops, then taking it down again as the lights go out.

All his life after that he will have fears. And, after that, Gabriel Emerson knows that all his life he must journey to conquer them, to find their source.

*

And now that Evelyn has died, giving birth to Gabriel, what of Walt Emerson?

I think it's too easy to say he loved her. He needed her.

That's different. I never loved a woman but long before I came to Laing I loved a *thing* and so I can say a little about what it's like. Needing is a tap that can't be turned off, or its allegiance switched. It's an outpouring of loss that isn't heard or seen or smelled even though it's there in the attic rooms of the third-class hotel each night while William, through in the small galley they have, warms a pan of stew or watches the kippers steam for supper and Walt readies himself for work and the wind blows at the windows from off the sea.

Walt had made no special demand about how or where Evelyn was to be buried. He wasn't bothered about the kind of service that was performed. He made only one request. Unknown to his two boys, he asked for a death mask of Evelyn to be made before she was interred in the coffin. He could think of no other way to survive the life he'd have without her than to have a representation of her face that in the darkness of his room he could run his fingers over. And so he did, and it did help him, and in quiet moments he took the mask out and he moved his hands across the smooth shape of her features, reading love like braille in the contours of her face. One day Gabriel, trespassing as he liked to do, found the mask in amongst Walt's things and picked it up and looked into the stilled face of his Mama whom he'd never seen. Then he screamed. He sobbed for half a day, until Walt explained that it wasn't his Mama but a representation of her. It was enough to stop the boy from crying, but after that Gabriel was always made uneasy by any kind of mask which reminded him of what death had done to his Mama and how the mask of her wouldn't smile or yield to him and how it seemed to hide what she really was.

Walt held Gabriel to comfort him the way he had seen Evelyn hold William – though Walt always held Gabriel more in hope than expectation. When Gabriel had been a baby and Walt had needed to comfort him, Gabriel had always cried and settled himself in his own rhythm and not, it seemed, in accord with any bidding of Walt's. Is it different, he had wondered, to have carried a child in your own belly for nigh on a year? Is it that labour, that mutually dependent need, which banishes reticence and the dance of self-consciousness. He had asked Joannie Kilner, but all she'd told him was that she imagined everything would follow love and she was sure Walt loved the child – loved both of them.

Of course, Gabriel was close to Walt physically. It was inevitably so with one parent gone, and the mother at that. But when Gabriel sat playing with Walt's big fingers, pulling them through his hands, or resting against Walt's bulk in a chair in an unthought-out moment, it was always at Gabriel's own bidding and not at Walt's.

The war is out there, of course, for the five-year-old Gabriel – surreal, marvellous, foggy on the half-believed horizon everywhere. Two bombs left over from German air raids on Barrow or Heysham drop on the town. One hits an empty bus stop under cover of darkness, the other falls on a field six months later and kills a cow outright. A siren winds itself sluggishly over Laing into a bullet sound some nights. The hotel's cellar becomes womb to two boys and their tentative father on air raid nights. The world is telescoped into a procession of newsreel images flicking on to the screen of a child's outer life. A man brings up two sons alone in the town.

The only real sign, though, that war has impinged on Laing, the only sign that matters – not bits of rationing or men somewhere on the wireless reporting battles – is the transformation of part of Henry Kyle's colony out on the fells into a detention camp for German and Italian nationals. Brock Spivey, who's serving in the Territorial Army, is employed as a guard at the camp. The authorities ship them out of the camp in batches to the colonies, to Canada and Australia. One man hanged himself, thinking they were sending him back to Germany, and Brock Spivey claimed the gramophone the man had owned, and now Brock Spivey takes the gramophone everywhere he goes in his clattering truck. When he stops anywhere, he plays records that the man had and his two dogs howl and yelp in the back of the truck and Brock Spivey stands watching the world go by with a big grin on his face.

The camp where Brock Spivey is a guard is small – smaller than the prisoner of war camp for real soldiers at Grizedale further east across the fells. Those who are interned there have been held since the summer of 1940 when a wave of concern had spread through the country about fifth columnists at large. The Women's Protection League in Laing had sent a letter to the regional commissioner, taking up the cry of some national newspapers in encouraging the Government to *Act! Act! Act!* Brock Spivey says that the camp at Henry Kyle's colony where internees are held is for spies who've all been caught, and it seems possible. One or two Laing men have, miraculously, seen the real soldiers, those real POWs, face to face in the Grizedale camp behind the wire that, equally miraculously, holds them. The foreign nationals held in the detention camp, whatever Brock Spivey says about them, must seem less impressive since they are not real soldiers. They are still the enemy, though. They still lack some essential human-ness which their custody only accentuates.

Apart from the camp for the internees, the land all about Laing is largely untouched by war. Its men are, for the most part, safe at home in reserved occupations – mining and fish-ing. The people of Laing seem to remain blessed in an orderly universe in which elsewhere it is rumoured (rumour is untrustworthy) there is chaos and rage and randomness. It makes them, so they'd believe, a chosen people. Good things (marriage, sex, wages, solidarity) happen here to men and women because of it (just as, unless their luck is bad, people everywhere think this). Here in Laing the Kyles, in an act of will, arch across the landscape in a sky of clear glass, a roof across the world, an enclosure. The whole thing is known. The whole picture. Contained by the Kyles who refract small pieces of it down into the lives of ordinary men.

On Sundays, which is the day that Gabriel's Dada doesn't work, the two boys walk with him over the black sand of the beach. They are a familiar sight. Their footsteps, side by side, leak wetness from where the moisture lies just underground. Seagulls flying low around them cry in the wind. The sand blows from the beach over the marram grass and across the town. Water blows fast over the sandbanks into the harbour where metal cranes like storks are gathered in twos and threes. The moving water is not the tide but the speed and the strength of the wind that blows white horses off the tops of the water and blows the sand as well and blows in the boys' faces and smells of kelp and sea-salt and reminds them that they are alive and necessary. They walk for miles along the beach in the wind, Gabriel making up tales out of his head, William listening, Dada listening, asking questions, watching. Gabriel's Dada has no friends in Laing except for Joannie Kilner who is in her late forties and is disappointed at how she came to find the world, and except for the girls at the hotel who mother him when they are in a suitable frame of mind. Sometimes, when his sons are asleep, when there are air raids and they are huddled together – the three of them – when he thinks no one is looking, he will watch them, study Gabriel in awe and fear of the promise of the boy, and be cowed by it. Evelyn would have known what to do. Evelyn would have known.

'I'll be sad with you today, Dada,' Gabriel will say as they walk across the wet black sand. And the three of them on Sundays throw stones into the sea. Walt has a dream of the sea that often comes back to him. He confides it once to Joannie Kilner. He's dreamed it several times. A young boy stands on the sands shouting desperately at the sea to make it go back. An older man above him on the rocks looks on. Later, the man sits awake, troubled by what he's seen. The boy sleeps soundly.

The folk of Laing give Walt advice on how to bring up sons. The Women's Protection League take a passing interest. He never asks for help. He listens patiently, though, to people talking. Quell them, they say, talking about Walt's boys to him. Shape them as you would clay. Round off the edges. Give them a backbone. Have them fear God and the Kyles. But Walt can only love them.

'What d'you do today, Gabriel?' Walt will ask if the boys have been to school.

'I said roll call to the prisoners, Dada. One has blue eyes. They're so real, Dada. Take up space. D'you understand me?'

'I understand, Gabriel.'

Walt will sit near the fire, closes his eyes a little though he isn't tired. Gabriel will help to straighten his Dada's jacket and polish his shoes one by one and set them by the fire.

'Don't leave the shoes there,' William will say, coming in to lay the table. William's toy soldiers always stand neatly in rows on the table. He packs them away in the wooden box he keeps them in. He is the kind of boy, I think, who is happiest setting out his soldiers in steady ranks, in some established pattern, ready for some war, some life, that will be met bravely but neatly.

'Don't nag so, Bubba,' Gabriel will say, though William's nagging doesn't bother him. William likes the chores. Likes the punctuation of them. William's an old woman with nothing learned. William is eight. He's too amenable, too smoothed down – an old woman nurturing by instinct and begrudging small elements of his day.

The two brothers sit on the harbour wall, on the promontory that separates the grey sand beach from the harbour where the coal boats set out for Liverpool. William seems happy in Gabriel's company, though sometimes he will wander off with the town boys, with Rolf Stent and Morton Filbin and the Tillotson boys from the miners' cottages, and will come back bruised and sullen after Rolf Stent's teasing, will leave them alone for a while and then be drawn back, as if all along it's meant to be that he'll end up with them. Gabriel is already ahead of William at school, eating knowledge, dreaming dreams. William, three years older than Gabriel, is a steady, somnolent boy, big-built like the miners' boys, and slow about the place.

'Come on, Bubba. Hurry, Bubba.'

William's not as wick as Gabriel. Not as buttery and alive. I believe by the time Gabriel was three, the older William was following him around. Loved him. Like? Like a brother. William is a born follower, a steady boy, not made of magic like Gabriel, eating his way to a satisfaction with the world. Days like this, they watch the boats go out through the small slapping sea. Their heels drum at the stones of the quayside. The sea tastes on their boys' mouths. The younger boy likes to stand on the plinth of an old sea monument which had been raised by the people of Laing. The monument is gone now but the plinth still stands. The sailor's name is still visible, carved into the stone plinth, though few people can remember why or where he sailed any more.

Sometimes Gabriel wonders about him – pictures him – this man who sailed from Laing. He wonders why men built a monument for him then let it fall. Walt has a story he tells the boys as they walk over the black sand of the beach on Sundays in their day together before Joannie Kilner's evening dance back at the third-class hotel. It didn't seem like a Walt kind of story. That's what Joannie Kilner said. It seemed, she said, more like a tale that Evelyn would have told. Perhaps it was. Perhaps that was where Walt first heard it. Perhaps he heard Evelyn tell it to her unborn child whilst William dozed with his head on her lap and the fire snapped vaguely over bent logs in the hearth. Perhaps it is Walt's way of keeping Evelyn alive for them. She must have seen the plinth. She must have known about the sailor who sailed from Laing.

'There was a sailor who had a son and who sailed to the edge of the world,' Walt would say.

'Was there, Dada?' the boys would ask.

91

And Walt would tell them that the men paid for his ship, because they hoped to become wealthy if he succeeded. Those men who paid for the ship were happy to stay safe at home. They believed in their hearts he'd fall off the edge, or else fall prey to the sea dragons who lived in the northern waters where he wanted to go on his way to China, to palaces made of gold, he said; to islands of silver, he said; to things, he said, so wonderful that dull men couldn't even imagine them.

They built the sailor a statue that used to stand on the plinth looking out from Laing. *Your* plinth, boys, Walt says – where you stand on the harbour – and one day the sailor sailed off in a fine ship built by the men of the town. They said that when he came back from the edge of the world – if he came back – they'd take their hats off to him. They said if he came back, they'd make him King of Laing.

'When did he sail, Dada? When did he sail?'

And Walt will search for the answer in the tale, search for the answer that Evelyn used to give.

'He is always sailing,' Walt will say. 'Always trying to make it home.'

And even thinking of it now, I know this to be Evelyn's tale. I know her to have told it to her unborn child, to the swell of her belly cradled in her fine hands.

Gabriel looks out to the horizon. Beyond the curve of the earth, beyond where the ships sail over mines dug under-ground which run three miles out, an hour out for the fishing boats of Laing, the sea fades into the fallen sky and a line that marks the beginning of imagining. The boy will shout across to passing boats from the harbour's edge as they chug out beyond the shelter of the land towards the open sea.

'Where are you headed?'

Men will shout back, their words lost amid the noises of the engines and the clatter of the day all around them. Gabriel watches them go, standing on the plinth by the harbour wall. Sometimes, when the boats have gone, he'll read the name which can still – just – be made out at the foot of the plinth. The name on the plinth facing the sea from Laing is Gabriel Emerson.

Maybe Evelyn knew.

Storms in Greenland; fogs that damp down even sudden sounds

They sail beyond the blue Atlantic, into the dull brown of the ice stream. It is not until they have passed John Davis's final landing place of Godthaab that they weigh anchor. They have sailed for six weeks with no sight of land and then, rounding Julianehaab, five days up the west side of Greenland. But to understand its scale, better think of them journeying six years rather than six weeks. Imagine astronauts journeying six years away from the Earth they know. Imagine the alienness of things now – and the distance from home; so, six years from home it is in Gabriel's mind.

A landing party is made up with the hope of hunting down seals around the inlet. Two days ago the crew of the *Endeavour* had fought to catch a horse whale offshore. The animal was fierce in its resistance. Even speared through the heart, it fought like a devil. Finally, it had escaped, badly wounded, leaving blood in the sea all around, and mystery that anything could fight like that.

Inland, Gabriel writes, there is the most remarkable saw-toothed mountain visible from the ships. The mountain top is ice-covered. Down in the valleys, though, there is vegetation. A river of melt-ice runs down to the shoreline, cutting through grey shale banks that crack to splinters when the men walk across them. It is early July, and they observe that even this barren edge of God's world feels the mercy of a summer. Gabriel, sat below deck aboard his own *Endeavour*, copies the words he knows Emerson to have written, though I know the sun he feels and the way he feels it are his own.

There are two row boats landed on the shore, one sent under Emerson's own command, and one under his first lieutenant on board the *Endeavour*. The row boats land on the shore and the men haul the boats in. Athol goes south down the shoreline. Emerson leads his group inland over the rise that runs down to the sea.

'We are as children,' Emerson will write in the log that will not be found for amost four hundred years. 'We take in the world about us with an innocent and an unobstructed eye, believing ourselves the first Christian men to set eyes on all of this around us, watchful for fabulous beasts or in case a second sun might rise matter-of-factly in the sky. Slabs of granite, grown over in places with smooth lichen, are laid about us. It forms the land in pressed sheets. I am indeed persuaded that this is the oldest rock in the world. Stunted birches, willows, dwarf rowans barely risen to the men's waists, have forced themselves through cracks and fissures in the rock. The man ahead turns and shouts from the next rise. We hurry up the slope to where he stands. And in truth, in all my life I never saw anything before nor will again that moves me to sombre thought as does the sight which lies awaiting me down in the next valley. And a notion comes over me that, for all our banging of drums and strutting and warring with other men, we are in the end only tenants of this earth we would win mastery over, taking with us when we go the paltry few pre-conceptions we have amassed and what little knowledge we have worked from the earth.'

The remains and scattered stones of the church lie close to an embankment where a European longhouse stands. What might have been a cow byre stands broken to its bottom stones in places. The farmland around it was once tilled. It is marked out by dandelions and cat-tails growing readily in the thin soil above the permafrost. There are no human remains, no signs of life despite the searches of the men, though there is evidence that a settlement had taken root here. Generations of men had clung to life in this place at some time in the past. Now they were unremembered. Only these bleak remains, preserved in the cold, dry air, stand testimony to them.

Clear of the farmstead they find a single gravestone. Maybe there were others. Perhaps the weather has claimed them. The one standing looks too old, in truth, too weary, to be still pre-served. They cannot read the symbols that perhaps were words for these people carved on the stone. Gabriel remembers what he once read or was told about the Vikings: that for the Norsemen who sailed the northern waters in search of territo-ries to farm, every animal, every plant, every piece of water, had a soul to fill the emptiness they had to contend with.

'If it is true,' Emerson writes, 'that the Norse Vikings came here in times lost, then I will say that the Vikings of Greenland vanished into the emptiness into which they came and settled and sometimes feared as if it stalked them in their patient, stubborn dreams, and one day it rose up and swal-lowed them. And I say that in the end only memory is a

defence against death. Plain men like these die and are forgotten. Only rich men's lives make history.'

They take off their hats at Emerson's bidding and say a
prayer for the souls of those who were buried here, whose
tombstones, even whose memories, are lost here. Somewhere
in the higher ground a fox is barking, unseen. The men walk
on, retracing their steps. Up the shoreline, a thousand yards
away, there is a commotion arising. It is the second group
from the ship. They have killed a ring seal.

The seals in the inlet swim close by the ships. They swim
sideways, propelled by the stroke of their hind flippers. Athol's
group have stumbled across a group of them on the beach.
Most of the seals had made it back into the water, out of danger, but the chasing men reached one and struck it until it lay
still.

Athol cuts it up, takes out the gall bladder as Emerson
instructs him to so that it will not explode and taint the meat,
then clears the creature's thin intestines and leaves them as
carrion on the beach, keeping the sweetmeats for the dog
onboard the *Endeavour*. They take the carcass back in one of
the row boats.

The biggest of the storms strikes them as they sail far up the
western coast of Greenland, approaching the line that marks
the territory of the Arctic.

The helmsman's fingers are by now showing early signs of
frostbite. They have begun swelling and darkening at the tips,
but the helmsman is kept at his post through days when the
wind is up and a gale is threatening. This is how Ingerman's
fingers, exposed for five days as he steers north, have become
affected.

The storm, when it comes, lasts a night and a day. Sometimes it does not look like water at all, but great green cliffs falling on them. It is only the sureness of their cause, Emerson believes, that sees them through, compels them to stay fast. The sea falling over them is so huge that it covers the ships across the poop and quarter decks. Waves striking the *Endeavour* sound like a hundred guns. At one point Ingerman is thrown from the wheelhouse. At times they doubt whether they will survive at all. The ships are separated from each other. Men pray at their posts. As the *Endeavour* rises and falls they are forced to make fast the sail, seeing only water above them and water below, and the noise so much that they can barely hear the shouts of other men beside them. Or so it all seems to Gabriel, spending nights in the Icehouse and days in the stupor of remembering.

I watch them stumbling out afterwards into the new day, big all around them. The sky has been washed clean. There is red on the horizon, clouds bunched vertically in segments like a retreating army a great distance away. Overhead, it is a cold, firm blue.

There is a different, more settled quiet outside the Icehouse than the silence which cloaks them each night as they sail. Ingerman had to shimmy halfway up the foremast during the night when some of the rigging came down on top of them. It frightened him, not knowing what it was, just hearing the crash in the dark all around and above him. Ingerman won't settle below deck. He can't sleep. He prefers to stay up in the wheelhouse they have built for him. At night the others hear him pacing the wooden deck boards above them, on lookout against the things that trouble him. Now his ears ring from the cold that feels like a sucking pressure on him in the nights above deck. The temperature in the Icehouse is down to minus ten, set to the temperature Emerson must feel at this latitude. Ingerman's fingertips are discoloured and swollen from the cold and from gripping the metal struts which, stinging, cling to the soft loose skin of his palms each time he lifts his hands from the frozen steel to find another grip. As they walk back across the colony, Ingerman holds his hands out in front of him to look at them as if examining meat.

In the Bear Pit later, Gabriel fills in his record of the night's sailing. He mentions Ingerman's climbing the foremast. Athol has calculated their position for him, based on the speeds he supposes the *Endeavour* to have made travelling north up the unknown quarter of John Davis's strait. Gabriel notes this calculated position and records it, bent over as he completes his notes. The angel sits close by in the high-backed chair, watching him, patient, seeing him busy. I am not always close enough to hear what she is saying. I imagine that Gabriel has told her about the other Emerson's voyage long ago, the one he likes to imagine in his head, the one he draws, the one he dreams about. Gabriel sees her more now; sometimes he will talk to her about the voyage. She seems reluctant, though, to talk about a broken man's obsession with some fragment of history. I know she is interested in *him*, though. I know she's asked about his life here. I know for sure that she has asked him, for example, if he has ever left the colony. She must have wondered whether in all the long years here he has seen anything of the world. Perhaps she'd wondered just what it is he saw with those crisp blue eyes. Perhaps she was looking to find a way to *see* him. Perhaps she was looking for a way in. He seemed to think about the question when she asked him whether he had ever left the colony, and paused before answering, and then drifted back into whatever he was doing beforehand. He did not say. I could have told her that long after Henry Kyle had died and security around the colony was disappearing and in theory we had ceased to be captives held against our will and the only thing that kept men here any longer was a fear of the world beyond the wall that surrounded us – Gabriel disappeared. He walked away. Twice.

Both times, he returned. Both times he resumed the life that Henry Kyle had given him.

Rose is asking why they are sometimes choosing to miss the resocialization programme. Although I myself am still careful to scurry back from my perch in the rafters of the Icehouse in order to take my place at all of Rose's sessions, the voyagers themselves do not always attend. Rose doesn't much care about what it is that they are doing. She can't imagine that it's anything worth her interest, I don't suppose, and after all we are all nominally free men. But she knows that the repeated absences of the four of them are proving a disrupting influence on the rest of us. Their disobedience is in conflict with the picture she has of herself as the good therapist, accruing steady gains.

It's certainly true that the voyage is taking its toll. I feel that Gabriel and the others are becoming detached from the rest of us. They are coming adrift. Maybe that's why for this meeting Rose has made sure that everyone attends – even those four. She told us that the meeting had to do with the fire regulations. She said it was mostly health and safety, and that therefore everyone from the dormitory had to turn up. But now we're here, we can see that in reality it's Rose's last chance to haul the four miscreants back on board before she loses them for good, perhaps to start a bigger mutiny. That's her fear.

The group sits in its circle. Men, heavy with reluctance and temazepam and torpor, on the edge of their chairs, sit planning their escape from the room. No one dares to speak. The silence is a chill pressed on them. It never reached Gabriel before the way it seems to now, a catch of breath on his heavy heart, and he is curious. Gabriel looks down at his hands. They are gripping the arms of the chair in the high room in the colony and they are white at the knuckles and the rest of us keep our heads down and Fat Rose is waiting.

Sometimes in the night Gabriel dreams that men wake him and ask him questions. They take him to a tall room. There are beams across the arched ceiling. The light is too poor to see too well. Gabriel doesn't recognize the men.

What do they ask him? It's hard to remember afterwards. They want to know what he saw. They refer to him as Emerson. As Gabriel Emerson. They're wary of him. He has knowledge that they lack. They must think he's Emerson the voyager, these men who come at night to the dormitory and take him to the big room. They bring him back and he sleeps – then, roused, he finds that he is sweating as he remembers it.

Rose is questioning Ingerman patiently. She knows there's something up. She's wooing him. She knows that some of us, at least, are not her little boys any more. Ingerman is the weak link. The least defended of them. Ingerman has rope burns on his hands and insufficient sleep. She homes in on him using the pressure of the group, and the silence, and the pause that she creates and then welds into a club to strike him with. Ingerman swings one big, clumsy-footed crossed leg back and forth in a low arc, keeping the rest of his body still. Don't say anything about the Icehouse, men, pray; don't give the game away; don't give way to her, Ingerman.

'There is so much tension in that leg,' Rose observes.

Ingerman says nothing.

'Why are you letting us down?' Rose asks him. 'How else will you be able to accomplish anything before you die other than by letting me help you prepare for a fresh start when you leave the colony?'

Rose smells blood, concentration flat to the wall like a strong light, circling him.

And suddenly Gabriel sits up and looks at her and I can see that he knows. That she's a terragot. And Gabriel's heart is going boom-de-boom.

'Only memory defends us against death,' Gabriel says.

'What?' she says.

'It was Gabriel. He said it.'

'Gabriel? Did you say something? What did you say?'

And Gabriel repeats his thought. 'Only memory defends us against death.'

'Without my help,' she says more loudly, 'what will you do? What will you *do*?'

But Rose's spell is broken, as if a small current has passed through them all with Gabriel's interruption, and Ingerman doesn't break and no one tells her about the Icehouse.

Sometimes the noise of the eskimos from the shoreline reaches them. It comes in through the curtains of fog hung all around. Gabriel hears it. Maybe the others do too, Peary and Ingerman and Athol. The noise of the eskimos somewhere beyond their sight is like the howling of wolves a distance away through the fog.

The crews had traded with the Greenland eskimos in settlements around Godthaab. Emerson himself had traded one of the eskimo tents made of animal hide for some ships' provisions, some nails and rope. Officers had eaten with two eskimos aboard the *Endeavour* and exchanged gifts. The eskimos who were encountered by Emerson had wide faces with noses flat to their faces. They were oriental in the shape of their eyes. The look of the natives encouraged the belief that the Orient, which was sought through the North-West Passage, was not so many weeks away, that maybe the eskimos could be of help in locating the Passage. But within days a state of virtual war had come to exist between the two ships' crews and the natives. Three of the eskimos were killed. They were accused by the miners on board the second ship of pilfering their tools, of taking any metal object they could lay their hands on. There had been a confrontation. The captain of the second ship, negotiating with the eskimos for the return of the miners' tools, said the eskimos had no sense of the proper way of conducting business, nor any desire to learn. They were only interested in scavenging. Before Emerson could intervene, shots were fired repeatedly over the heads of the remaining eskimos who hovered close to the shore. What Gabriel hears is the howling on shore of men at war and afraid.

Rose is annoyed because Ingerman won't do his programme any more. Because Peary has come off his aversion therapy to persuade him out into the world from under his hood. Because the gerbils and their cage have been taken. Because Athol's libido and temper are evident again and because Gabriel is wandering. She is annoyed because all four of them, she's sure, aren't taking the medication they collect each day, (mariners need clear heads and steady hearts). She is annoyed because she has no authority to do anything other than to cajole, now that they are no longer detained against their will as they were in Henry Kyle's day, now that they are simply waiting, clinging to the wreckage of Henry Kyle's liner. Because Sallis the director cannot see her. Because she is fat and losing weight but not fast enough for Sallis to notice her amid the schoolboyish excitement of his writing and his archive, and the playing up of residents in her charge isn't helping. And love, warm romantic love – the kind that sparkles – is so very far away.

The room is still.

None of us speak. Gabriel's assertion and Rose's retort leave us hanging.

In the distance, beyond the fog, beyond the lives in whose smallness we struggle, each towards an imagined light, is a distant howling like wolves or men at war and afraid.

Some of the bergs are pinnacled, church spires and Persian mosques cast adrift in the sea.

'The noise of the ice,' says the log, 'is a thing that breeds strange conceits and images in us, so that it is possible to believe the place to be vast, and void of all sensible vegetation and creatures.'

The bergs are blue-white and phosphorescent on dull days but shine when the sun turns the sky lighter through the mist. When the sun breaks clean through on to them, it lights up their massive ruined forms in refracted colours. Gabriel marvels at them, sits patiently in the Bear Pit sketching them.

The coast of Baffin Island rolls in high screes down to the water. Icebergs ride into the fjords. On the morning that they sight Baffin Island, three snow buntings hang like plovers over the boats in a sky dull as the coalsmoke sky above Laing. One of them is surely Gabriel, looking down on the voyage, seeing things from his bird's blue eye. Gabriel – feeling the wind in his face – watches the buntings soar, then sees a man below him on the quarterdeck hacking a chunk from the ice with a knife as the ship moves quietly past a berg in water cold and still as stone. Every few moments there is a sudden noise, like a pistol crack or a clapping of big hands, as the *Endeavour* glances drift-ice and clips it out of her way. There was a sound in the night when a small berg capsized on impact with the boat. The berg sank. Men's hearts settled in the fog. The *Endeavour* held firm and kept her course.

'What did they do when they got there? Your Captain Emerson and his crew?'

The angel is curious. The angel has unearthly knowledge of him, Gabriel believes. It is knowledge, he believes, that only an angel could have. The angel knows about his dreams, about the black sand dreams, about the way he wakes with the taste of salt like a kiss on his mouth.

'What will you do when you get there?'

'Get there?'

It seems to be tiring, holding the angel there in his imagination. It affects his concentration. It makes him drowsy.

'As far as the *Endeavour* sailed.'

Gabriel's mind is high over the water.

'I don't know,' he says.

Sometimes it is hard to remember what the angel knows because it is a thing that Gabriel has told her, and what is known divinely. Perhaps it puzzles him that she knows so little of the colony and so much of his secret dreams. Maybe some places are invisible to Heaven, he reasons.

'Ask Henry Kyle,' Gabriel says each time the angel asks him about the colony, about what it had been like – about its *purpose*.

It's true, of course. It's all in Henry Kyle's records. In the archives that are being catalogued for Texas. But the angel wants to hear it from Gabriel.

'Won't you talk about it even now at the end?' the angel says.

But Gabriel drifts away, back to the bergs, more and more conjoined with the mariner he'd rather be, cajoling his crew through the waters off Baffin Island, wondering if there will be time. Gabriel knows that men were wrong to tear down his monument. He has to be redeemed. By Gabriel. He sketches some more. Leaning across a little, I can see that he is sketching a rowing boat being landed by a group of men. The angel, his angel, unhurried, watches what he is doing.

'Why did he land men on Baffin Island?'

He is forced for a moment to look at her, the flawless skin on her shining against the light of the window.

'Why did he put men ashore,' she repeats, 'if he was so keen to find the Passage before the winter came?'

'They thought there was gold on Baffin. That was the deal. The ship in return for the gold he'd steer them to along the way.'

'And was there? Gold?'

'Not really gold. It looked real. The miners they took spent a week digging it out of the rocks.'

And all the while Emerson waited and bided his time and saw the summer reach its height and pass beyond the equinox, because this was the necessary price he'd had to pay.

'What was it?'

'Amphibolite,' Gabriel says.

All the books say it was amphibolite. It's true. A yellow mineral in Baffin's igneous rock. A crystalline copper sulphide that shone like gold and was set visible in the rocks above ground. Fool's gold. It was fool's gold they sent back to Laing in the expedition's second ship.

Gabriel's angel has keen eyes that show a fleeting frustration with the way he sees the world. She tries again to ask him about Henry Kyle, but Gabriel is reluctant to be drawn away from the dreams of his northern world of ice and snow in which his sailor sails.

'It's necessary,' she says. 'As part of my errand.'

'Errand?'

'You, Gabriel. You are my errand.'

He looks up at her.

'Why wouldn't you talk to me for so long when I first came?' she asks.

'I didn't see you,' Gabriel says.

'And now?'

'Now I see you.'

But when he shifts his mind away from the voyage like this, Gabriel loses focus. She talks on and on. They are not questions. Maybe it's not a time for questions any more. Her sounds, the way she strings them together – they're more like words tossed high and far into the air, like boys throw sticks to see if the far bank of a river can be reached. The words fall in between. The river runs by, ignorant of things and hard and hurrying.

The first time Gabriel left the colony, he somehow travelled to Yorkshire, maybe caught the first train he'd come across. There, Gabriel laid low for a while.

It's difficult to be sure because I was not there to keep an eye on him – to watch over him – but it seems he followed a man named Peretta, spied on him (this much was confirmed by the police), became him. Became the man he had spied on, or at least another version of him in the next district. He took the man's name. Set himself up in lodgings, claiming plausibly to have a wife and two daughters just as this man Peretta had. Found a job as a warehouseman just like the other man. He dressed like him. Learned his mannerisms. Drank like a fish just like the man whose life he assiduously reproduced, which is how things fell apart and eventually the police became involved. He was finally returned to the colony a shell of a man, all trace of the character he had played gone from him.

He drifted off again. This time it took longer, months, before he was unearthed living as a man named Brolin. All efforts to trace his movements had yielded nothing until he surfaced replicating the life of this second man. Tom Brolin was an English teacher in Lancaster in his mid-forties and in the early stages of prostate cancer. He was being treated at a Manchester clinic where Gabriel followed him and his wife week after week, learning how to be him. Three months later, Gabriel was himself registered under a local GP and diagnosed in the records which surfaced afterwards as suffering from the early onset of cancer of the prostate. It was the search for any previous medical history which led them back to the colony.

In the colony they were more cautious with him after that. They were able to turn up his medication and any semblance of a living, beating, troublesome human being faded and then vanished for some years, and there were no more episodes embarrassing to the colony's staff.

An examination five days after his last return to the colony showed that the cancer which had taken hold of Gabriel's prostate was in complete remission.

'Do you remember Bubba, Gabriel?' she says.

The river washes the sticks and words away. Somehow I can tell that he is aware that she fills space, that she has a perfume – that angels fill real space. Athol appears, standing at the door, watching him, watching her, and for the first time Gabriel realizes that he is not the only person who can see the angel. Athol can see. Athol is impressed with her, sensing flesh and promise, the smell of a young girl and not an angel. Then, as the angel and Athol talk, from some space inside of him that Gabriel has fallen into comes the word 'Brolin'.

'What's that you're saying?' Athol says.

'Who is Brolin?' Gabriel asks.

The angel, anxious, looks at him from the door where she has been making ready to leave.

'Brolin?' she says.

'And Harold Friegang. And Peretta,' Gabriel says. 'They were men, and I knew them. And Kasperl.' He looks across at Athol who is not looking at him but at the angel. And at the far end of the room, I have gone cold. The expression my mother would have used when I was little for such a feeling is that someone had just walked over my grave.

Gabriel waits for her to speak. She is real for an angel, and she has, at the end, it seems, been sent by Bubba to save him – and there is so little time.

Later, when Gabriel has drifted away again into his private world, I tell the angel that I knew Brolin. I knew the others. And so we talk, the angel and I, about Gabriel, about Laing, about the third-class hotel with no name.

8

The third-class hotel

The boy thinks of Joannie Kilner as someone who had something and has somehow lost it, the way a small part of his Dada has been lost – the way a part of his Dada below the ankle has been mislaid in Flanders. And so, as a kind of consolation, Joannie Kilner has the third-class hotel which is set back from the harbour in Laing, which has with it a resident night porter and an overdraft – and a piece of her (as Gabriel has suspected) is missing.

Gabriel wanders alone from floor to floor – through the kitchens where the first-floor women cook with big supperpots or make cakes through the night as an alternative to sleep; through the fine, sweet smells and squabbles of the third floor, and through the intervening second-floor straggle of lone, uncommunicative men with white faces, cheap suits and heavy cases. When there is no one about to talk to or no cake to beg for, Gabriel goes up another floor to Joannie Kilner's top-floor flat at the back of the hotel to sit with her for as long as she will tolerate his questions, or until it is time to wake his Dada who sleeps through the day and lives, big-eyed and patient, through the night.

William is often out, anxious not to lose his place in Rolf

Stent's gang of whooping young soldiers, nervous of the casual ruthlessness that boys with a little authority over others seem to exercise. Dull William, though, is dogged as ever. He will come back to the hotel at suppertime, resolute and uncommunicative, hungry and wishing Morton Filbin or Rolf Stent dead, or wishing he could murder toads as easily as Rolf Stent or as imaginatively as Morton Filbin. But the next day he will be off again with them and, as a result, Gabriel has the run of the hotel on his own.

'Were you happy, before?' Gabriel asks Joannie Kilner.

'Before what?' she wonders. Gabriel's presence reminds Joannie Kilner that there is a different way of seeing things.

'Before now,' Gabriel says. 'Were you happy?'

'I would say I was distracted,' she tells him.

Joannie Kilner had never run a hotel before. She took it after Stent's offer to help her organize how she'd use her suddenly deceased husband's life insurance monies. That dry as chalk voice that Stent had. That quest for impartiality, even with the wife of his dead partner.

'A piece of property,' Stent had apparently said. 'That would be better for you than just laying money up in a bank.'

Such a purchase would be a more secure investment for the years ahead. Later it turned out that he was involved in finding buyers for a number of properties whose owners he was representing. He never said as much. Never even thought it in all probability. To have thought it would have been improper, and Stent was always proper. Now that he had been appointed town clerk – the authority always appointed a prominent local lawyer to the post – propriety was even more necessary. I think that propriety was a kind of religion to Stent. And like other religions, propriety encourages fanaticism and threatens damnation if the rules are breached.

'What kind of property?'

'Anything that would serve as an investment. The firm would deal with the conveyancing, of course. A house, a piece of land, something whose value would be sure to increase.'

He said he hoped to drive her around the district to show her. He hoped, I think, to saddle her with one of the large and poorly maintained villas on the seafront heading out of Laing.

'The third-class hotel,' Joannie Kilner said quite suddenly, before Stent had a chance to name any sort of place himself.

The third-class hotel – (the people at the other two hotels in Laing always referred to it as 'the boarding house') – was a dark, narrow, four-storey building with properties close to it on either side. It was decaying slowly, tucked away out of sight of the harbour from which the town's two real hotels had views out to sea. The doors of the hotel, facing down six stone steps on to the street, were too heavy for its hinges and slammed each time someone forgot to hold them back in place. It was one of several jobs which had never seemed to get done and which, after a while, people had simply come to accept as part of the fabric of the place. The previous owners, who had run the place half their lives, had been a crabby old couple who, knowing they would eventually inherit money from various relatives, had let the hotel slide and, having failed to sell, retired and settled on the shores of Windermere. From there they had arranged for the hotel to be managed for them whilst their agents had sought unsuccessfully to off-load it. Meanwhile the couple resolutely refused to cut their asking price. Finally, leaking cash, the couple had agreed to close the place and so the hotel had been boarded up, and slowly the price came down until it was low enough for Joannie Kilner with the money coming from her husband's death to make an offer.

'It's been up for sale for years,' Stent said.

'Will my money go near enough to buying it if I can borrow the rest?'

'Why do you want a boarding house?' he asked her.

'A hotel,' she had corrected him.

'Very well. The point remains. You have never in your life been involved in such a business venture. Why that? Why now?'

I can imagine there being no curiosity in his voice as he asked her. There would be only careful modulation in the way he wished to challenge her proposal. He wouldn't, anyway, understand her answer when it came. Stent agreed, though, to find out whether they might be prepared to accept an offer, and whether she could afford to buy it. She believed she could trust him in this, and that Stent would never cheat her – not in a way any accountant could pin down. In this at least she had his measure.

Sometimes, apparently random acts create their own small momentum, as if the energy required generates a kind of magnetism that other people nearby are susceptible to. When, after some months of quiet business for the hotel which had no name, it happened that the first woman turned up needing a room for a night, with no money and no baggage and asking for shelter, it seemed natural that Joannie Kilner, with all those rooms to spare, should take the woman in. I believe that Joannie Kilner came to imagine in the end that this was what she'd meant to do all along without realizing it at the time.

'I lack the faith to go out and deal with the world any more,' she had said as her answer to Stent. 'I want the world to come to me instead.' Stent would have frowned. Stent understood only what could be touched or counted – the rest, to him, was piffle, though propriety never allowed him to say so out loud.

'What would you call the place?' Stent had said while he was seeking under mild protest to secure the place for her.

'I don't believe I'll give it a name,' she'd said. 'I think, like me, the hotel will make its passage through the world indistinctly and anonymous.'

But everyone in Laing had heard of Joannie Kilner. Joannie Kilner was a familiar story. The children had a song about her. And the woman who came for shelter, without the resources to pay, had heard of Joannie Kilner too. The woman who had arrived with no money or baggage still screams sometimes in her sleep. Gabriel often sees her as he meanders through the hotel looking for people, for wisdom, for cake. Gabriel knows her. She's been here a long time, longer than Walt. She makes fine cake. There were no bruises, no physical marks on her when she arrived unannounced all that time ago at the door. He had been too clever for that, too much of a disciple of his religion. Sometimes, when Alice Stent cries or screams in her sleep, Gabriel, hearing her, knows that she dreams of terragots. Maybe Stent believed his first wife's dreams were piffle. Maybe he was sceptical of dreams because they could not be touched or reckoned up.

It was, therefore, only in a particular sense an accident that one complete floor of Joannie Kilner's hotel gradually became a form of refuge for women, not charging rent for those who couldn't pay. And it was a similar kind of accident that another floor would develop a different specialism, though Joannie Kilner would only ever refer to it as the *third-floor business*.

The number of real customers generated by Joannie Kilner's hotel was never great. The hotel had never managed to establish a particular reputation. No one specific class of person had come to see it as their particular kind of hotel. It was not an established family guest house of a hotel; it was not a 'grand' hotel, prominent on the sea front like the Crescent. It would forever be dependent on picking up the crumbs left by the other two hotels in Laing, by single men travelling through the town on vague business which generally involved suitcases or insurance or, as one of them put it to Joannie Kilner, the chance of a good thing somewhere down the line. But as the business of the refuge on the first floor increased, so the *real* business of the hotel suffered. Fewer salesmen came to stay, not wishing to be disturbed by insomniacs, to have to share their breakfast with waifs and strays, or to be surrounded by women drawing up cooking rosters, baking cakes or taking minutes of resolutions. Those paying guests who did still come tended to be first-timers, outsiders passing through Laing for one night who frequently woke in the night startled by the sound of a woman screaming as if a death had occurred below them on the first floor, or by the sound of cooking pots being dragged across the floor in the dead of night. Joannie Kilner herself never heard any of this. She was a good sleeper. She had a different dream to the one that stalked Alice Stent.

Joannie Kilner's dream, which she dreamed often, was of herself in a fine blue dress. She recognized the dress each time she had the dream as the one she had worn as a girl at the public dance in Laing to which her mother had taken her each Sunday. The ballroom which staged the public dance each week wasn't as large or as grand as the one in the Crescent Hotel whose floor, it was reputed, was polished, buffed and sanded daily. But there was enough small magic about it for a girl who loved dancing and had taken classes. The dance was held in the small ballroom on the ground floor of the third-class hotel in Laing. The practice of holding a public dance ended when the crabby old couple, whose passion in life had been ballroom dancing, had retired to Windermere. Not many people in Laing even remembered that the hotel had once held a public dance each Sunday evening – let alone that it had been held in the now down-at-heel third-class hotel being run by Joannie Kilner.

There was a puzzle about Joannie Kilner's dream. Each time she dreamed the dream, although she was always dressed immaculately and wore her proper dancing shoes and knew the steps and arrived on time, she was somehow never able to dance. Something was preventing her. And then, for no apparent reason, the music played by the orchestra in her dream began to wind down like a tired gramophone record, slower and slower, until she could bear the sound no longer and hurried from the ballroom. And in the dream she never knew why. Before another week was through she would have had the same dream again, as if her whole life comprised the same single repeated obsession to which she returned over and over and to which all else yielded.

The guests who stayed on in the third-class hotel by and large didn't pay anything. They were women who were there as Joannie Kilner's guests, having been offered the kind of asylum that an underbooked and unnamed hotel may offer. It was inevitable that the bills would mount. There was no reserve of capital for her to fall back on. It seemed that Stent was right about her lack of business acumen. Finally, Joannie Kilner was forced to announce to her regular (mostly non-paying) guests that she would have to do something. She said she might have to consider closing down the hotel, maybe for the winter. Maybe she would just open as a summer hotel. It saddened her greatly, she said, but it was hard, business being so bad, to see an alternative. No one said much.

Later, one of the non-paying guests came to see her privately. She had a proposal for Joannie Kilner to consider. She said she knew of a way in which she herself would be able to pay a rent to Joannie Kilner. The girl came to ask if she could have the use of a room on a different floor for an hour or two each night, perhaps on the quiet third floor, which didn't often have bookings as there was only one bathroom on the whole floor and all the rooms were double or family rooms and not many families or couples booked into the hotel. If she could have use of a room, just for an hour or two, she'd be able to pay some kind of rent to Joannie Kilner from the extra that the men would pay her for sex in a good room in a clean hotel, and that could help to keep the hotel open all year round.

Her name was Emily. She was a short, squat girl. She had a pleasant, olive colouring to her good skin which made up, to a degree, for her plainness. She had an indent in her top lip, as if the two halves had once been press-studded into place but now had parted. She said she knew one or two other girls who would like to do the same if they were allowed. Some were already at the hotel, using the first-floor refuge. Others had once been in and had moved on. They were girls with children, with no husbands, or with husbands who drank; girls who risked walking off with a man to find some quiet place around the harbour; girls who went off in a motor car with one of the weekend guests of the Kyles or with one of the Needs Committee out along the estuary road to conduct their business; girls who would be safer coming to Joannie Kilner's hotel to use a room on the third floor for half an hour and get a properly reckoned return and pay Joannie Kilner a percentage of the room fee if it helped to keep the place going.

'What sort of return?' Joannie Kilner had asked.

'The brass. The money,' Emily had explained. 'The going rate.'

'And you *want* to do that?' Joannie Kilner asked. She meant the sex.

'No. I want to stay *here*,' the girl said, laying the emphasis carefully. 'And I can charge more doing it here, in a proper room, than out on the harbour. And it'll be safer. And there's less chance of getting arrested and getting harried by the Women's Protection League whose husbands are the ones who make up half the trade.'

'How long will you carry on doing this?' Joannie Kilner asked her. She meant the sex again.

'Until I'm free of it,' she said. 'Until I've made enough not to do it. It's not forever. It's until I can get out of Laing. It's a means to an end.'

That is how Joannie Kilner later explained it. It was a means to an end. And so they came, gradually, suspiciously (because they all knew Joannie Kilner's story), a dozen of them in total, perhaps, Emily's friends most of whom, like her, had come from the Heights of Abraham, taking up their business on the third floor. Some were nice; some were hard as nails; some were as bleak and difficult to fathom as a Laing fog. All

119

were content to have the relative safety of Joannie Kilner's hotel in which to operate in the evenings. Emily herself had once had a run-in at the back of the town where she'd gone with Sam Wormold, an acquaintance of Stent's on the Needs Committee. She and Wormold had argued over how much he owed. For her time, he'd left her an alternative return. He'd left it with a small knife. He'd left it carved into her top lip. And so all of them were grateful for the safety which was offered to them through the use of Joannie Kilner's hotel.

Which is how Joannie Kilner came to need a night porter for her third-class hotel, with a refuge for a first floor and with the third-floor activities being conducted by Emily and her friends, and the salesmen and the one-nighters sandwiched unknowingly (until Alice Stent's screams broke the air) in between them both. Joannie Kilner needed a night porter to keep an eye on things in the evening, to direct people (usually men) around, to keep the few legitimate guests separate from the first-floor refuge and the third-floor business. Beyond these three floors, of course, Walt had the rooms right at the top, under the roof. That left the ground floor: the kitchen (filled with the smell of ginger and cinnamon from the cakes), the lobby (with the clumping Walt holding sway resolutely and good-naturedly through the long and vaguely busy nights), and the ballroom.

At the outset, Joannie Kilner had worried about whether they would mix, about whether such a cocktail of waifs and strays would work. In truth there was a kind of stand-off between the first and third floors. There were some things both floors had in common, of course. The main one, they agreed, was that generally it was men who stood between them and the world they'd wish for. But it was only when

120

Joannie Kilner resurrected the tradition by which, each Sunday, the hotel put on a public dance in the ballroom that the lines of demarcation between first floor and third floor were broken. Then, the two sets of women met simply as residents of Joannie Kilner's hotel with no other labels attached to them. The refuge women felt safe because there were rarely any men around – just Walt on duty (the consoling smack of his fitted shoe on the wooden floors about the place) and the boy Gabriel and the odd nervous and outnumbered salesman from the second floor – and the third-floor girls felt relaxed and languorous because they weren't on duty yet and this was time off before business generally began in earnest some time after nine o'clock.

In Joannie Kilner's childhood, of course, there'd been Sunday dances here. She'd worn the blue dress the first time she'd actually been old enough to take the floor and take part herself in the act of dancing rather than merely watching from the side. The dress had been let out by then to its full hem length. She had danced with several handsome men, and once with a young and nervous Henry Kyle when he was a new officer who had recently been commissioned on his nineteenth birthday in the Cumberland and Westmorlands and who'd come to town with friends to celebrate. She really had danced with such men, and with a young Henry Kyle. It was only in her dream that she was never able to dance. It was only in the dream she had that the orchestra wound down and that she fled, running, until the dream was over.

9

Passing Baffin

The sea and the sky and the land are a milky whole, as if they dream it. The sea mist is an animal. The icing-up is the deposit left over from its breathing. It is a hard, grey ice a millimetre thick. It is bitter enough in the rafters where I am wrapped heavily against the cold, but my discomfort is nothing to that which claws at the voyagers forty feet down below me where the refrigeration unit blasts freezing air at pace across the length of the Icehouse.

The rigging drips with milky lines of the ice left by the breath of the animal, of the sly, invisible terragot which stalks them (which this time is no simple light, no dream to be flailed at). The terragot says they are not men at all. It says they should return to their smaller lives. It says they will not conclude the voyage just as Gabriel Emerson never concluded it. The terragot says it has their measure, says they will turn tail and run.

The damp generated by the ice in the air is incessant now. It has a weight to it. Since on the voyage they use only what they have taken with them from the start, the bits of spare clothing they have hang suspended from the beams in an effort to dry them out. Then the dampness in them freezes at night so that the ice has to be beaten from them before they can be used. The gerbils have perished in the cold. Ingerman has a rash on his legs and his back which Athol says is from his damp clothes and the way they freeze to him at night when he is pacing the decks above them.

They are far beyond the furthest point reached by John Davis on any of his voyages. Baffin sailed further north (to seventy-nine degrees) but stayed hugging the western shore of Greenland. Long before now Hudson's crew, fearful less of what lay ahead than of what their imaginations made of it, had pitched their leader overboard and made a mad, desperate scramble for home, reduced in the end to eating candlewax and birdskins before they made it back to Europe. Every day now, every hour, is a new creation as they sail west over the top of Baffin Island – over the world – in search of the Passage. Every day is an invention, is a feat of believing.

Cliffs rise six hundred feet out of the Sound through which they sail. The *Endeavour* pushes by through shards of field ice. The cliffs are lined white with strips of hardened snow and grey with shale. The next day, the land – as if willed to do so in an idle moment by these few first men – rises more gently through a series of ridges. Wild, random flowers – in immediate and unexpected colour, reds, yellows – grow low in the earth; a stream cuts through grey gravel. Cliffs set further back rise to a flat plateau from which (Gabriel watching over them knows) land to the north is visible when the fog lifts for an hour or sinks and sets below the level of the summit of land.

Daylight is with them constantly now as they sail. The lights in the Icehouse stay on through each night. There are no days and no nights for Gabriel to separate; there is only a dull and incessant sheen of whiteness reflected on them which makes sleep difficult but navigation a straightforward matter for Ingerman at the helm. And then in the new day the morning outside the Icehouse fills out as if the sun, by some feat of imagination, has begun to rise again without ever sinking, without allowing the previous day to fold and die so that they merge one into the other in a single, unbroken, dizzying thread of light.

The death on board ship of the dog is reported as August begins. Athol suspects some form of poisoning from the offal of the seal they caught recently. Already, the flowers which were evident a week ago growing on land have gone. Six inches into the ground, as they dig to bury the dog, the cement-like hardness of the permafrost takes hold. They try to break the ground with two pickaxes left over from the miners who set sail for home a month ago, but they cannot. They settle for constructing a shallow pit of earth from the top soil which is the only part that can be dug, and they form a mound with it to bury the animal. Later in the day, back on board the *Endeavour* as they prepare to set sail, they see a bear on a raise of land jutting out into the Sound near to the position of the buried dog. Maybe the bear has smelled the dog. Athol fires two shots at the creature from the deck rail of the *Endeavour* – brilliant cracks of sound in the wet and heavy air – but the bear holds its ground, and stands, and sees the boat pass.

They change course on the last day of August. The log records that they have rounded an extensive promontory of land and have found open water to the south, a wide channel with the movement of water suggesting that this is the route of the passage leading to a wider tidal sea. They turn south. They give thanks. They hold a small celebration with a bottle of wine Athol has held in store. They drink on deck, watch the tide slide by. They give name to this stretch of water – Gabriel Sound. It will be two hundred years before the water is found and named afresh. Then, when men finally reach this place once more, it will be rechristened McLintock Sound. This time it will be reported back and the name will stay.

It is now that they first hear the song. Like a finger tracing the line of a glass over the mountains, a hollow vibrant song, sweet, like death, like a foretaste of death, like an angel's song – the song of the beluga. They gather in small groups off the ship, these unearthly white whales, cousin to the narwhal that they saw the eskimos hunt around Davis Strait, sleek under the water then breaking the surface and breathing with a sound like air forced through long, narrow pipes when they are close to the boat. Gabriel listens on deck to the sound of the belugas. The final letter found on the voyager, to his son, will make reference to the belugas, to their sound, to their white, miraculous bodies, to the way they accompany the *Endeavour* through the Sound. The animals somehow know the shifting patterns of the world around them, somehow survive under the ice, having the faith and instinct that, somewhere beyond the deep passage of water they have chosen, will be a hole at the surface to breathe in time to stay alive, and one to follow that, on and on, to allow them to press on in this, the most unbelievable of kingdoms. It is a kingdom, Emerson writes to his patient, waiting son back in Laing, that a man might dream in a long sleep that he would never awake from. And the final sound he would hear? The song of the white beluga coming from the deep to breathe and to sing and then to dive again.

Once in a handful of years the belugas are trapped in a *savs-sat* – an eskimo name. Once in a handful of years, the act of faith men call judgement defeats them. While they are feeding deep in some fjord, the calm, narrow mouth of the fjord begins to freeze over. The ice-bridge across the opening holds, then expands inwards. Eventually, it expands too far for the beluga to swim under the surface ice in a single breath. The whales are crowded into a smaller and smaller space of water, between the sea ice and the shorefast ice. Then their song deserts them and they wail and cry like stricken calves, crashing from the water through the shrinking ice holes in turns in search of air, craving a fracturing of the ice, or death.

Each day now Gabriel's task is to force the ice clear of the boat, to imagine that the *Endeavour* could have sailed clean through the sea of ice in the Sound. Each morning they break clear the riggings, all the ropes and lines singed with films of ice breathed on them by the terragot with its sour-breathed ill-will, its mockery. Sometimes the sea about them turns heavy and slow to mush, as if it were setting already. Then the path of the boat gets clogged by this field ice swelling up around them. They press on, in the knowledge that now the boat is sailing south, away from the pole, waiting for sight of the channel opening out again, waiting for the ice like fields of white ash to thin and for water once again to slip noiselessly past the hull and to cease rubbing and grinding the steel plates. The tiny ship forces south through the Passage. It is, Emerson says to his son, like threading the eye of a needle.

Gabriel's mind can see it.

Gabriel's heart can believe it.

But the heart is a tremulous thing – as promissory and indistinct as the song of the belugas who dare to live between long breaths under the moving ice.

The skies are wide as plains. They meet the sea where the mist like smoke lifts clear of the water. The water thickens, like oil, fibrous and slopping at the mouth of the boat. It struggles to roll. The water, mucid, films over and folds, films and folds and compacts into mush that swills about the moving vessel. It holds together in pieces, in plates, in rims of frazil ice, in floes, in fields of white ash that are pushed and harvested by the boat. The ice compacts and glazes in the water. The pack ice forms into walls a foot deep lying unstable and unconsolidated. Gabriel's *Endeavour* forces on, the big iceman Athol standing by, the helmsman Ingerman and the lookout Peary straining for sight of the end of the Sound, the start of the open sea and safety and the land of Anian.

The sun drops late in the day. Night creeps up on them. It is still weak and easily vanquished. It is less sturdy than the ice. But the night is alive again. Each hour is a battle to seek open water. Some nights the Sound, the world, is motionless.

They keep the mainsail set so they can utilize any breath of wind. They stay ready for any sudden chance to move when the ice breaks and gives way to the ship. Athol and Ingerman aim blows at the ice. They hack and stab to keep their single small channel of water open. Peary organizes an occasional charge of gunpowder when the plates of ice pack too hard and will not give way to the blows of spades and the miners' axes. Sometimes they are held in for an hour, held in one spot despite the wind cradled in the sail, and the efforts to free themselves from these temporary pauses become desperate and savage. They must keep clear – Gabriel must believe it or his doubts will harden and be frozen by the breath of the terragot and the ship will hold fast, and still there is no sighting yet of the Anian Strait that will see them through safely to the sea and Cathay. They work frantically through the night, breaking the boat free. Athol and Ingerman fire blow after blow at the encroaching ice walls forming low in the water. But no sooner are they cut free than the plates of ice are rewelded together around the ship, and their striking out at the ice must begin all over again from the bow of the ship outwards to the slim channel of water ahead. In the end, the rudder freezes fast. In the end, the ice turns hard and stills. All the world is composed of one thing and one thing alone, and that one thing holds them fast. The mainsail tugs and catches at the wind, useless and mocking. They are stuck fast.

The wind dies. The ice is endless now. There is nothing to see and the nothing is set in the profoundest silence. The days grow shorter and the land and the sea (which is no longer sea at all) has taken them in. Each night the sun blazes down in a cold far fire and sinks and they have not moved and the ice has not broken yet. Now they must wait and pray. Now they must battle with their fears – the terragots. Dare they walk? Dare they leave the ship? Dare they set out, like belugas do under the ice, having a faith that what is left can be traversed?

Stillness can be the worst of all conditions, demanding, in the way that it hangs and overpowers the human heart, that men listen to their fears. Numbing their ability to act, their knowledge of how that first step might be taken. It is the fear of losing life, of missing love (small fissures, pockets, like water to a thirsty man), of being absent from the world, of ceasing to be.

Emerson still writes his letter of love. What would a man write to the son he has abandoned for this, trapped at the end of the world, unable to go back, fearful yet of what going forward might mean? What message would he send? What act of consolation could he make? What to do?

After that last night of frenzy, smashing clear the ship and seeing the ice take hold again and again, stronger, more certainly, the ship wedged in ice, they lie, dreamy with exhaustion, on the deck. Panting like dogs. Their arms and legs burned, a lead-heavy, desultory pain. It did not help them. The one sound left, as they come and sit in the boat each night now and wait, is the straining of the ice pressing, when it shifts, against the boat. Maybe it's the refrigeration motors. Now, in the small, growing Arctic nights, the terragots hover.

Have they the heart to go on?

Are they men?

They wait. Each night in the Icehouse, they wait.

The world has ceased turning.

How far to Anian?

10

The dance alone

During the week, in the hotel that Joannie Kilner owns, the ballroom lies dark and cavernous, an obstacle around which people must skirt to reach the stairs to the first floor or to reach the kitchens at the back. On Sundays, Joannie Kilner pays for a five-man orchestra to come and play on the box stage at the front of the ballroom and she has the room lit with a revolving ball-mirror fitted to the ceiling so that the light spills across the darkened floor.

Of course, it is never quite the same as it had once been, at least not in the mind's eye of Joannie Kilner. And of course no one comes to the dance from the town as people had done in her youth. No one with position. No one who *means* anything in Laing. People know about Joannie Kilner and what she's been up to. And they know about the third-class hotel.

Those at the dance now are women from the refuge on the floor above the ballroom, the friends of Emily who use the hotel with Joannie Kilner's consent to ply their trade of sex, and the few salesmen passing through Laing who are, out of ignorance, staying at the hotel. Later, of course, there will also be the former internees led by Jacob Brolin.

Sometimes, oddly selected couples will dance for a while.

130

More often the floor will be empty while the small five-piece orchestra plays. Joannie Kilner will appear part-way through the evening and watch from a side table. She will thank the orchestra. She will take the floor and she will dance a single dance alone on the hard-shined wood under the splints of light. And after the night of the dance the ballroom will be left in darkness for another week, unused, while people navigate around it and the third-class hotel's other business goes on.

And the thing that Joannie Kilner lost? The part of her?

Her virginity.

To a man young enough not to know better than to force it, and well-connected enough to avoid the consequences. It was Stent who tidied things up. It was Stent who, seeking to mediate, persuaded the girl's parents as quietly as was Stent's way that there really was insufficient evidence for her to pursue the case of rape in court as she herself had hoped. So instead, in the aftermath of the affair, Joannie Kilner had married the solicitor who'd been involved, an older man who before long would inherit Stent as a partner, a man as dry as Stent but taller and with an interest in fishing. It was Stent who, three months after the incident, was asked to help again and arranged for Sam Wormold from the Needs Committee, a medical man, to locate someone he knew would see to the abortion.

In the two days that the local police searched for it (before they had been persuaded that the whole thing had been a mis-understanding), there had been no sign of the blue dress she was wearing.

Walt Emerson did not realize at first what the business of the third floor was; that the girls, who seldom seemed to *live* in the rooms on the floor below him and who were restlessly nocturnal – even more so than those of the first floor – sold sex; that the men who entered the hotel in the evening through the old-fashioned door that opened out from the hotel on to the street were their clients. These men arrived through the evening to the sound of the huge door slamming on its weak hinge. They tended to be men who would forget about the door and who would let it slam. It was the punctuation of the night into the early hours. Brock Spivey was the worst culprit. He could never remember to hold the door as it fell back into place, though he always apologized to Walt for it.

'Shit, Walt, I'm sorry,' he'd say. 'I'm just up to see the girls.'

Brock Spivey tended to come on a Friday. Usually it was late on. Usually he was drunk. His dogs would be yelping distantly in the back of his truck parked in the alley at the back of the hotel. He would arrive noisy and would leave remorseful.

'Shit, Walt, I'm a shit. I'm a terrible shit to that girl of mine.' But Walt never understood what he meant.

Walt always meant to repair the door and its hinge which had been weakened by its sheer weight and size and usage over the years, but he never did. It seemed indicative of how Walt always floated on the edge of things. It seemed to demonstrate how Walt was never wholly part of the lives lived out around him – how he was never quite *there*. He was as much on the edge of Gabriel's life as he was on that of the hotel's. He could no more get around to repairing the hotel door than he could get around to sharing what he felt for Gabriel with the boy himself. It's what it reminded me of each time I heard the door swing open then slam shut.

All this time, I think, Walt truly didn't realize what the

third floor was about. It was William who first said it. William had been beaten up in a fight at school. Gabriel was still very young at the time, and was being looked after during the day by Joannie Kilner and by Emily, the youngest of the girls who moved in and out of the hotel like evening fireflies but who liked to help with Gabriel during the day whilst Walt slept. Mrs Ingol, the Parish School reception teacher, had brought William home. It was her first day back at school. She'd been off for a while after the news of her son's death in the war. She wouldn't go into the hotel. She left him at the door. Gabriel afterwards had asked Joannie Kilner why Mrs Ingol wouldn't come in. Joannie Kilner said it was because her son had died and it had made her sad and angry about things. William had returned with bruising and a bloodied face. Walt asked him what had happened. William said that Rolf Stent had made fun of him. There'd been a fight. Walt asked why. At first William wouldn't say. Walt asked again. It turned out it was because they'd said William lived in a whorehouse. Because William Emerson's Dada worked in a whorehouse.

'You mean you didn't know, pet?' Joannie Kilner said when he told her. 'What did you think all the toing and froing on the third floor was?'

'I thought they were,' and Walt thought about it, '. . . restless.'

'What'll you do now?' Emily asked. Emily was twenty-two, though of course she looked much older. She was not very pretty, Walt thought, but she treated him well. She didn't tease him as some of the other girls did. If she did, I never saw it when I was there.

'How do you mean?' Walt said.

'Well, I like looking after your boys when it's needed.

133

They're the only things I love. I mean, Joannie's nice. Joannie's hotel saved me. But she's hardened in the middle. Something's made her hard. It makes me feel, you know, proper, when your boys are around. Like I belong to something. Like I'm necessary. Are you going to take the boys away, now?'

'Why should I do that?' Walt asked.

'I thought. Maybe . . . I don't know.'

'Me neither,' Walt said.

'Does anyone say anything to you about Emily and the others?' Walt will ask Gabriel when the boy has been at school for a while. By then Gabriel will be a frequent visitor to the third floor. The girls won't mind. He will sit amid the scents of sex like a small buddha while each man in turn arrives and chooses a girl and disappears with her down the corridor. Gabriel's presence will be a restraint on the men who come, a damper on their fecklessness, on the need that drives them here. He will calm men. He will come to know more at the age of six from simple observation than Walt ever will about the mechanics of how a diaphragm is fitted, how women can throw a switch to occupy a different and temporary mood, how to fix hair curlers, how to swear, and how crying (when it is necessary) can be a fine thing.

'Sometimes,' Gabriel will say. 'Sometimes they say things.'

'What do they say?' Walt will ask.

'They say I live in a whorehouse where Hun spies come to fuck,' Gabriel will say.

'What do you say?' Walt will ask him.

'I say Walter Friegang has a soldier's knife,' Gabriel will say. 'I say that Emily's the prettiest girl in Laing.'

*

War is enacted with vigour by Morton Filbin and Joseph Tillotson and by Rolf Stent with his father's gun holster strapped to his waist. It is war as they imagine it – two lines of men, bang bang, then break for dinner. William has to play the enemy. When they capture him, they make him roll in nettles pretending he's been shot, and eat grass in the prison camp they contrive for him. Afterwards they follow William, thirsty, grazed, into the big, cool kitchen of the hotel. Joannie Kilner will pour them lemonade and they gasp as they drink fast. They are polite and ferocious as she watches them proprietorially from a high stool.

'My brother says the Germans have tunnels under the sea,' Joseph Tillotson says.

'How does he know?' Rolf Stent says. 'He's an imbecile.'

'I'll tell him that. He's older than you is our Billy. He'll smack you one.'

'I'm not afraid of your Billy.'

'He will, you know.'

'Then my father will sue him, and then what will he do in court?'

Joseph shrugs. They see less of Joseph's brother Billy now. He's fourteen. He's walking out with a girl from the next street. Rolf Stent and the gang whistle at them from a safe distance. Billy Tillotson grins foolishly at them.

'They'll come over when our soldiers are over there and rape people's sisters.'

'Who will?'

'The Germans.'

'What's rape?' Morton Filbin asks.

'It's like arguing,' Rolf Stent tells him. 'It's disputes.'

'I haven't got a sister.'

135

'Your Mam then.'

'Not your Mam. Nobody'd dare say anything to your Mam.'

'My Mam says we daren't talk to the internees. They're spies. That's why they got arrested first of all. We might give stuff away for when the Germans come.'

A work party from the detention camp is being bussed into Laing now. The men are brought in to work around the harbour. Those in the work party are volunteers from the camp. They are category 'B' internees, neither *enemy* nor *friendly* aliens but somewhere in between. They are content to work in return for a change of scene, a glimpse of the sea and of the real world.

Gabriel, on the harbour wall, watches them return on the first day of their labour at the harbour, heading past towards the truck that has brought them down into Laing and will take them back to the camp. Gulls wheel and bicker overhead. Weak sunshine spills down on the town. Laing smells of industry and of the sea. The internees near him, one by one, are in line. Not marching, just walking. They are not soldiers.

'Gabriel Emerson!' the boy calls out, saluting as the line goes by him.

'Jacob Brolin!' The first man, older than the others, with thinning hair, nods as he gives his name, serious, enjoying, it seems, the brief passing game with the child. To see a child is uplifting enough for Brolin.

'Gabriel Emerson!'

'Walter Friegang.' Friegang is a short man, overweight, red-faced. Far from a soldier.

'Gabriel Emerson!'

'Donato Peretta.' Peretta is younger, handsome. Italian. He winks at the boy.

'Gabriel Emerson!'

And on and on.

At the back is the youth, Kasperl, who juggles four balls the size of large eggs. They are pieces of clay which have been shaped and baked and then painted and polished with patience into perfect round shiny spheres. Kasperl doesn't seem to notice Gabriel, or the town around him, or his countrymen walking their poor men's march in front of him through Laing; only his four shiny painted clay balls which he is always juggling – sometimes in loops, sometimes in columns of balls, sometimes cascades with balls running narrow and wide, narrow and wide, but always, like magic, falling back down into his big hands whenever Gabriel sees him. When Rolf Stent's gang see Kasperl they dance behind him in the line.

'He's like a question mark,' Joseph Tillotson says.

'He's like a coat-hanger,' Morton Filbin says.

'He's like an idiot,' Rolf Stent says.

Representatives from the Women's Protection League, led by Stent's second wife (a Tillotson before she was married, fatter and plainer now and cheated about what life has done so casually to her), have protested about them being let out into Laing in this way. Surely they represent a danger to Laing, the League says. Surely our own children deserve better protection than to have men like this free to roam around our town. These people are not like us; the Kyles oughtn't to let them in. But the mines' management is under instruction from the Kyles to use all available manpower to help get the coal moved from the pit to the harbour and away to Liverpool for the war effort, to fulfil their production contract with the authorities.

And so the need for labour is paramount. The internees are not real soldiers, and they are under escort at all times. At night they are taken back to the camp. And so they work on like this through the winter and the spring.

Women watching the internees take pleasure in telling them about the bombing of German cities. They tell them the RAF is busy bombing Germany every night.

'It's your fault,' they say, 'you started it. Men like you started the war.'

Friegang asks about Leipzig. He has family there. Someone says Leipzig's been bombed to pieces. Brolin tells him not to worry, that no one really knows.

'It's all right for you,' Friegang says to Brolin. 'They are bound to bomb Leipzig. You're all right. You're from Dresden. Who's going to bomb Dresden?'

One day a woman spits in Kasperl's face. Kasperl is still young. What does he understand? He looks up in astonishment from the back of the line of men and drops his juggling balls. Kasperl sees the woman. It's the Parish School teacher, Mrs Ingol. He sees the bereavement in her face channelled hard into anger. Her son was a clerk working for the Borough Treasurer's Department. He died in North Africa. She has only her mother who lives with her left. They bicker each night across the tea table because her mother's legs don't work and she wants to be taken here and there and they quarrel about it. Everyone in Laing knows about Mrs Ingol and her mother. Kasperl wipes the spit from his boy's face. He picks up the four balls from the ground and wipes them clean, but he does not juggle for the rest of the day.

When the truck brings the internees into work each day, the people of Laing stop what they are doing and watch them go past, rest their tools, let conversations hang still momentarily, eye the trailer lorry with the men in the back. There is quiet as the lorry drives through to the harbour, then afterwards the townspeople take up their lives again, knowing for sure in their own minds how the world is divided between good and evil, into purpose and chaos; how some things are bread and others are brick.

Every day now, after school is over, Gabriel does his roll call with the internees as they finish for the day and trek back to the truck that will take them from Laing, imagining all the while, as children do, that day follows day follows day without ending or beginning until eventually the circle is complete and men begin again and Gabriel will, each time, take his place and run his roll call with Friegang and Brolin and the others by the harbour wall of Laing with a little sunshine above and the war being won and the world running true to course and familiar as a shore tide.

This is how Gabriel sees it. And childhood will always be there as a sheet-anchor and will be the way in which, no matter what has transpired before, everyone on Sundays seems to dance – lost women, and men selling shoeshine from hard cases, and whores, and exiles from a war that has just passed, and grievances and sins are put aside in a ballroom over a hard, wood-shined floor flecked with splinted, turning light and nearsighted dreams and longings.

Unlike the real POWs at Grizedale thirty miles away, who will remain in custody until the war is over, the internees held in a section of Henry Kyle's colony are gradually released from detention. A policy of shipping some of them abroad to the colonies had reduced the numbers greatly early in the war. Then, those classed as enemy aliens (those who were category 'A' internees) are moved to a camp on the Isle of Man. Finally, there is the release of 'C' category detainees (friendly aliens) and, in dribs and drabs, those in the 'B' category from 1941. The internees in the work party who have been bussed into Laing are in this category.

Some of them, like Friegang, had lived and worked in England for many years before the war and their internment, and they are happy to stay. Friegang hopes that the regulations for former internees will soon lapse, that other jobs will become available, office jobs, that the war will go away, that the old life he had will come back. Friegang had enjoyed his time in the camp, early on at least. He was smart and official-looking, and the Camp Commandant made him Hut Captain. He was also happy to mill around with the few real Nazi supporters in the camp, to make the salutes and sing the songs even though he wasn't really a Nazi, he was just an administrative clerk working for a company whose office had been in Marylebone and whose little flat had been in Islington. But Peretta and a couple of former gravediggers from Hamburg who took exception to Friegang had organized a campaign of non-cooperation against the orders he kept giving. They protested against the rotas for this and that which he kept sticking up in the hut, and about the rules for sluicing the showers and folding the bedding, and about the way the hut jobs were divided, and in the end no one listened to him barking out his little orders. After that he drifted away from the small and noisy Nazi contingent in the camp, or maybe they had shut him out themselves, and he had sulked a lot and played with the Prussian army knife he kept for show.

Peretta, who had organized the coup in the hut against

Friegang, is one of the Italians from the camp. Peretta came to Scotland from Italy when he was a boy of twelve. His family ran an ice-cream business in Glasgow. All of them were interned when Italy entered the war. Peretta is young, but still older than Kasperl. He is handsome and a little sure of himself. In the camp he is popular, always taking up causes, always useful because of the English he speaks (a fixed-together, workaday Italian English, not the careful, educated language of Brolin).

As for Kasperl, he had been part of a circus. He is a clown, a real clown, and a fine juggler, part of a small travelling circus all of whom had been interned at the camp, though only Kasperl is left now. The Circus Prenzlau toured Holland and France and the south of England – Sussex and the hop field towns of Kent – through the summers of the twenties and thirties. For many years, Circus Prenzlau had not toured Germany so much. German people, especially in the provinces, did not like circuses as much as the Dutch or especially the English. They were a famous sight at summer fairs on the greens of southern England. They were a small circus and they travelled together in six horse-pulled caravans. The first caravan was Heimy's. He ran the circus. Heimy was not quite a dwarf, though everyone said he was. He loved Mozart. He loved vodka. He loved his dog, a small, whitish mongrel, with only three legs and a bad habit of letting off wind. The dog had been trained to perform as one of the acts because Heimy could not afford anything more exotic than dwarfs and jugglers and three-legged dogs.

Everywhere the Circus Prenzlau toured, Heimy took his wind-up gramophone and each night, when the circus had finished its performance, he played music and drank vodka

141

and talked loudly to his dog about the state of the Weimar Republic and the 'fucking Nazi pansy boys' as he insisted on calling them. His favourite trick was to hang down from a bar to make himself taller. He'd hang there trying to stretch an extra inch from his small torso, ranting about the Nazis, hectoring the others over by the camp fire while the dog farted as it snoozed and Kasperl sat running up a cascade of six small balls in his big hands.

After the Nazis came to power, Heimy found himself arrested and put in a work camp. He was, the new authorities said, a recidivist. The rest of the circus carried on as best it could. When he was released after a year, Heimy made the decision to move Circus Prenzlau permanently to England where it was most popular. England was where good money could be made during the summer. They stayed in an old white oast house in a village by a river that ran through flat fields into the cathedral town of Canterbury, and they never went back. They became a continental circus based permanently in England, doing a little street theatre in the winter months around the narrow streets of Canterbury, the dog dancing on its three legs to the music of Heimy's wind-up gramophone in the square by the Cathedral Gate, and odd-jobbing on the orchard farms around the town. Then every Easter, Circus Prenzlau set out touring in their six canvas-roofed caravans.

Kasperl can juggle anything. He practises continually in Laing, as if he's hoping that one day the Circus Prenzlau will pass by on the road going over the fells and he'll rejoin them. But they never come. They never will. All the circus folk were interned together. They were arrested one night after a performance. One by one they were all released until only Heimy and Kasperl were left in the camp. Kasperl's problem is that the other performers were classified as category 'C', but Kasperl was given a 'B'. Perhaps it was his appearance that earned him the distinction. Whatever the reason, with all of them gone – including Heimy now – Kasperl, the youth, the juggler, the idiot, has come to be dependant on Brolin. Kasperl's English is poor and Brolin, who helped teach classes in the camp to pass the days, has been teaching Kasperl. Kasperl is not a realist. He is a dreamer. His head is in the clouds. He needs looking after, and it is Brolin who looks after him.

Brolin is the eldest of the internees sent to Laing. He is in his forties, and greying a little. He carries small books with him that he keeps in his pockets. A little poetry, a little prose – some Dante, some Schiller, a book on architecture. Brolin is a widower now. Brolin was in the camp with his wife (with whom he had come to England originally). He had persuaded her to take the place he had been allotted by the camp commandant on one of the passenger ships, the *Dunera*, which was due to transport a batch of internees to Australia in July 1940. The camp had been allotted one hundred of the places on the *Dunera* and Brolin had been selected as one of those to go, though not his wife.

'You should go on this ship,' Brolin had told his wife, convincing her that she should take his place. Such swaps were possible if the commandant could be persuaded that it would make for an easier life.

'A new life,' he had told her, 'is six weeks away. Europe is no place for us any more. You take my place and I'll follow after. I'll get myself on the next list. Six weeks, and our *Dunera* will bring you to a new life – Australia.'

But she was not as strong as she had been when Brolin had first courted and married her, when he'd still been apprenticed in Dresden as a stonemason. The journey had proved too much for her. She had died of a heart attack on board the ship. The commandant had notified him. Now Brolin is alone. He looks after Kasperl and seems sadder than the times when he and Heimy sat listening to Mozart in the camp on Heimy's gramophone, with tears in his eyes listening to the singing of the German soprano, Anna Mutter. 'My other love,' Brolin always said to Heimy, 'My one true other love', whilst his wife darned clothes and Kasperl, out in the compound, practised his juggling.

Since the work that they did before their arrest is not classed as 'useful to the nation' – which is the phrase the authorities use – the internees are not allowed to return home or to go where they wish. They are told work has been found for them in Laing. They are sent to see the town clerk in Laing, who is Stent the solicitor. They line up, a little shabby, a little worn. Kasperl, in particular, looks ill-kempt. His pale chequered jacket is grubby after a year in the camp. He is tall and thin and stooping. He wears brown boots that clank on the floor, his hair has grown long and curly like a girl's. He smells, and he scratches at the fleas living on his skin.

Stent is writing notes.

Brolin says to Stent, 'May I speak with you?'

Stent looks up and waits for him to speak.

'As for me,' Brolin says, 'I do not mind where I am, what I do, until war ends. The others have families, businesses. Not me but the others. Can those men not go back to their homes? They have suffered enough, surely?'

'You are . . .' Stent says, looking down at the papers on his desk, '. . . an ice-cream maker, a circus performer, a stonemason, a travel agency clerk. We are unlikely, I think, to be able to categorize such things as useful to the nation. Therefore, it has been decided that you will work here in Laing. You will work for the mining company, carrying out the work prescribed for you.'

'And if we do not agree to this?' Peretta asks from the end of the line.

'There is a war on,' Stent says patiently. 'There is a shortage of labour for the mines. You will agree to this. If you fail to comply to any aspect of your work, you will be detained once more and be classified as 'A' category enemy aliens.'

'Why not like it was before internment,' Peretta says. 'Why isn't it like the tribunals when the panel says I can go home. Live at home. Go home. Work in my business. Why not this now?'

'What happened before is immaterial. You are category 'B' aliens. You have been released from internment at the discretion of the regional Commissioner for the purpose of assisting with the war effort. Which is, after all, all that any of us is doing. Is it not? You will be billeted in Laing. You will report each day to the police station. Any letters that you write should be handed into me for the Commissioner's office to forward. You may not travel beyond Laing without permission, and without a necessary permit. Do you understand?'

'And if we complain?'

'There are no complaints.'

'You think this is right?' Peretta says.

Stent is looking for something on the sheets of paper in front of him.

'I say, you think this is right?'

145

Brolin, standing next to him, without raising his eyes from the floor, without looking around, puts his hand quietly on Peretta's shoulder.

Stent reads from his papers. 'You are Donato Peretta. Italian. Twenty-four years old. And you were . . .'

'My family make ice-cream. Good ice-cream. It is business. In Glasgow.'

'And now you dig coal. For England.'

'I know nothing about coal. I am ice-cream. My family is ice-cream.'

'I spoke to the commandant at the camp,' Stent says. 'I gather you were trouble there as well. I gather you were . . .' He looks at the sheet in front of him again. '. . . hot-headed. I gather this is why, in your particular case, release from internment took as long as it did.'

'Hot-head? Trouble? Who says this?'

'The commandant reports that you caused trouble over the death of one of the internees.'

'I just spoke up for the ones who were not treated well on the ship. I felt bad for them. For Brolin, too. For what happened to his wife on the ship. He should tell you.'

'You protested about it to the International Red Cross when a delegation visited the camp? You put the commandant into a difficult position.'

'Yes.'

'Even though you had been told by the commandant that an investigation into the incident you raised had been commissioned?'

'Yes. I did this. It was right.'

'You chose to ignore that it is a criminal offence to do anything that is prejudicial to the efficient prosecution of the war.

146

You think that a year or two of making ice-cream qualifies you to make unfounded accusations against the British Government? Against the country that afforded you an upbringing?'

'I was right to say these things. I think also I am right to say I would like if possible to go home. To see my family. What should I tell my family if you say no? What to tell them if you will not allow it even though we have been released. Even though we are no danger any more, not to be locked up.'

'Tell them you are working for England. Tell them you are working to win the war.'

There are concerns in Laing about the foreigners coming to work in the pits. Joe Filbin from the union tells his men that his hands are tied, that they have no right of strike over it, that the only concession he has wrung from the Kyles is to keep the one who is an idiot away from the underground work. The internees had been given medicals before they had been signed on to work in the pit. Joe Filbin had seen the men he was getting from the internment camp. Surface work is girls' work, old men's work. Joe Filbin will not have the idiot Kasperl working underground. So Kasperl is given women's work on the surface, sweeping and cleaning, and collecting the dog tags from the miners going underground for each shift, whilst Brolin and Peretta and Friegang work underground loading the newly cut coal into the containers at the coalface and ferrying them back to the winding shafts.

Some shops will not sell goods to the internees. The harbour pubs – the Seven Stars and the Harbour Inn – will not serve them. Traders who do choose to deal with them sometimes have swastikas daubed on their door during the night or their shop window broken.

On the internees' first day at the pit, Brolin is told by Joe Filbin's men that they must have their hair cut. In the internment camp their hair has grown unkempt, Kasperl's especially. It will be dangerous, they are told, working around the pithead with women's hair and there is the danger of lice after their time in the camp – though everyone knows that in truth it is to see how they react. Everyone knows it is for sport.

Men gather round in the silence of first light at the pithead. First they hand out the uniforms; then they cut the internees' hair. They have an older miner cut the hair of each of the former internees in turn back to a short, back and sides. Kasperl is last. With Kasperl they make the most of it. They have given him pants that are too small and come down only to his shins, a miner's tunic that hangs shapelessly on him. They shave Kasperl until his head has only a blue stubble grazed across it. At one point Peretta rises as if to stop it, but Brolin holds him back. Kasperl sits in silence throughout the performance. When they have finished, he stands up. Men wait to see what the boy will do. Kasperl stands up to make his way across to the huts where he will work, where he will be responsible for handing out the lamps and hats and for collecting the tabs of miners going down for the new shift, and for washing out the showers and sweeping the changing huts – women's work. He pulls out four juggling balls from his tunic, and silently, bald-headed, pants hung about his shins, all the way across to the huts, he juggles.

The former internees are billeted by Stent at the boarding house – the third-class hotel in the town – and this is how

Donato Peretta's painstaking courtship of the sceptical Joannie Kilner begins.

'Will I get paid rent for taking them in?' Joannie Kilner had asked Stent.

'We must all do our bit for England,' Stent had said.

Donato Peretta begins his courtship of Joannie Kilner within a week of their moving in to a huddle of rooms at the back of the second floor. Peretta knows only that a large obstacle rests in the way of his courtship of Joannie Kilner, like an eclipse blocking out the light over a part of her. He will discover eventually the nature and shape of the object. He will come to think of it as having the shape and texture of a dreamed blue dress. He will find out, though not from Joannie Kilner, that she was raped. He will not find out the name of the man who was responsible. He will not find out that it was Henry Kyle.

11

Bubba's life

'Are you here, Gabriel?'

They are trapped in the ice.

Maybe all along Henry Kyle was right. Maybe they are not men, and have no right to dream. Maybe they must leave Emerson the mariner as he has been left for almost four hundred years. Perhaps the *Endeavour* cannot after all have passed through this piece of sea that chokes with ice at the end of every sudden summer. To believe that it could be done requires an act of faith too big for them to traverse. They know now that the only way Emerson could have made it to the Strait of Anian – the only way he could have seen it – was by walking some vast, unguessable distance.

'What do we do now?' Athol asks.

'We have to wait for the end of winter. We have to wait for the light to come, like Emerson did.'

'And then?'

Gabriel doesn't know. 'Will you wait with me?' he asks Athol.

'We all came this far.'

'What about you, Peary?'

'I'll stay.' Peary's still in search of his ending to write about.

As for Ingerman, there's no question but that he'll come. There's no life for Ingerman outside the colony. They'll all come, all wait for the end of the long polar night, all hold their breath like belugas under the ice in an act of faith that the far side, and pure air, can be reached. For now they wait.

But for what? For favourable tides? For courage?

'Gabriel?'

The angel's name is Evelyn. She wants him to call her Evelyn. I hear her laugh, amused, when Gabriel says she is an angel. She still comes to see him each afternoon for a short time, breaking him out of his daze, interrupting his arctic dreams, his waiting. He and Athol and Peary and Ingerman return to the Icehouse each night, but Gabriel isn't sure what is next. They wait, stilled in their hearts, trapped as Emerson is in the ice, waiting for the centre to crack, for things to give. (Unless it is the absence of medication taking effect; unless it is the physical strain of the voyage beginning to tell on them.) Around them, at minus sixteen, the ice packs down and hardens and shines and the nights grow longer and the days less real.

'Bubba left a gift for you.'

'A gift?'

Her use of the name again draws him out from the vague arctic light which, away from the Icehouse, filters all his senses, thinning them down to simple watercolour washes. My calculation is that they have been three months voyaging.

'Yes – Bubba. But it's not time yet.'

Only Walt and William knew about the name, knew that from the age of two he called William 'Bubba', because an attempt at 'brother' was easier for the child than 'William' and it stuck.

'Bubba is here?'

151

'No.' She looks sad. The angel takes his hand. 'Bubba is dead. He died, Gabriel.'

He looks at her hand holding his. He thinks of his body as meat, as a vehicle for movement and pain and consumption. Not as a conductor for feeling, emotion.

'How did he die?'

'In his sleep, Gabriel. He died quietly after a long life.'

'It's a good way to die.'

'Yes,' she says, 'a good way to die.'

Henry Kyle had always said that it was the best way to die. Kyle's ambition for us, for his charges, and maybe for himself, was that we died quietly in our sleep; to die untroubled was a blessing to be bargained from God.

Yesterday he told her that Peretta had once courted Joannie Kilner. She had smiled. Evelyn had smiled at that.

'Do you know Peretta?' Gabriel had asked her.

'No, I don't,' she had said. 'Maybe you'll tell me about him one day. When you're out of this place. When the colony has closed down and you're making your fresh start away from here. Maybe you'll tell me about him then.'

Peretta had loved Joannie Kilner, Gabriel said. Peretta had told him. Peretta loved Joannie Kilner, and Walter Friegang had a dagger. And Evelyn was his mother's name.

She had leaned over and kissed him on the cheek after that; kissed by an angel, named Evelyn like his mother.

And he had taken her to see the Icehouse.

Bubba had moved away from Laing and become a printer's apprentice in Blackburn, Lancashire, and somehow lost the habit or the need to carry food around with him everywhere for comfort. He'd never said much about Laing. Never wanted to go back. Once, he'd visited the colony. It had been after his wife had died, when he'd discovered that the past he thought he'd buried had been there all the time, when he'd realised that the past had lain unframed, unspoken of, between him and his wife, tilting and unsettling them in an otherwise lasting and necessary marriage. The love they'd had was built around and straddling the thing he carried carefully, clumsily, for himself. When she died, he had apparently gone to the colony. Once. Henry Kyle was still running the colony at the time. William made mention of it in his will. He went once. He never went again and he didn't speak of it. After that, *it* had been this lesser, still resilient, dormant thing between William and the world, between William and the daughter he loved, who rang him most nights and reminded him to feed the dog and pay the bills and have a haircut. The bear of a thing clung to his back. Sometimes it mauled him; once in a while it grew restless and heavy; for a while it would make no movement at all, but always it was there, brooding and unwilling to let go. The daughter he had didn't know her father had a brother until he told her three days before he died. He knew he was dying when he told her.

He'd been a good printer. In the days when he set out, printing was a trade which required attention to detail and patience in organizing and checking and rechecking the weight and measure and density of the inks and the temperamental rollers and mechanisms of the presses. It required dexterity fiddling with the mechanics of the presses that needed constant attention and adjustment – each part feeding precariously into the next to form a whole process. It needed an acceptance of the smell of printers' ink ingrained on his fingers day and night, and a willingness to work long and unexpected hours finishing short-order jobs. (As a rule, he said, people always wanted their printing two days before it was possible.) He'd started up his own business and later ran it from the ground floor of the big house they bought opposite the corporation park. He made promises to customers that he kept by delivering orders even late at night to men's homes out of town if their offices were closed, and he worked hard and he was systematic and he was polite with the competition, and after his breakdown he was ripped off badly by the Rotarian who had a bigger printing firm in the town. The Rotarian bought William's business out and then re-employed him back afterwards to run it for him on a peppercorn wage and a commission on the work he'd already built up. Everyone knew that it was no longer William's firm despite the Rotarian's ruse of keeping William's name for the business, and the Rotarian revelled in the discovery that for such a little sum you could hold another man's life and well-being in your hand. They never argued. William accepted his fate, though one time he did break two small bones in his hand slamming his fist against a print table one night after the Rotarian had gone home. In Casualty, he said simply that he'd caught it in a press.

Even in the two months he spent in the hospital after the breakdown he didn't talk much about Laing. He joked to his daughter that he made a mean wicker basket in the rehab class. And he made a decent recovery. And they survived, as people sometimes do, in this case in a much smaller house with some garden, and he became a fine gardener and his wife complained half-heartedly that she could never get him in for supper because there was always one last damned job somewhere out there for him to do. And after she died, his daughter would sometimes ring him in the summer around ten o'clock to remind him to stop and to make himself something to eat because he would have forgotten tea. And when his own illness began, his sadness over it – like any joy he had accrued through his life – was contained and let out frugally (he could always see Gabriel in his mind's eye chiding him: 'Fly, Bubba – fly', but dull William never learned to fly) and he began to arrange his affairs as neatly, as soberly as his childhood self had once arranged his phalanx of toy soldiers, or the adult William had arranged his bedding plants, pipe clamped between his teeth, the long oval of his face solid in concentration.

The will made no direct reference to the magical brother he'd had. It said only that once he'd made a trip to West Cumbria to see a man called Henry Kyle who ran an institution, and that he wished to leave a gift to someone there who was in Kyle's charge. Somewhere in the instructions for his solicitors, separate to the will (in order to avoid his family knowing) were instructions for the despatch of a small package. The package was to be sent to a post office box number. It was the address to which all mail for the residents of the colony was sent in Henry Kyle's day (in order that the mail could be sifted and then passed on – or not). The package was sent, but in place of the parcel, an angel arrived.

Away in the administration block, I know that Sallis and Fat Rose sit and wonder what to do. Sallis, chain-smoking, keeps the light from his office with heavy blinds barred across the window. He had explained to Gabriel's visitor that there was a degree of sensitivity about the kind of files she had wanted to see. Notwithstanding the legal restraints on information about third parties, the records of residents were never kept with a view to being used as public documents. There was a chance of things in them being misconstrued if they were taken out of context. Did she understand? He felt sure that she did. (That's what he said. That's what she told me.) The assessments, the prognoses, the very language used in such records could so easily seem direct and unflinching, he had said – the way a family would deal sometimes abruptly with its own members within its own four private walls because it knew it was a family. Sallis, looking over the tint of his spectacles, drawing on his cigarette, hiding from the light, had smiled at her.

She had tried to find out about the men who Gabriel thought that he sometimes remembered. All she was able to discover was that the four had been internees in Laing, and that they had escaped from custody and fled Laing in a boat, sailing either to their deaths or back to Germany. It didn't seem to help her much but at least the effort, like her confronting Sallis in the colony, had made her feel better.

Angels should always be told the truth and so Gabriel shows her. He has not told Athol or the others about it. This is between him and his angel. She stands half a dozen steps into the bitter winter land of the Icehouse and listens as he tells her about the plinth by the harbour wall in Laing where he and Bubba had used to stand as boys, watching the boats go out in the small slapping sea. And how Gabriel Emerson became, has become, stuck in the ice flow, fallen short of his Anian Strait.

'What about the life you will have afterwards?' she asks him. 'Will you give up your game when the time comes?'

'This is not a game,' he says.

'No, of course. Your voyage. Will you end your voyage

when it's time to go? When it's time to begin again outside?'

He believes she is so young and sure of things, and dives true and unafraid, a beautiful white beluga (with her pale skin caught by the light of the ice around them) singing and sure of where to rise to breathe.

'Too late,' he says.

'How can it be too late, Gabriel?' she says. 'Bubba would hope it's not too late.'

'You don't understand,' he says slowly. He looks at the ship standing out there in front of him in the Icehouse. He looks at Ingerman's wheelhouse built of boxes and planks, at the lines of ice running on the rigging of the ship. All the colours of the white refracted sky are upon him. His heart, of course, the beating part of him, is far from here, in a narrow, ice-held strait. But how to make her understand?

'It's too late,' he repeats. 'This is our ending, here.'

Like Emerson – his heart frozen in the ice at the far edge of the world where he has sailed.

12

Courting Joannie Kilner

Donato Peretta courts Joannie Kilner like a man laying quiet siege to a castle. In the evenings, after their days as fillers working below ground at the pit – the three of them loading the conveyor belts after the blasting and the drilling ready for it to be brought in containers to the surface to be sent down to the harbour, and Kasperl cleaning the shower blocks and sweeping the locker huts – Friegang likes to have sex with one or other of the girls from the third floor (at least when he has the money from his wages to pay). Brolin is too busy with thoughts, too filled with memories – with *weltschmerz* – to want to join him. But Peretta has eyes only for Joannie Kilner who is ten years his senior. No one knows if Kasperl has a sex life. Kasperl has a spot outside the hotel. He sits on the stone steps that run down from the lobby to the street outside and juggles quietly there with his four clay balls. Sometimes a swastika appears, whitewashed on the big front door of the hotel during the night, perhaps left by children, and Walt has to wash it off with a long-handled brush he keeps for the task. Brolin has told Gabriel how Kasperl had been in a circus since he was ten, how he had applied in a letter written for him by one of his older sisters, to join the great state circus in Berlin.

But you needed a performer's permit to be allowed to join such a prestigious circus, and several years' experience with a smaller circus before you could even apply to join. That was how Kasperl came to join Circus Prenzlau – in order to get his permit, and his experience, so that he could eventually apply to join the state circus. Kasperl had plans, Brolin had told Gabriel. Kasperl wanted to be a fine juggler, the best juggler. His touring with the Circus Prenzlau, Brolin said, was a means to an end.

Brolin said he knew that this was the single thing Kasperl wanted to do – to become a fine juggler and be allowed in the end to join the state circus in Berlin. He sought no other trade. He had no schooling to speak of, save what the other circus folk had taught him. That was how Brolin had come to teach Kasperl to read and write in German and in English.

Sometimes William's friends like to tease Kasperl on their way past in the evenings. Sometimes Morton Filbin and the bespectacled Joseph Tillotson and Rolf Stent like to try to distract him, to make him drop his four painted clay balls so that they fall and strike the steps and Kasperl has to pick them up and dust them and inspect them minutely to see if they are cracked or chipped before he begins cautiously juggling them again in his big hands. Meantime, Jacob Brolin sits sketching idly in the small pocket sketchbook he carries around every-where with him, resting after his day's work in the shadow of the ballroom, waiting for Gabriel and a game of Austrian rummy and the boy's tales of the mariner who'd sailed from Laing. And Peretta, with flowers, goes courting Joannie Kilner.

She has given Peretta no signal that he is ever progressing. Not even that she is interested. But still he persists, pursuing her with patience and forbearance and with Brolin's poetry and with an utter conviction in his cause.

'Men are donkeys,' Joannie Kilner tells him. 'Except when they are on heat, at which time they are like dogs. Are you on heat, Peretta?'

Donato Peretta shrugs his shoulders, happy that she is talking to him.

'You would be better with the girls on the third floor,' Joannie Kilner says. 'They will give you what you need.'

He treats it like some elaborate test of his character, and each snub he receives he seems to regard as proof that the prize he seeks is all the greater and more necessary. Peretta will have no truck with the prostitutes. He is civil with them, of course. He gets on well with the button-lipped Emily who gives him advice as best she can about how he might woo Joannie Kilner. 'Give up with Joanne Kilner, Peretta,' she has said, though, more than once, '– her heart has gone away.'

Some of the other third-floor girls tease Peretta about his endeavour when Joannie Kilner is out of earshot.

'There's nothing there for you, Peretta,' they will say. 'When you eventually get there you'll find she's all dried up.'

But Peretta only smiles benignly. Once a week he brings her flowers. He engages her in conversation; offers to walk her down to dinner each night in the hotel's dining room in which she eats at one of the several vacant tables. Resolutely he asks her each Sunday evening, when she materializes in the ballroom, if she will have her single dance with him. But Joannie Kilner always dances alone. Gabriel, watching him, surely believes that Peretta is hunting down the missing part of her, stolen by the terragots, and is trying to bring it back.

*

Jacob Brolin has taught Gabriel how to play Austrian rummy. He has taught William, too, but William finds cards too frivolous to enjoy for long. Brolin and Gabriel play cards squatting cross-legged on the ballroom floor after Brolin is back from registering his continued presence along with his compatriots at the police station in the town square as they must do each day after work. Brolin, coughing up a little coal dust from the shift the internees have just finished, cuts the pack and deals. The cards slip across the wooden floor as he flips them – one to Gabriel, one to him. Gabriel is emptying one world of maths and grammar and filling up with his own private dreams again now he's back home from school. He likes Brolin's company, I know. He is comfortable with Brolin. Brolin never tries to impress him the way grown men can sometimes do with boys. Brolin is happy for Gabriel, for anyone, to take him at face value. To take him as he is – a stonemason who spent his apprenticeship and the first ten years of his profession as part of the team of masons restoring the great Dresden cathedral of St Trinitas to its medieval splendour – a stonemason and an artist, a man living in exile in an adopted land. Brolin has shown Gabriel the sketches of his colleagues, of the internment camp, of Joannie Kilner's hotel, of Gabriel himself. There are several of Gabriel. They have been drawn fast. They have caught the movement and the instinct of the hour they were done. They breathe life.

'You don't pretend,' Gabriel has said to him.

'Pretend?'

'For other people.'

'No – only for me.'

'Like Dada, but in the daylight.'

'You think?'

'Dada can just be himself, but only at night.'

Gabriel looks at his cards and fans them out carefully. His hands are so small he can barely hold all fifteen cards. He needs two hands to hold them all.

'Your father is asleep, yes?' Brolin asks.

Gabriel nods.

'Your father is like a night creature; a fox – no, maybe a badger. Your father snuffles through the night around this place, yes?'

'Yes, like a badger.'

Gabriel likes to think of his Dada snuffling through the hotel at night. It makes him feel safe – like his Dada is snuffling the corners of each night in search of terragots to keep safe the world, to keep safe Gabriel.

Outside the hotel, Kasperl the youth is quietly juggling in his big hands. Rolf Stent and Morton Filbin and Joseph Tillotson are there, standing watching as Kasperl sits and juggles at the bottom of the steps.

'My Da says it's full of whores,' Morton Filbin says.

Rolf Stent asks Kasperl, 'Do all the women here fuck like gypsies?'

Kasperl watches them cautiously from his step, saying nothing, throwing his four balls up in a steady and consoling rhythm.

'You're very good,' Rolf Stent says, watching Kasperl continue to juggle. 'Show us how?'

'Go make balls and practise,' Kasperl says.

'We want to practise with your balls,' Rolf Stent says.

'Go make balls and practise,' Kasperl says again.

Rolf Stent stands there in front of him. At that moment the door of the hotel which had opened quietly slams shut on its weak hinge, making a loud bang. It is William who has spotted the three boys down on the street and come out to see if they will let him play. Kasperl's head shoots around to see what's made the sudden bang, to see who's crashed the door at his back. Two of his juggling balls fall to the floor, and yet something of the juggler in him keeps juggling with the remaining two balls. In a trice, Rolf Stent has grabbed hold of the two fallen clay balls. He steps back away into the street with the balls. Kasperl, leaning to grab him, drops the other two balls. Morton Filbin nips in and picks them both up. He backs off.

'They're fine juggling balls,' Rolf Stent says as holds the two balls up to the light, examining them. 'Did you paint them yourself?'

'Give me a throw,' Joseph Tillotson pleads. But he is the smallest. His only authority derives from having a bigger brother who sometimes plays with them. Billy will start at the pit in the spring. He's not around today and Joseph Tillotson's plea is ignored and Rolf Stent and Morton Filbin still keep two balls each. Morton Filbin throws his two balls from one hand to the other in a laboured impression of juggling, all the while keeping an eye on Kasperl, keeping a safe distance from him with the two balls he has captured.

'You steal them,' Kasperl says. 'You give to me the balls.'

'We just want to look,' Rolf Stent says.

'Are you a real juggler?'

'Yes, I am juggling.'

'In a circus?'

'Circus Prenzlau.'

'Do some more tricks then?' Rolf Stent asks.

'Please, my juggling balls please.'

'How can we get good like you if we have to give them back without a practice?'

'You give to me the balls.'

'Do us a trick and you can have your balls back. Can you do handstands? Do a handstand.'

Kasperl moves down two steps towards them and holds one big hand out. 'My balls back please.'

But the boys are quick on their feet. They step easily away, keeping out of reach of Kasperl. With his big, lead-soled boots and the coaldust still on his face, Kasperl seems the clown in all of this, now dashing from one boy to the other trying to reclaim his balls. Kasperl finally grabs at Morton Filbin. The boy throws the balls away towards Joseph Tillotson who swoops on them happily and gathers them and darts back out of reach. Kasperl pushes Morton Filbin away in frustration. The boy falls to the ground. Kasperl turns to William who stands watching on the hotel's top step.

'You ask them give the balls back,' he says.

But William can only stand and watch as Rolf Stent and Morton Filbin (who is now back on his feet) and Joseph Tillotson loop the balls to each other in the street a safe distance away from the steps of Joannie Kilner's hotel and wait for Kasperl the juggler to do a trick for them in return for his four painted, polished clay balls. Kasperl makes one final lunge at Rolf Stent who darts away. Kasperl falls. He swears angrily in German at them. They run, laughing, leaving William standing watching on the top step of the hotel.

I can picture how Joannie Kilner must stand at the door to her room on the fourth floor of the hotel when she sees the flowers. The door is perhaps just a little ajar, as if she is wary that the flowers on the table in the corridor from Peretta may be a trap. There is a small note with them. There is no sign of Peretta. She will open the envelope still standing out on the landing and read over the words on the paper:

> *'Io M'aggio posto incoro a Dio servire*
> *com' io potesse gire in paradiso.*
> *Sanza mia donna non voria gire*
> *quells c'ha blonda testa e claro viso,*
> *che sanza lei non poteria gaudere*
> *estanda da la mia donna diviso.'*

Perhaps she folds the paper back in half before she takes up the flowers from the table in the corridor, goes back into the room, and closes the door.

Friegang hangs around the girls as is his way. Even when the girls don't want to know, even when they are not taking business, Friegang is always there.

'Do you love me, Emily?' Friegang will ask.

'I love you like I'd love a big dog,' I hear Emily say to him whenever he asks.

He is forever polishing his glasses, or polishing his knife which he will draw from its scabbard when he is with the girls, and he will try to tell the girls that he has fought in a war with this knife.

'Does your weapon impress the boys?' Emily will ask him. 'It does little for us. Eh, girls?'

Her sentiment makes Friegang angry. He will pretend not to hear. He will continue polishing the blade, more privately, hoping some other girl will remark upon it, but they seldom do. The sheath knife had not been issued to him. Friegang is no more a real soldier than the rest of them. It was an old, Prussian cavalry sheath knife and it was blunted. Friegang had bought it before the war in an antique shop in London where he worked in the office of an Anglo-German travel company who specialized in arranging walking tours of the continent. He never imagined then that one day he would labour in coal mines with illiterate circus performers and Italian ice-cream makers.

Friegang was allowed to keep the knife in the internment camp only because he was such a figure of fun and because the knife was blunt and useless. He was allowed to keep it because the idea of a roly-poly, pasty-faced administrative clerk actually doing something with the sheath knife – using it as a weapon – was too preposterous to contemplate and so he was allowed to keep it.

Brolin waits for Gabriel to take his turn. Gabriel has two runs of spades and a set of sixes which he still holds. He also has two jacks. He decides to lay down one of the jacks but gets nothing to help him from the new card that he picks up. Brolin takes up the jack that Gabriel has laid down, then sets down his cards, leaving Gabriel caught holding a full hand.

'You play too adventurous,' Brolin says, marking the score then sweeping up the cards. 'You should have laid some sets down already instead of trying to surprise me with a full hand.'

'I always want to win too well,' Gabriel says.

'Compromise will come,' Brolin says. 'Not too much, please God. Just a little. Just a touch on the rudder like your sailor Gabriel, then you will be away, straight and true.'

He cuts the cards and begins to deal again. A woman floats

by silently on the edge of the ballroom, heading to the kitchens. It is Alice Stent. Ever since she arrived at Joannie Kilner's hotel, she has taken to wearing only white. Gabriel has asked her before now why she wears white but perhaps she is unable to tell him. Perhaps she is unable to tell anyone – except for Joannie Kilner. I am sure that she will have told Joannie Kilner.

'Why does she do that?' Gabriel asks Brolin.

'Do what, boy?'

'She always wears white. Why does she do that?'

Brolin shrugs, and continues to deal. 'Maybe out of craziness. Or out of hope. People do things; other people can't tell why. Then men like you and I are left to pick up the pieces.'

'Kasperl is crazy,' Gabriel says.

'The boys make him crazy, teasing him. Kasperl is so young – a young man with only one great skill. One passion. One purpose. To juggle. Even his name shows his passion.'

'How can just a name do that?'

'It is a stage name he uses with Circus Prenzlau. "Kasperl" is famous puppet character. Like your "Mr Punch". He is Mr Punch all his life. He is Kasperl the Juggler. That is his life. After that he is nothing.'

'Is Peretta crazy?' Gabriel asks. 'Joannie Kilner says so.'

'Crazy, or in love,' Brolin says. 'Life without loving is a dry thing – bread with no taste.'

'Dada was in love with my Mama but she died when she was having me.'

'Sometimes love is sad,' Brolin says. 'Necessary but sad. Dante says this.'

'The other men say you had a wife and she died.'

'Yes.'

'Does it hurt?'

'It hurts. But I'm glad that it hurts.'

'How can you be glad?'

'Because it shows how good she was for me. It shows I found love. Some people don't. Not everybody does.'

'So why does the lady dressed in white not talk to people? She'll not find any love if she doesn't say things.'

'Maybe she has the white instead of the loving,' Brolin says. 'Now you play cards. My head is sore with questions.'

They take up their cards. The woman in white has passed them by and is gone into the kitchens. More cake, Gabriel knows. One of the equations of the hotel in which he's lived his life is that unhappiness in women makes for good cakes. Brolin looks to see what kind of hand he has dealt himself and lays down his spare card.

Each evening, Peretta asks Joannie Kilner if he may sit with her at her table in the dining room for dinner. Each evening, she declines.

'Your young friend is on heat again,' she says to Brolin as she passes him.

'He wishes only to dine with you, lady.'

She shrugs. She produces the note Peretta had sent to her rooms along with the flowers.

'You gave him this so he could give it to me?'

Brolin nods. 'He wishes to impress you. He wishes to give you poetry, but he knows none himself. So I give him poetry, but I tell him just to be himself, and then, one day, maybe – who knows.'

'What does this mean?' she asks. 'It is in Italian. I do not speak Italian.'

'That is a sadness,' Brolin says.

'The poem, Brolin.'

'Ah, the poem – yes! It is an old poem. Older than Dante, who is the finest of all poets. The poem says that the man has proposed in his heart to serve God so that he might one day enter Paradise. But, without his lady – the one of the fair head and clear face – he does not wish to go to Heaven. This is because he can take no pleasure from anything whilst he is separated from his lady.'

'Then he is a fool, Brolin.'

'Jacopo da Lentini a fool? Surely, no! He is a wise man, madam. The master, Dante, he think so. I think so, especially since Peretta surely feels as Jacopo feels. He sends the poem because this is how he feels. Because it says what he feels and in the language of his ancestors. He wishes to tell you how he feels, but his knowledge of poetry is not so good and so he came to me.'

'He would be better giving sweet words to Kasperl,' Joannie Kilner says. 'Some boys have stolen his juggling balls and he is like a dog who has lost his bark. Go and tell Peretta to care for him.'

'And if I say that in the florist shop today the woman shouts at him – will you care more? While Peretta was buying the flowers for you, the woman who sold him flowers shouts at him because her son died in the war. What will you say if I say that? If I say the price to bring you flowers is that a woman shouts into his face each time?'

'I will say to forget it, Brolin. I will say she is a stupid woman. I will say he would better spend his time going to talk to Kasperl the juggler – go see to the dog who has no bark.'

13

Waiting for courage and the spring

They nurse and console each other through. In the winter that passes, Ingerman grows vague and weaker, and Athol – removed from Prozac and from the light – sometimes grows sour and difficult to persuade. Sometimes his patience deserts him. Sometimes he puts his big hands together and prays in fierce words to a god who abandoned him to Henry Kyle. Gabriel grips Athol by the shoulders, telling him, 'Faith, Athol, we will see this through.' They sleep as best they can, so cold to the bone and damp on their skins. Sometimes they talk. Peary writes, hoarding words, hoarding his view of the world about him and his search for a way to end things properly. Only Gabriel seems made for this, growing in confidence as the days, such as they are, pass by over their heads – becoming Gabriel Emerson the mariner day by day, seeing to the ship, nurturing his crew.

In the wilderness outside, there are no true days left any more that they can reckon. Light has to be imagined. The only movement is the breathing of the ice – the way it sometimes shifts and cracks unseen around them. They are prey to this incomprehensible winter which stalks them outside the *Endeavour*. The ice has lifted the ship like a child's toy proud of the sea level. It shows how they are at the mercy of forces outside their control. All the seamanship in the world cannot help them any more. Now, there is only a bare and rudimentary faith – an instinct – to survive by.

Gradually, the ship has become a kind of womb, a single space into which the four of them withdraw, moving less and less, suspended in a pause which is broken periodically by a burst of temper or of madness. They have small tasks on board ship set them by Gabriel, they have routine, but they cannot hide from the reality of their lives - from the prison that this terrible season has become. Only Gabriel seems consoled. Only Gabriel seems to grow more real as the days become less so.

In the short days that preceded full winter, they hunted. They wandered the kingdom around the ship – the flat, irregular ice of the frozen sea and, further away, the land, dressed in snow and ice, rising imperiously a mile away. The sun blazed in long regretful sunsets which came earlier and earlier. The winds came and went. The caribou and the ptarmigan slowly disappeared, perhaps moving south for the winter, away from the *Endeavour's* trapped position. Only the wolves seemed prepared to stay, and even they were seen less often. The log notes the migration of the animals, the abandonment, the exile that they felt being left like this. The crew wandered their small land alone, staying within sight of the ship, watching the miracle of lights in the northern sky, watching for storms, for fogs, for the belly growl in the earth that preceded the winds that blew until the timber of the ship's stem sang like a tuning fork and set Ingerman howling and Peary deep into his hood. Until finally they were driven completely below deck by the snowstorms. And by mid-

November the sun had gone for good and the inky, grey-blue sky held its single breath over them and the noise of the compressing ice racked the timbers of the ship. There was fog, and wind, and wolves picking at the bones of the land, and the menace of the big white bears that were frightened of nothing and owned the world around them.

The temperature drops to minus forty. Snow drives hard against the land. Though there is heat from the stove below deck, the heat rises and the temperature down at the floor level remains below zero. The cabin walls are stiff with ice which Gabriel and Athol work regularly to hack clear. The ice forms from condensation and from their breathing. The others have to work to persuade Ingerman not to leave the ship during this long winter. He has fallen once already out on deck. The fall gashed him down his side and restricts his movement for the time being. The wound is bathed and redressed frequently by Athol who brought some small medical supplies from the infirmary when they first set out.

A wall of ice is wedged against the timbers of the *Endeavour*. The temperature outside is unbearable. A few minutes out there in the obscene cold is more than anyone can bear. And anyway, Ingerman's condition is too precarious for him to go out through the worst of the winter. Sometimes he grows delirious. Sometimes he sleeps, still, like a corpse, not like Ingerman used to do at all. They are all sick, full of headaches from the cold and the damp and the sameness of each day, full of warning aches in their limbs and spines.

'Are we home?' Ingerman says.

'We're going home,' Gabriel says, cradling Ingerman's head. Gabriel can feel Ingerman's pain, and draws it out of him. Ingerman is coughing blood.

They lie like babies, listening to the noises of the compressing ice around the ship through the polar night, fear like a stillness on them. And in the stillness, memories.

Henry Kyle's message to them was simple: you are not men; the lives you had are forfeit. There should be a *tabula rasa*, he informed his Board of Trustees each time a man came – a clean slate – when a man took up residence in the colony and was given an identical uniform, a blue boiler suit. Each man could keep only the kind of mementoes of a past life that would fit into a bedside cabinet. A past life was thought to interfere with successful integration into the running of the colony, where each act, each incident, was recorded. Henry Kyle kept bathing books, bowel books, menstruation books, punishment books, treatment books. Henry Kyle spent forty years charting the minutiae of the world that was his creation. Residents querying the colony's system, or its purpose, had their behaviour charted and treatment for it recorded. The resistance or aggression of residents was recorded. So was passivity, and undue inquisitiveness, and sexual behaviour. And all behaviours were corrected by the use of the sideroom - the punishment cell attached to each dormitory. How else could so many men together be controlled? How else could Henry Kyle see his work through?

Each sideroom measured eight feet by six. A flap opened at floor level in the door to allow food to be passed in and the shitbowl out. Athol would shout abuse through the flap. Peary would bang on the door and walls for hours and days until the palms of his hands were black and swollen. Ingerman would sing. The sideroom was the only place Ingerman ever sang. He had fine pitch; his ethereal voice would drift across the

173

colony sometimes from the vents in the sideroom. The noises – the shouts, the bangs, the cries and the singing, the defiance – would carry on for hours. It would sometimes continue for days. But always, in the end, a silence fell. Always, in the end, there was an acquiescence which took over – although Athol and Peary and Ingerman and Gabriel held out for longer than the rest of us, held out each time they were assigned to the sideroom. It was they who retained some shreds of identity, some hope, some rebellion, some need to stay the man each had once been. It was these four who Henry Kyle found the hardest to break, who spent the most time in the sideroom, who sought shelter in crevices and dreams he could not reach, who are still here at the death, so long after Henry Kyle has gone, still breathing in and out, in and out, still clinging, still dreaming dreams.

Evelyn sat with him for week after week. At first, I came to believe, she had come out of nothing but curiosity about the creature she had found. Later, she came, I am sure, to help him. In the beginning I watched her willing him to speak, to acknowledge her, but initially Gabriel seemed not to see her. He could be like that. She thought that if she demonstrated her willingness to keep coming, he would eventually trust her. But he said nothing. She would look at her watch and grow anxious.

'Maybe it is me?' I could see her wondering. 'Maybe I am doing something wrong?' And she would leave, disappointed. But something brought her back the following week. Finally, she stopped being anxious. She seemed no longer to expect anything from him. Time became unimportant. She seemed no longer to expect him to *do* things – to perform. She sat for hours with him, making no demands – on him or on herself –

and one day he said to her, 'Sometimes, this far away, the only thing I see is the shape of a man pulling through the snow and ice – I can see him quite clearly – and I wonder where he is going, and if he will return.'

After that, he said nothing again for weeks. I know that she told the director, Sallis, about it – how she had sat with Gabriel for many months and that, after showing no sign of acknowledging her, he had suddenly spoken clearly to her one day, once, in a single complete sentence, before falling back into silence. Sallis had said it probably meant nothing. It could have been a reflex action, Sallis had said. It was then that she had asked if she could see Gabriel's records which Henry Kyle had kept. But Sallis had explained about the records.

'What happened to your sailor?' the angel asks.

Some days they play cards, he and his angel. A little Austrian rummy when she visits him in the afternoons. Gabriel is examining the fan of his cards.

'After he got trapped in the ice through the winter,' she continues. 'What happened after that, when the spring came?'

Gabriel picks the top card up from the pack lying face down on the table. His hands are stiff and awkward, poisoned by the Icehouse cold. His face is bleached, a little pockmarked where sores have crusted. 'He walked,' Gabriel says. 'He waited for the spring light and then he walked.'

'Walked how? How did he walk?'

Gabriel examines the card he has picked up. It is a two of hearts. He slots it in alongside another pair of twos somewhere in the middle of his hand, then throws away an unwanted jack.

'Over the ice,' Gabriel says.

Gabriel knows that they walked over the ice to the Anian Strait. It was possible. They could have done it. And died on the return journey to the boat, not merely fleeing in panic from the ship (which all the while lay frozen hard in the ice) as scholars had suggested. Emerson was better than that. Emerson's journal said he found what he was looking for. It said he *saw* the Strait – the blue still sea of Anian. The position of their bodies when they were eventually found meant that if this was true they must have been making their way back to the ship for several weeks when exhaustion and the cold finally overcame them. Their plan had been to make it back to the ship on foot, then when the ice broke in June or July to sail for home. That way, they would return to England having confirmed that the North-West Passage was a reality. Then they could organize a return the next year in bigger ships – a fleet of ships – strong enough to sail through the summer ice and through the Strait to Cathay. Then Gabriel Emerson would be as remarkable as Columbus or Marco Polo. Then he would be the man who, a century after Columbus found America, became the man who found the Passage over the Americas to the Orient, and not the poor wretch time has made him. He would have been complete.

'But they never made it back to the ship?' the angel asks.

'No, they never made it back,' Gabriel says. 'Until now. Now they will make it back.'

Below deck Peary is writing, down the long tunnel of his hood. The candle he writes by is enough to throw a weak light on to the paper he writes on, and a yellow patina around him that gives way to darkness.

'What do you write, Peary?'

Peary lifts his head. His eyes are difficult to see. You have to imagine them. Gabriel, wrapped against the bitter cold, has come down from the deck. It has been quiet above. The blue grey sky, pressed with stars, is lit with the reflection of the ice all around the ship. They have taken to standing watch on deck in the early hours. They are scouting for any possible rim of light that could suggest dawn might be near after the long wait. An end to the polar night. But there has been nothing. Just the same still constant dark.

'I always wondered what it is you write about,' Gabriel says. 'I never asked before.'

'They took it off me when they found bits of things that I'd written,' Peary says, 'but I kept writing. I always wrote. Ever since I came.'

'What about?' Gabriel asks.

'About the colony. About what they did.'

'Who?'

'Henry Kyle, the others. Even now. Fat Rose's charts. Everything.'

'You wrote about the colony? About Henry Kyle?'

'All my life.' Peary says. 'You never knew this. Every day they did things. Every day I wrote. I saved everything I wrote. Your voyage, my books – it's the same thing.'

'No one else knows what you wrote all this time?' Gabriel asks.

'Henry Kyle knew.'

'Henry Kyle knew? What did he do?' Gabriel asks.

'You know what he did. You know. He put me in the side-room. He gave me treatment. He called it treatment.'

'What about Rose? Did Rose know?'

'I kept it hidden. Till Roland found out. Roland found where they were hidden – all my notebooks.'

'What happened to Roland, Peary?'

'They took him away. He tried to sell my notebooks to Sallis. Roland thought it would get him a better kind of place to live after the colony. You know – nice nurses. Lawns. No bedsit with drunks. You would think after all those years he'd have stopped believing what they promised, but he carried right on. Athol beat the hell out of him. They just moved Roland out one day, quietly. And Sallis doesn't bother me any more. Except I think I bother him. I'm the only one who wrote it all down. That's why they keep me and Athol here, saying they can't find the right placements for us yet, saying we're difficult placements – Athol because he killed a man a long time ago and nearly did the same to Roland, me because they hope I'll die in here so all my writing for forty years will die too. They think only Henry Kyle's story should make history. Only Sallis's. They think only *their* story should get told. Not mine. Not ours.'

They have waited weeks for the sun to reappear, standing watch for the light which was taken from them three months ago. They are the first white men to have known the possibility of days – not nights – filled with stars. They are the first to have seen a single, constant black night stretching an entire season.

A faint light grows on them day by day. Not sunlight, because there is still no sign of the sun. But the tone in the air is less dense than it has been through their winter. It becomes enough for them to see their way around the *Endeavour* without the aid of candles. It is a grey kind of twilight that allows them to see each other as they are now – pale, creatures drawn with the privations of the big winter, sitting talking through the last of the long night.

'The landlady we were given in Laing made us pray each night,' Athol says. 'She told the town clerk it had to be a condition of our getting a room in her house. So we had to pray to keep our room. She used to tell us that she'd suffered like Jesus. She said that this was how people got to Heaven – through suffering.'

'When I was small,' Gabriel says, 'I thought Heaven was a farm. I thought: when I go, I won't know what to do, how to milk the cows or feed the hens; I'll be no good in Heaven.' Gabriel smiles at himself.

'Why did you think of a farm?'

'I knew that God had lambs, so he must have been a farmer.'

'How could you know that?'

'It was in the prayers. The Lamb of God. Nobody said what it meant. They just said it.'

'Do you still believe in Heaven?' Athol asks.

'No.'

Outside, it is snowing down from the big pale sky.

'Why not?' Athol says.

'There is no Heaven, apart from what we make it. My Dada when I told him said it wasn't a farm, it was whatever you wanted it to be.'

'What did you want it to be?'

'A hotel. A big, big hotel for everyone, with lots of rooms. And a big ballroom, for everyone to dance.'

'You, Peary? You think there is Heaven?'

'No,' Peary says. 'No Heaven. Only Hell. Henry Kyle's colony is Hell. Afterwards, there is nothing.'

179

'But if there is no Heaven,' Athol says, 'how can a man wind up his life after being in this place? If afterwards is nothing, how can a man *finish* a life that was nothing before?'

'Vasco de Gama sailed around the unknown cape to India,' Gabriel tells him. 'He said men should have no unfinished business at the end.'

'How can we four have unfinished business?' Athol says. 'We have had no lives. Life was nothing. Afterwards is nothing. What have we to finish off?'

'I have unfinished business,' Peary says.

'You? What business.'

'With Henry Kyle,' Peary says. 'My unfinished business is with him. So is yours.'

'Henry Kyle is dead,' Athol tells him. 'Dead and gone.'

'Dead but not gone. No more than Gabriel Emerson the sailor has gone.'

'The cold has got to your head,' Athol says impatiently.

'You think your business with Kyle is over, big man? You think anybody's is? Everything that was of me, Kyle took. He laughs at me, still. He has me.'

'He hasn't got me. I don't go hiding in some cave of a hood like a hibernating animal.'

'Believe me – he has all of us.'

'So what do you plan to do, Peary? You go to Henry Kyle and shout "Boo!" and you're going to frighten him to death. Ha ha!'

'No more now,' Gabriel says.

'You're going to say you're a ghost in that fucking hood of yours. And Henry Kyle, he's going to see you and say "Shitfuck, a ghost", and he's going to drop down dead even though he's been dead for more years than I can count?'

'Enough. There shouldn't be fighting between us. Peary is right.'

'Ah, fuck him.'

'He's right, Athol.'

'So what are you going to do? We should conclude lives that Henry Kyle stole from us. So what do we do?'

On the last day of March, a sudden solar corona becomes visible from the ship. The men stand together on deck to watch it. A layer of thin cloud passes over the sun and lights up in tints of yellows and greens and blues. It is the first natural light they have seen from the ship since the previous November closed over them.

The new landscape around the ship excites and frightens them. The winter has twisted and buckled the ice high up around the ship. Big shards of ice have cracked the flat line of the sea all the way to the far land they had been fighting towards for shelter when the *Endeavour* had become frozen in the ice. The shards rise like buildings out into the air and strike them dumb. It leaves them wondering at the authority that commanded the scene of apparent revolution as far as they can see in the grey half-light.

But no matter what is there, at least now they can see it. Now they know that they have almost seen off the polar night. They pray. They clutch each other. They wonder what lies ahead beyond their small salvation of light.

Two days later, the sun itself rides out above the horizon briefly for an hour – a solid gold disc of light setting fire to the new sky. The crew stand silently on deck in the brilliant cold watching the first sunrise of the polar spring. Peary lifts off his long hood, the better to see the new sky. His hairless head (even his eyebrows have fallen out), is criss-crossed with scratches and pock-marks where life's boils had erupted. No one speaks. Later, back down below deck, they will hear Ingerman singing – some sweet boy's song he had long since forgotten. Athol brews tea on the stove, and Peary takes it through to Ingerman and changes his dressing.

'Bubba wanted to send you something in secret,' Evelyn, his angel, says. 'I don't believe it was his intention that his family should know of you. Not for their sake but for yours. As part of his will, he left instructions with his solicitors that after his death a package was to be sent to you. They sent the package to the post office box number which Henry Kyle used for mail intended for residents of the colony. But of course Henry Kyle was long since dead by this time. The post office box number was no longer in use. The package was returned to the sender – to the firm of solicitors.'

She pulls out a small package from the shoulder bag she carries. The parcel is wrapped in simple brown paper. She passes it to him.

'You know what it is?'

He feels the shape of it. After a moment he nods.

He takes it from her and opens it cautiously. It is pocket-sized. The cracked leather cover has a small crest in the bottom corner. The corners have frayed through the hard cover to the cardboard innards underneath.

The book has the sour cream smell of must. Gabriel flicks through the pages which are heavy, rough. The pencil and charcoal drawings, despite the smell of faint decay from the paper, are firm and clear.

'You know who they are?' the angel asks him.

'That one is a sketch of Peretta,' Gabriel tells her, pointing out a handsome man with a big straight nose and dark eyes. 'Friegang there, with the glasses. One of Kasperl sitting on the steps of the hotel juggling with balls. Rolf Stent stole the balls from him. Just one of Joannie Kilner – see.'

Joannie Kilner always threatened that if she found Brolin sketching her, she would kill him. 'You stick to drawing that big, dumb Italian Peretta,' she had said to Brolin. 'Or the girls of the third floor. They like to be drawn, to be flattered. Go flatter them. You draw me and I'll kill you, Brolin.' And only once in the time they were there had he drawn her. In the sketch of Joannie Kilner, she is dancing on a ballroom floor amongst other dancers. But she, unlike the other few couples in the background, is dancing alone. Most of the sketches in the book, though, are not of the third-floor girls, or of the internees. Most of the sketches are of Gabriel. He is six or seven years old at the time. He seems oblivious each time to the sketcher close at hand. Sometimes he is with William, sometimes alone. One shows him asleep on a couch; around him, carrying out small tasks or passing the time, are Emily and the other girls from the third floor – like a Lautrec sketch of the girls of the Montmartre, with a young, fair-headed boy asleep amongst the whores.

Gabriel folds shut the sketchbook. Holds it.

'Athol says that Henry Kyle's archive is being sent away,' he says.

'Yes.'

'Where?'

'America.'

'America?'

'To a university in Texas.'

'What will they do with it?'

'I don't know. Add it to their collection. People will study it. Use it for research.'

'Where is the archive now?'

'The administration block somewhere, I think. I don't know. Why? Dr Sallis told me it was to be shipped to America in just a few weeks.'

'Do you know where in the block?'

She shakes her head. 'No, not really. Why do you want to know, Gabriel?'

'There are some things that belong to us. To me, to Athol, Ingerman, Peary. We want them back. They are part of the archive and we want them back.'

'Why don't you ask Dr Sallis?'

'No.'

'Why not. If they are yours . . .'

'Sallis wouldn't understand. They are ours, but Sallis wouldn't understand that. We have to take them, but Sallis mustn't know about it. Will you find out for me where the archive is. Whether it is locked up?'

'Gabriel, you can't go taking things.'

'Only what's ours. Nothing else. Only what's ours.'

'Will you tell me something, Gabriel?'

He waits for her question.

'What did Henry Kyle do?'

He doesn't answer.

'I want to know. Really.'

'It's in the files,' Gabriel says. 'Everything is in the files. Help me. Bubba would want you to help me. Will you help me?'

'You're asking me to break my word to Dr Sallis?'

'Yes.'

She is surprised by his bluntness. 'Will you let me think about it? About what you're asking?'

'Think about it,' Gabriel says. 'Then help me. Help us.'

'May I look at the sketchbook?' she says.

Gabriel passes it to her. She flicks through the pages one by one. On the flyleaf of the book is an inscription:

'To Gabriel the Sailor. Good voyaging, boy. Good health. Good luck. Good life. Jacob Brolin.'

She flicks through the pages of the sketchbook, looking at Brolin's work.

'There's one page missing,' she says.

'Yes,' Gabriel says, 'one page missing. I had to give it to Peretta.'

She looks quietly through the rest of the sketches. 'I can't help thinking,' she says, 'that I was not meant to see these. But for an accident, I would not have seen them. But for the package Bubba left after his death being addressed to a discontinued post office box number and being returned to his solicitor, I would not have come here.'

'Were you there when Bubba died?' Gabriel asks her.

'Yes,' she says.

There is always an angel present each time someone's life ends; an angel or Death.

'He was my father,' she says. 'I was there when Bubba died.'

14

The day the world must end should be a Sunday

Even the day the world will end must begin like any other – a little weak and wasteful sunshine over the house of Laing, perhaps a wind off the harbour. A day like any other. A day like this.

Even the day the world will end may begin with routine and mindlessness. Men, sniffing and scratching, rising in the first poor light, shaving in cold water, in clean silence, pulling their shirts over white, goose-pimpled flesh. Women lighting fires and making breakfast and running through preparations still needed for the Laing Fair. Miners, made dull by sleep, walking to the pit heads and down to the harbour to the crying gulls and the breeze off the fast sea and the smells of brine and potash, carry food wraps, tobacco, cold tea flasks. Two boats put out looking for Shetland cod hoping to make it back in time for the Laing Fair. William sets off early with Rolf Stent's gang, laughing and kicking at the air as boys do; women pound dough to make bread, and air rooms; old men sit out after church and watch the sea. The day runs on.

'Are you losing heart, donkey, that you come down less often to see me?' Joannie Kilner asks.

It is true that Peretta has seen her less often recently. It is harder to see her now that they are out at Salem Turn. They moved to Salem Turn at Brolin's insistence. They moved out after the pit-fall.

There had been a smell of gas around in the bottom chamber. For several days, after the night blasting, the former internees and the other morning fillers – the men who filled the moving conveyor belts with shovelfuls of coal previously cut and blasted loose – had been testing each crevice with their lamps, nervous of the gas, watching to see if the flame would turn tell-tale blue. Even with the wick turned up, the flame some-times burned blue. It had been reported twice by Peretta who had grown nervous of it. But when someone was sent down to check, it had seemed OK. It seemed a fuss was being made over nothing. That's what Joe Filbin said afterwards. What was he to do, he said – call the men out on the say-so of one filler, and lose the men a week's bonus on the strength of it and risk facing a charge for organizing the illegal withholding of labour? It seemed a fuss over nothing. After all, there was always gas around in the atmosphere of the pit. And it was never easy to detect. It wasn't always distributed evenly, that was the thing.

Maybe all it took on the morning of the explosion was a spark from someone's pickaxe striking a stone. Just a fluke. A build-up of gas in one small corner. They got everyone out who'd left a tag on the surface, including the three internees who'd been working underground and those who'd been injured in the blast. They thought they'd got everybody out, but when all the tags were checked someone said there were still some missing. And so they organized a recount. It turned out after the recount there were two of the boys listed on the shift whose tags Kasperl should have had but didn't. And everyone knew that Joe Filbin had told Kasperl that it was his fault. Everyone knew that Joe Filbin told Kasperl he'd have him hung in a butcher's shop if the delay they'd suffered led to anything bad when they went back underground to look for the two missing boys.

The two missing miners were both Bevan boys – conscripts to the mines. They weren't from Laing. They were twins. They kept themselves to themselves. They had been talking to each other, sharing some joke or remark and they had neglected to hand in the necessary segment of their dog-tags after collecting their lamps at the start of the shift. They had been busy with each other and they had simply forgotten about the tags.

Half-way through the dig to find the two boys who were believed to be down there still, part of the bottom gallery gave way and the sea came in like thunder. The pressure of water burst past the weakened dam of the collapse and the sea hammered through, taking everything in its path. Most made it to the surface. One of the Bevan boys – one of the twins – died. One Laing man drowned in the failed rescue.

Kasperl, the youth, in his too-big trousers and his flapping jacket and the hair shorn to the scalp on his skull, put his head in his hands and cried. The rescue teams came up in the cage ten at a time after that, gasping at clean air, coughing out the raining coal dust and the sweet sickness of the spent gas and the stench of the sea. Peretta, who'd gone down with them, knelt and kissed the ground. Around the hill, miners were silent. The internees stood away from the main body of men, watching.

They were told that they should not attend the funeral. So, on the day the Laing man was buried and the mines were closed, the internees stood on the harbour to watch the people go by. There had been an argument. Someone had said they should not be here, even to watch the cortège go past. Some people still blamed the youth Kasperl for the mix-up with the identity tags that cost the life of a man and of one of the Bevan boys who'd accidentally been left down there when it was thought the pit had been cleared.

'You speak to Joe Filbin,' Peretta had said in the end. 'You people will spend a day closing the mine to bury your dead, but not a day closing the mine to prevent it. Everyone knew there was gas. He should have told men not to go down instead of finding an outsider to lay the blame on, instead of blaming Kasperl.'

There had been a scuffle. A punch had been thrown. Peretta wouldn't back down. He had floored a man with a single blow, then walked away. People backed off. The cortège moved on, towards Laing's cemetery.

After the Wellington Pit had been shut down because of the flood and the internees had been laid off, they went to live at Salem Turn. Joannie Kilner had arranged it through Stent. Stent knew of a run-down gamekeeper's lodge on one of the Kyle estates for lease. Joannie Kilner had agreed with Brolin, who acted as their spokesman, that it was probably for the best for the time being after the death of the Laing miner and the Bevan boy.

The day the world may end should be a Sunday so that the world may first dance. Then, as now, Joannie Kilner's small orchestra may play quietly. A few people will be dancing as they do here; others will sit at tables around the edge of the dark ballroom in the third-class hotel with no name. And only then, when people have danced and loved and made whispered confessions, will a kind of fire take hold around the edges and be spun by the wind until it engulfs even the still centre of things.

Donato Peretta is here. Brolin is here, drawing fitfully in charcoal on the sketchpad resting small in his lap. Friegang is here too, somewhere. It is Sunday. It is the night of the dance and they are all down from Salem Turn. They come into Laing when they need to register their presence at the police station in accordance with Regulation 18B which Stent had instructed them in, and they come down each Sunday for the public dance at Joannie Kilner's hotel, but otherwise they keep to themselves. They do odd jobs around the Kyles' gaming estate beyond Salem Turn and they dig beach coal now and then for pin money. The pitfall has shown them that they will always be outsiders. In the pits, men are back at work in all except the Wellington Pit, which has been sealed after the recent flood and the gas explosion which had precipitated it, and which till then had been the most productive of the Laing pits. The internees drive back and forth between Salem Turn and Laing in the truck belonging to the hotel. A couple of times a week, Brolin and Peretta drive into Laing to fetch supplies for Joannie Kilner's hotel. Apart from that, and the Sunday dance, and registering as aliens, they stay away. It is safer that way, whilst people still feel bad about the men who died.

Peretta sits alone, wondering about love. Gabriel sits with Brolin at their own small table in the ballroom. There is no sign of William. William has not yet returned from playing with Rolf Stent and Morton Filbin. This isn't unusual. On Sundays, William knows that Kasperl will be waiting for him to ask him – to beg him – for news of his juggling balls. And so William will not come back to the hotel until late, so that he can avoid poor Kasperl.

At first, Kasperl had chased after each child who passed, wanting to know if they'd seen the two boys who had stolen his juggling balls and where they might have put them. Once, he had frightened William half to death, grabbing him by the scruff of the neck and shaking him for an answer. But Brolin had warned off Kasperl from chasing boys out on to the street and frightening them, and so Kasperl has settled for shouting out at any boy who passes, asking them whether they know the whereabouts of Rolf Stent and Morton Filbin and his juggling balls, and Brolin has to bring him in and sit him down in the ballroom or else Kasperl will stand and wait on the steps all night as if in his head he were hoping for the circus itself to pass by.

Peretta looks up from his table and sees Joannie Kilner watching him.

'You wish to sit, madam?'

She shakes her head.

'You are neglecting us, Peretta,' she says.

'It is for the best, madam. After the deaths – the mine – Brolin says it is for the best. You have the flowers I bring for you today?'

'Yes,' she says. She has the flowers. 'Will you come to the Fair next week?'

'I think not. Brolin says not. Not while things are difficult.'

'And the woman in the florist's shop? The teacher who lost her son? She's still angry? She still shouts?'

Peretta shrugs. 'Is always. Is best to talk of other things.'

She looks around the ballroom. Then she sits. 'I see your friend is entertaining the boy again.'

'Brolin likes the boy's company. It is good for Gabriel whilst his father works.'

'Brolin doesn't like the company of women?'

'He had a wife. She died after they came to England. He is alone now, no family here. His father is a communist. There are many communists in Germany when Germany is so poor in the twenties when money is nothing, when people go hungry, when the fascists are throwing their big weight around in bars and on the street marches. His father is in prison after the Blackshirts take him. His father dies and Brolin comes to England with his wife. Sadness stays on him.'

'He would still do better with a woman for company again. He thinks too much.'

'I think he worries about what things are for.'

'What sort of things?'

'Him. His life. He worries what his life is for. He sees he is getting older and he wonders now what are things for. His wife died on a ship taking internees to Australia. She was beaten by the soldiers on the ship. The internees were starved. They have belongings stolen from them. Lot of them are beaten up. She has all her things stolen by the guards. That's how she has a heart attack. That's how she died. I try to protest, to the Commandant, to Red Cross, to Stent when we come to Laing, but nothing happens. Now Brolin wonders what there is of him to give that is worth giving.'

'And Kasperl, the dog with no bark? Is he still patrolling

the steps of my hotel? While Brolin draws pictures and wonders about things, and while the other one goes rummaging amongst the whores, and you speak Italian nonsense at me, is the dog with no bark on guard outside my hotel?'

'Hush, or he'll hear you. Look at him over there by himself. He is so young – so deft with skittles, so clumsy still with the world. Brolin has brought him inside, away from the cold, and the boys who torment him. He will learn.'

'And you, Peretta. You never learn. You send me poetry again.'

'I ask Brolin to teach me poetry. Brolin knows about these things. He teaches me poetry so I can give it for you.'

'I don't speak Italian, Peretta. You might as well write to a donkey as write to me in a language that I don't understand.'

'That is because the real beauty, Brolin says, is in the saying it. But if I cannot speak poetry as it should be done, then I must write it.'

'So speak it.'

She hands him back the sheet of paper on which the poem has been written down by Brolin and signed by Peretta.

'You will have me speak it to you?'

'Yes, you speak it to me, donkey.'

'I cannot. Brolin will speak it. But I do not speak classical Italian. Not poetry. Not Dante. I am not an educated man like Brolin. I only ask Brolin for a poem to say how I feel.'

'And how do you feel?'

'As the poem. The poem says.'

'Speak it, donkey, for me. To make me happy.'

'This would make you happy?'

'Maybe,' she says. 'Maybe it will make me happy.'

And so Peretta, uneasy, intense and concentrating on the

unfamiliar words and cadence, reads the poem to Joannie Kilner – Dante's love poem, written down for Peretta in Italian by Jacob Brolin who watches him across the floor of the third-class hotel.

'Così m'hai concio, Amore, in mezzo l'alpi,
ne la valle del fiume
lungo il qual sempre sopra me se' forte:
qui vivo e morte, come vuoi, mi palpi,
merzé del fiero lume
che sfolgorando fa via a la morte.'

'*Amore* is love?' she says.
'Sì.'
'*Morte* is death?'
'Sì. *Morte* is death.'

Brolin and Gabriel sit on the far side of the room, close to the kitchens. They watch people go to and fro through the evening of the dance, watch the inhabitants of the first-floor refuge baking in relays and the women of the third floor tease and yawp at each other.

'Will they be in love in the end?' Gabriel asks.

'Who knows,' Brolin says. 'When I was young – a little older than you, perhaps – I heard Anna Mutter sing. She came to Dresden. She sang arias. My uncles took me, because my father said that it was frivolous to spend so much money on tickets for a mere performer. And I fell in love. A love can only be so simple, so complete when you are a child. A love like that, later, you have to fight to keep alive. Sometimes it dies. Sometimes it perishes in the first cold wind that strikes.'

'She's letting him talk to her,' Gabriel says.

'I can see.'

'Is it them you're sketching?'

'Maybe,' Brolin says.

'Together?' Gabriel asks.

'You must have patience. You must let things be. Now, you tell me. Will you be going to this fair they are having on the beach?'

'No.'

'Why not? Everyone talks about it.'

'My Dada says I was frightened when he took me before the war. I didn't like the masks all the people held to their faces. Once, I found the mask my Dada had made of Mama to remind him of her. I cried.'

'You don't like the masks?'

Gabriel shakes his head. He is watching Brolin form the swift shapes of his subjects. When he is finished, he tears the page out and gives it to Gabriel.

'You will give this to Peretta,' he says.

'Not to her?'

'No, give it to Peretta. If she is curious, she will ask him if she may look at it.'

There is no sign of William. It is supposed at this time that he's away with Rolf Stent and his gang, simply keeping out of the way of Kasperl, but it will be several days before he returns. By then the dry winds of fear and apprehension, like a reckless mistral, will have begun to blow about the town, scattering leaves and shaking the tiles of roofs and searching for flames to fan and will catch them and take them up and burn and burn till finally it is weak and spent.

In the ballroom, Gabriel's head rests on the table, asleep. Kasperl sits watching, curious. Soon Walt will come from the desk in the lobby and nod shyly to Brolin and to Kasperl and will carry the boy up the stairs, clumping three flights to lay him on a bed and kiss him and deliver his nightly benediction to his son, 'Goodnight, my King of Laing,' and set him to sleep, safe for now from all the terragots.

Brolin has stopped sketching now, eyeing the world through a glass of weak beer. Another year, or less, Brolin is surely thinking, and maybe war will be done and we can break free of this place; another year and we will have set sail like the sailor, like Gabriel's mariner – the one his clumping, gentle father tells him about in stories on the beach as they look out to the sea.

Maybe Peretta would wish to stay here, with his love. Maybe Friegang might stay for the easy way he could go on fucking the third-floor girls. Maybe even Kasperl would be tempted to stay, if no Circus Prenzlau arrived to take him away back on to the road. But no, Kasperl would not stay. Kasperl had dreams. Brolin and Kasperl would set sail – and one day Kasperl would find some circus, some street theatre, and take up his life again. And Brolin would look for a life even now to take up, a cause to find, maybe one day a woman to love – an Anna Mutter to sing for him – and children – boys – to breathe life and hope into this world and set them on their way.

Brolin finishes his beer, tries to confess his thoughts to the idiot youth Kasperl who will not understand but who will listen. And under the splintered light of the ballroom, Peretta dances with Joannie Kilner. And if it were true that this were the day the world would end, then the last line in their heads would be from the poem that Peretta translates for Joannie Kilner as they dance her one dance together in the third-class hotel in Laing – *To this state, Love, you have reduced me, among the mountains, in the valley of the river along which you are always strong over me; here, just as you will, you knead me, both alive and dead, thanks to the fierce light that – flashing – opens the road to death.*

15

A single cause

What can reduce men to despair is that which also gives them hope – time passing.

For forty years there have been no clocks within the colony, visible to us residents. Time had little meaning for us. Instead of time, which is a personal thing, we had a rhythm, with Henry Kyle conducting. No clocks: no time passing. No hope and no despair. This has been a frozen continent – which is how, I think, Henry Kyle had planned it when he made this place his life's work.

The absence of visitors always added to our sense of having been becalmed. Even the occasional visitor who did arrive, like Ingerman's mother who came to watch him patiently through her thick brown spectacles, only ever exacerbated our sense of distance from the beating heart of possibilities, from things passing, from time itself. Henry Kyle had truly succeeded in excluding us from the world. And so it seems all the more vivid now, so long after Kyle's death, to find within those few of us still here a quiet rolling sense that time *is* passing, that things *are* happening.

Another ten or twelve residents have gone from the colony this last week. Those of us who are left have no wish to go, however. We cling like limpets to the small things that we know as life. Apart from Gabriel that is. Apart from Gabriel, and apart from the three others for whom he has created a bigger purpose.

I remember Henry Kyle as a small, unspectacular man. He wore marble spectacles. He wore a three-piece suit and a pocket watch which hung from his waistcoat and pinged every hour. I never saw him dressed in any other way. I never saw him unshaven, even when he had been called out for some emergency in the dead of night, when he would appear in a neat tweed suit, stiff-collared shirt and tie. He would take his exercise walking slowly around the colony, hands held behind his back, head up – like a small Tsar. He rarely raised his voice. He believed utterly in God, in God's plan – in the plan that he, Henry Kyle, and God had arrived at between them. He worked long hours. He never took holidays to my knowledge – that is, he never spent time away from the colony for all of the years that he presided over us unless it was in connection with the colony's business. He took his meals each day in the Great Hall along with the residents; he had his own table at which he ate alone on the raised stage of the hall, looking down upon us. Even after his death, his presence is still said to be with us. It is said that the ghost of Henry Kyle can still be seen some nights stalking the empty, secured buildings of the colony – as if he is reluctant even now to leave us to the mercies of the world he kept us from.

I would say, that to a young man like Kyle, anxious to make his mark on the world, the Mental Deficiency Act must have seemed like manna from Heaven. Knowing what I know now, I have no doubt that he must have fallen upon it as if it were the Word of God. Which it may well have been. For, at the time that I first came across him, he seemed to me, to most of us, to be the resurrection of some Old Testament prophet in his inability to picture the world in any way other than his own; in the way he and God had agreed how the world was and what was necessary for it.

I know now, of course, that things can seem one thing and be another. I know that Ingerman can stare, bug-eyed at some apparently random pattern in front of him and that he, looking at the same component parts as I, can see something utterly different; that Ingerman can see one thing and I another without either of us lying. I know that good and evil can be like this also. I was brought up as a boy in the Lutheran belief that good and evil are like bread and bricks – always constant and easily distinguished. I thought that some men – important men, well-respected men, men who had acquired *position* – were simply better than others at identifying which was which and saying so; at leading us all through a sometimes foggy but well-mapped and uncontested country. They are not. I know now that the real battle is in hearing other men's pain. The real battle is in listening for the possible screams of distant lives.

Henry Kyle was twenty-five when he established a colony for the feeble-minded, and when it fell to him to set about capturing certain kinds of people from the towns and villages of Cumberland and to set them apart in a colony, both for their own benefit and for that of the communities from which they came. Each of us taken in this way was put into the uniform of the colony. Each of us duly failed the diagnostic tests which were required before we could be admitted against our wills. Of course the tests were rigged to ensure that none of us could pass them. We learned that when you have God on your side – when you *know* that it is a good thing to lock a particular man up and evil to allow him back into the community at large – then such things are surely permitted. So in turn, over the years, Athol and Ingerman and Peary and Gabriel, and I, along with all the others, arrived and one by one failed the diagnostic tests which confirmed the legitimacy of our incarceration.

There was an appeals system, of course. The Act demanded that an appeals system be set in place. Residents were allowed to petition against their confinement. Fewer appealed than made the simpler attempt to flee. Of those who made attempts to escape out in the kept-clean world, the one who tried most often was Roland. Each time, though, he was hunted down by Henry Kyle's black Ford which seemed to lurk on the edge of so many street corners, in so many towns, that people believed there was a whole fleet of them under Henry Kyle's control. In the end, even Roland gave up and accepted his fate. Those who did petition against the decision to confine them in the colony were allowed to bring their families or others to support the petition. The only one I ever knew who had someone with him for an appeal was Ingerman. Ingerman's mother, squinting through her thick brown spectacles, came to his petition and pleaded with Henry Kyle to allow her son home. But no one ever won their petition. What chance against the Word of God?

The Mental Deficiency Act, passed by Parliament in 1913, established four categories of persons who could be unilaterally locked away from society. One of these – the one in which Henry Kyle came to specialize – was the *feeble-minded*.

Kyle's residents were a cross-section of people with a single common thread of experience: they were those whose difficulties with the world led them to stand out from the larger crowd, people whose lives lacked a steady, unaffecting tick. They were, in the words of the Act which lay on the statute book in England until 1959, people who were *defective*. They were those who exhibited anti-social tendencies without actually having broken the law. They were farm-workers who were slow; they were women who'd given birth outside marriage or who were easy sexual prey; they were those with speech impediments or congenital diseases. They were people who were odd. They were people who were different from the general mould which, it was imagined, God (Henry Kyle's God, Stent's God, the Women's Protection League's God) had used in fashioning humanity. I know what Brolin would have said. Big people dealing with little people – the story of the world, Brolin would have said. But at the time that Henry Kyle was discovering the Word of his God, Brolin was just a boy living a boy's gentle life in the old medieval city of Dresden (and being moved sufficiently by the city's public architecture to consider taking up an apprenticeship in stone-masonry at the Cathedral in the heart of the city.)

Henry Kyle's notion – the vision that informed and guided his life – was that the people he collected from the towns of Cumberland represented an identifiable genus whose social behaviour, whose differences from the norm, could be traced back to a single neurological disorder. It became Henry Kyle's work to find the link that would connect all of the forms of feeble-mindedness represented by the residents within his – and other – such colonies. It became his work to find this single cause.

A single cause would help in the treatment of those who were afflicted. A single cause would delineate an entire class of people who both deserved looking after and needed separating from the mainstream of men. A single cause would happily confirm the majority of people once and for all to be normal, and would set them apart from a small and uncurable element of humanity who were in need of confinement. In between these two categories, Henry Kyle posited an unsurmountable barrier, a wall which could not be straddled in either direction. Once he had found his single cause, all men would be shown to reside inexorably in one category or the other. Men at birth would be damned, or they would be saved.

The legacy of Henry Kyle, after forty-seven years, amounts to one hundred and seventeen crates of information: files, records, diagnoses, measurements (of foreheads and craniums and spinal columns and eyes and feet and teeth and bowel movements and leg stride and dietary allergies and voice cadences and musical pitch and inner ear vibration and temperamental humours and skeletal shapes and so on), and data books and photographs and records of the punishments which aimed to annul all individuality – to ensure control – and work registers and bowel books and menstruation books and bath books and roll calls and sickness records. All of these will shortly be loaded on to two transporter lorries on the first leg of their journey to Texas to form part of a university library collection.

Believe me when I say that Henry Kyle left no stone unturned in his search for a single cause. At the time of his death he believed, according to the notes which he left, that he had narrowed down his search to the two possibilities which remained for a single cause: perhaps some neurological symptom he had yet to come across – some virus or germ within the brain, or else a hereditary element to the condition, a single element which nevertheless manifested itself in a vast array of social deviancies. He noted everything in his search. He missed almost nothing. Among those he confided in, among his fellow professionals, he was renowned for missing nothing. There was only one thing that he did miss in his search and that was a sound he did not hear. It was a feeling he did not sense, because he was so distanced from any pain that was not his own. He did not hear the possible screams of distant lives; he did not feel the pain that was manifest in the men all around him whom he sought to judge.

Henry Kyle's search for a single cause would elude him to his death. He would search for it in the unflinching and committed way that men once searched for new continents – for a New World, for Cathay, for a snow-covered mountain in the heart of Africa, for a sea route to India, for a North-West Passage. Poor Henry Kyle must have thought that the map of the world he had forged would last forever. He must have believed that the work he instituted would prove as solid and as steadfast as Jacob Brolin had believed the massive medieval stone buttresses of the Dresden Cathedral of St Trinitas to be. He must have believed that his work would prove to be as permanent and enduring as the statue of Gabriel Emerson promised to be to the citizens of Laing when the *Endeavour* set out from Laing's harbour in the spring of 1620.

Athol is out somewhere organizing supplies. Peary and Ingerman, I know, are at work in the Icehouse since shortly it will play host to a different kind of drama. They are building the walk they will take. They are constructing a circuit around the circumference of the building. The uneven ground is being manufactured using wooden planks laid on the ground over lumps of concrete from the already cracked and broken Icehouse floor. It's over this that they'll drag their supplies. It's over this that they'll show that it was possible that Emerson could have found his Anian Strait.

And Gabriel? Gabriel is with Evelyn - his angel - in the Bear Pit, but the time for playing cards - for their games of Austrian rummy - is over. Time passes. Hope is in the air.

I sense a different relationship between them now. As though Evelyn - the angel - has become the junior of the two. As though she defers to him. Maybe it's because he knows her now to be his brother's child. Maybe that knowledge brings a perspective to both of them. Whatever the reasons, there is more a sense of stature, of patience, about him - a sense of him rising to a single defining act. Soon, the Arctic light will shine for several hours a day, enough to permit them to begin their walk across the tundra ice, towards the North-West Passage which they believe is due south, some way beyond the trapped *Endeavour* harboured in ice.

'I told Dr Sallis I wanted to see him,' Evelyn says.

'What did you talk about?' Gabriel asks slowly.

'Oh, you, I suppose. I don't know. I didn't want to mention his archives - your things - too openly in case it aroused his suspicion. I just wanted an excuse to get in there. After a while, I told him I wanted to visit the Ladies Room and left his office. I must have spent a good ten minutes nosying around the rooms in the administration block, all the offices, without anybody stopping me. There's not many people left working there now.'

'Did you see anything?'

'No, not really. When I went back into his office, Dr Sallis was on the phone to America through in the secretariat. I looked around for keys or key cupboards. I found a shipping order for the archives that Dr Sallis had signed. They are being sent to Texas at the end of the month. That's two weeks. You wouldn't believe how much they're paying for it. And for Dr Sallis to travel out with it. Is it just files? What's in it that a university would pay so much money for it to Henry Kyle's estate?'

'There are no documents then?' Gabriel asks, ignoring Evelyn's question.

She shakes her head. 'I'm sorry. I tried. I really did. I tried to think of anywhere in there that the archive might be. When Dr Sallis came back into the room I even began asking him about the archive more directly to see if I could find anything out that way. Did you know he is planning to write a book about the colony himself? He has a publisher and everything.'

'What did you say?'

'I told him I thought it was wrong. I told him it wasn't right that he, or Henry Kyle – or his family – should make money out of it all now. I told him all of his efforts should be on helping those people who'd spent their lives here and not on making money and writing books. He just smoked his little cigar and looked at me through the tint of his glasses and smiled. He said I was just coming in from the outside. He said that I couldn't possibly understand about it. I'm sorry. I don't think I've been of much help to you.'

I know that when she left Sallis's office, Evelyn had reached to snap up the sun blind as she'd passed it on her way to the door. The pulley string had ravelled up the blind in a flurry, winding it fast to the top of the window, allowing the sun outside to pour into the cool office, making Sallis squint in the sudden, direct light falling on him.

'My brother was so cautious,' Gabriel says. 'He mightn't have tried.'

'Bubba would have tried – for you. I think if he thought he had the chance he would.'

'Did Bubba have a good life?'

'Yes, I think so,' Evelyn says. 'Sometimes he was troubled. I think he blamed himself all of his life for whatever happened. But by and large I think he had a good life. He found some happiness and he clung to it.'

'Was it Bubba who taught you how to play Austrian rummy?' Gabriel asks.

'He taught my mum too. We used to play on holidays when I was little. He was in hospital for a time – I played a lot with him then. It used to help us to talk. My father was never an easy talker, unless you got him started. The cards helped. But even then, he never talked about you.'

'Brolin taught us both how to play – me and Bubba. In the hotel. Brolin was a good teacher. He was patient. Brolin taught people to read and write. He helped Emily to read, and Kasperl the juggler who had been in a circus from ten years old; he couldn't read either. And Brolin taught Austrian rummy to me and to Bubba. He liked to play.'

'What happened? To Brolin and the others?'

'They died.'

'All of them?'

'Yes, all. It was a long time ago. In the war they died. Brolin was sad. I liked him. I remember what he said to me. He said the story of the world was the story of how big men dealt with little men. He said the story of the world was the same in every small town – it was how the big men dealt with the little men, and the consequences of it.'

'What will you do now?' she asks.

'It's done,' Gabriel says. He means it's set in motion and there is no going back now. I think he also means that he knows now where the archive is being stored. Gabriel tells her about the key which was left for him unannounced in his cupboard in the dormitory with a note attached to it. The note tells Gabriel how the Great Hall has been used this last six months to catalogue Henry Kyle's archives. It explains how the floorspace is presently taken up with storage of the now-catalogued records of the colony going back to 1922. How they are set out inside the locked hall in row upon row on the long tables we had spent so many years eating from, whilst Henry Kyle looked down upon us from his own high table.

Gabriel wonders if he may ask her something. Of course, she says. He asks her if she will look after Brolin's sketchbook for him.

'For safe keeping?' she asks him, wondering.

He tells her yes, for safe keeping. That's it. For safe keeping. She agrees. She says she will look after it for Gabriel. She says that she knows of a good home for the sketchbook if Gabriel has no use for it afterwards – when it's all over.

She means me. If Gabriel has no use for the sketchbook afterwards, I know that she means me.

16

The search

There are five boys missing. They have not been seen since
Sunday, since the day that Peretta had danced with Joannie
Kilner. Men walking their dogs have made cursory searches of
the wet land along the estuary and of the beach, but there is
no trace of the missing boys, no sign of anything amiss.

Teams of miners are spoken to together in the changing
blocks at the start of shifts to see if anyone has seen the boys,
but no one has seen anything of them. People are organized
by Stent to go around the town door-to-door asking if there's
been any sight of them. Four men are even sent out to Salem
Turn to ask the former internees.

The internees are waiting to be reassigned work. It seems
as though eventually, if the war lasts that long, they'll be sent
to work in pits further north in Whitehaven, or in Lancashire
at Wigan. No one much from the town, outside Joannie
Kilner's third-class hotel, has seen them for several weeks,
and so Stent sends four men out to ask if they know anything
about the missing boys.

Friegang has been drinking and is asleep. Peretta won't
deal with them.

'You talk to them,' Peretta says to Brolin. 'They don't listen. They don't hear what you say.'

It is Brolin who comes out alone to speak to the men who've come from Laing. Brolin explains that his compatriots have seen nothing of the missing boys. He says that if they are needed, even though they have been laid off from working at the pit, they will be happy to help with the search for the boys.

'You don't think you've created enough trouble?' Joe Filbin says to Brolin.

'Peretta said what he thought should be said on the day of the funeral,' Brolin says. 'Perhaps he was only wrong to do it like he did. He is young. Not so diplomatic. Full of, what? Vigour?'

'Full of shit,' one of the Tillotsons says.

'What he meant was surely right,' Brolin says.

'You're expert about right and wrong now as well?' Joe Filbin says. 'Five boys from the town are missing and you want to be a lawyer.'

Brolin shrugs. 'We have still seen nothing of the boys. But we will watch for them. We will come to tell you if we see anything of them.'

'What about the idiot?'

'Kasperl?'

'Yes, him. Has he seen anything? People keep seeing him wandering on the beach, on the fells on his own. He must have seen something.'

Brolin shrugs again. 'He says nothing. But I will ask him.'

'We'll ask him out here.'

Brolin watches them. 'As you say,' he says finally.

Brolin goes inside. He exchanges words with Peretta who

210

has stood watching the conversation from the window. They argue. Brolin talks him down. Peretta disappears from the view of the Laing men. After a few moments, Kasperl is sent out from the house.

The men from Laing ask their questions. They tell Kasperl that they know how he goes off alone. They say people have seen him walking over and over out on the fells and so he must surely have seen the boys who've gone missing. And it's true that Kasperl does walk, and he is often seen vague and cold at sunset, trying to find his way back to the gamekeeper's lodge at Salem Turn, having searched and failed again to catch sight of any circus, having turned back. But he shakes his head. He is wary of the men who ask questions whilst Brolin and Peretta watch on from the lodge. He is wary of the way they ask their questions. They say he'd better be telling the truth. They ask him if he knows what will happen if he's not telling them the truth, if there's things he should be telling them that he's not saying? But Kasperl's head is full of Circus Prenzlau not of Laing, or of boys. How to tell them this? He cannot. He shakes his head. He shakes it to everything. To their whole welter of sentences. To all their questions, until he is sick and dizzy with it all. And eventually they finish. They signal to Brolin. He nods. They turn and leave. Brolin comes out and he leads Kasperl back inside.

The men of Laing organize a search. It is decided to call on every available hand in the town. The search will sweep in a single line of men from the beach, moving beyond the houses on the Heights of Abraham and on to the fells. And so men gather in the square in Laing: people from the town, men from the union commanded by Joe Filbin, men from the Needs Committee led by Sam Wormold, brothers and cousins and uncles of the boys and the other searchers, and the miners who drink in the harbour pubs, and the men who visit Joannie Kilner's third-class hotel for sex with the third-floor girls, and the mountainous Brock Spivey down from his small-holding, towering over everyone, grinning and being egged on by men from the Harbour Inn and the Seven Stars with his two big dogs yelping on their tight leashes held fast in his fists. And in with them all, on the edge, watching, pensive, waiting for news of William, is Walt Emerson, drugged with lack of sleep – a sedate night creature dragged into the light of day.

Children are kept in school, and out of the way until whatever, whoever, has taken the missing boys is confronted, searched out and destroyed. Of all the sounds and sights in the air around the cold square in Laing – the heavy feet of men, and coughs, and spirals of tobacco breath, and shouts of organization, and dogs, and whistles and low whispers – there are no children's sounds.

All of the men wait for their instructions from Stent who stands on a box to give the orders. To one side, a smaller group of women have gathered. Unlike the men, they do not hide their fears for the boys. Apprehension is pinched on their faces, and all the time the beat of the town becomes shallower and faster, and its appetites diminished, its heart dry and anxious for a resolution.

They search for twelve hours for the missing boys – for Rolf Stent, Morton Filbin, the Tillotson brothers and William Emerson – moving over the town and into the woods and the man-made slate caves where everyone knows ne'er-do-wells could hide out for weeks undetected, and out on to the fells. They are encouraged at least to be doing *something*, beating the land, shouting for the missing boys. The dogs bark. The day wears on. The short afternoon turns cold. The sky tilts briefly into orange as its December sun falls quickly. The men grow tired. The pace slackens. Breaths smoke and spiral. The shouting diminishes. They search until it is dark, for as long as they can until the last light is drained from the sky, but there is no sign of the boys.

Rolf Stent and William Emerson turn up in Laing, unaccompanied, the next morning. Word spreads quickly around the town, around the harbour pubs, through the Meeting House where women work together on the preparation for the fair.

The two boys are wet and cold and dirty, and they are frightened. They are given blankets, and tots of whisky are poured down them. They won't say what happened. They are taken to their homes. Rolf Stent eats and drinks and eats some more, then sleeps, then eats again.

'What happened?' his mother asks. 'Were you taken away?'

Rolf Stent nods but says no more.

The word in the town is that the internees were involved, but no one is sure if Rolf Stent has said it or whether it's come from someone else. Across town, in the third-class hotel, William will not sleep or eat for a day and a night. With his arms folded across his small chest, he rocks on the pivot of the chair legs where he sits as if the rocking might eventually soothe him. Walt sits with him but cannot get him to say what happened. At bedtime, Walt puts him with Gabriel in Joannie Kilner's big bed, and William begins finally to edge into sleep for a little while until he wakes startled and white-faced at some vague morning hour, his head on Gabriel's chest, Gabriel – his big eyes wide and watchful – stroking William's hair.

'It's all right, Dada,' Gabriel says later in the morning when William has been set chores in the hotel at Joannie Kilner's insistence to keep his mind occupied, '– it's all right.' And Walt is persuaded, though the pause, the waiting, still hangs over Laing like the cold breath of some invisible terragot lurking at the gates of the town.

People are erecting market stalls in the square. A group of men are piling up wood barracked in lines ready to be moved down to the beach for the bonfire. It will be the first bonfire since the outset of the war. The wood, bequeathed by the Kyles from their estate and from the pits, is stockpiled in the square as it has traditionally been done. In times past it would have been dragged down to the beach at low tide on the day of the bonfire by horses, but this time it will be three tractors which will be used. The men work diligently, at a pace brisk enough to keep the cold out of their bones. The sound that gradually disturbs their conscious work is that of men's laughter. It is the former internees, pot-bellied and stubbly, laughing and smoking cigarettes in the back of the truck Stent has sent to bring them into town.

Inside the truck, Kasperl clutches his handbell. He carries it with him everywhere like a talisman now his juggling balls are gone. He had asked Brolin if he could bring the bell when they'd been sent for by Stent to answer questions, and Brolin had said yes. Friegang had tutted, but Brolin had said it might bring them all luck with the town clerk. And now they are being driven into Laing, summonsed for selling beach coal – nothing more. It is on Stent's instructions. Maybe Stent thinks it likely that the internees know more than they are saying about the missing boys. Or maybe, as he will tell them himself, he thinks it best – safest (for everyone) – for them to be in custody whilst the situation remains unresolved.

The truck rattles and coughs around the tight corners of Laing. The noise grows more distinct to the men in the town square unloading pitprops from the colliery for the bonfire. The truck pulls into the square and draws up opposite the police station. The men around the square lay down their tools, slow or stop their fetching and carrying. It's then that the driver of the truck must notice the sudden silence which is growing out there in the square because his own tuneless whistle has evaporated. He must see the way that men's gazes have followed the truck through the square. He leaves the engine running.

'Stay there till I go in and sort things out,' he says in the back of the truck.

'Why?' Friegang says.

'Stay there.'

In the back of the truck the internees imagine that the police station is simply shut. They presume it's just that there is no reason to get out yet, and it's cold, so they are happy to stay inside. They imagine that the driver has simply gone to persuade the sergeant to finish his breakfast and get on with opening up the station doors so they can be ticked off for selling beach coal illegally after gavelling it out of the beach outcrops. They know they didn't sell so much, and didn't make much money on it, and what money they made has gone on simple provisions. It didn't seem such a terrible thing, and they could surely cope with a caution or a reprimand.

Inside the truck they cannot hear much. Men from the square gather round but still there is no real sound from them. The only firm sounds are those of the internees in the back of the truck, ignorant of the men in the square because of the

215

flap cover that hangs down to the tailgate. In the back of the truck Friegang and Brolin and Kasperl and Peretta continue to smoke and to speak in a mish-mash of German and English quietly amongst themselves, passing time, waiting for the policeman to come and open up, like this was any other day. It's then that Brolin glances out through the flapping side of the canvas to find out what's happening. He lets the flap fall back. He catches Kasperl's eye. It seems to Kasperl that Brolin's heart is running faster. It seems that all the dull morning passivity has bled from Brolin's white face. And still, from outside the truck, there is no noise. Men stand grouped around the truck which somehow begins to be rocked. No one afterwards will be sure how it began to be rocked, though some will say that maybe it was Brock Spivey – who had been helping with the wood – who began it. It is this motion which finally silences the sounds in the truck.

'Who is doing this?' Friegang says. Then, louder, 'What are they doing? Tell them to stop.'

'Stay inside the truck,' Brolin says.

'Why?'

'Stay inside.'

'What is it?' Peretta asks.

'I don't know,' Brolin says quietly.

The sergeant and his constable have come out from the station after being roused by the driver. The sergeant tells people to back off, to leave the truck alone, but this doesn't seem to help. The protest from the sergeant seems to set up a slightly faster rhythm which is satisfying to the people who gather tighter around the truck. Friegang lifts the back flap. He steps down from the truck. Does he do this through fear or bravery? The others have never thought of Friegang as a brave man. Perhaps it is only instinct. Maybe it is panic. Maybe it is the only thing he can think to do. Sometimes, there is only one thing which can seem a possibility and everything else is illusion. Friegang steps down into the gap between the tailgate and the ring of people who are being held back by the policemen a very few feet away.

Friegang, the former hut captain, protests to the sergeant.

'Make them stop the pushing of the truck,' Friegang says. 'They must not do this. We are only here to answer questions. Inside the truck the others are made uneasy by this.'

'Do you lot know something about the boys?' It is Joe Filbin. He is the group's spokesman. He asks the driver. 'Do they know about the boys? Is that why Stent's brought them in? If it is we should know.'

'We have said not,' Friegang says, pushing at the spectacles on the bridge of his nose. 'Brolin has said this – we know nothing of the missing boys. We are here for some stupid coal. Some stupid beach coal. Petty rules. Not for any boys.'

The young constable hardly seems to be a real policeman. He is too young. The sergeant seems too old and fat – a special, risen to sergeant in the absence of better men during the war he was too old to fight in. Leftovers, just like the men in the truck. Like Friegang, who is little more than a clerk – who bumbles on now with his protest as if he was querying some clerical error on a booking form in that clucking way he has about him. The sergeant whispers to the young constable to go back into the station and bring out the shotgun he keeps in the gun cabinet in his office, the one he's kept all these years in case of an invasion. He sees the look of concern on the boy's face. 'Just a precaution,' he says. 'Just in case.'

The boy goes. The sergeant, alone now, turns back to

Friegang and tells him to get back in the truck. He thinks this will help to calm the situation. Friegang refuses. He is too wary of the crowd, of the rocking of the truck. He will not climb back up into the truck. The sergeant shouts at him to climb back in. Doesn't he know, the sergeant says, that boys are still missing? Doesn't he know that things are difficult in the town?

'That has nothing to do with us,' Friegang says. 'They must not do this.'

This time it is Brolin who shouts at him from the back of the lorry: 'Get back in the truck.'

Friegang ignores him.

'Steig in den Lastwagen,' Brolin hisses.

'The war is not here for us,' Friegang says, ignoring Brolin. 'These men cannot do this.' He turns to the gang of men surrounding him. 'You must leave us be.'

The men press forward and Friegang pushes them away from him to keep a little space between them. Someone stumbles. Friegang says something in German. It sounds bad. It sounds hard. Men further back want to know what's happening. Too late, and suddenly concerned, Friegang tries to scramble back up to the safety of the truck. Two or three men close by grab at him. There's a tug of war as Peretta and Brolin in the back of the truck try to pull him in and men in the square pull at him to get him out again. Friegang stumbles out of the truck and falls to the floor. He struggles to his feet but even as he does men begin pushing him. A circle is formed and, in an instant, he becomes something to strike at. Someone aims a slap at him, surprising him, knocking his glasses from his face. Friegang moves towards the crowd. A dozen sets of strong arms reach for him and knock him over as if he was no more than a rag doll.

It's at that moment that Kasperl jumps down from the truck. Joe Filbin and the others look round and see Kasperl suddenly, remarkably, juggling. He has no juggling balls any more, of course. He is juggling only with large washer nuts he has found in the back of the truck, and the handbell he has brought in to Laing, and with his hat. Laboriously he keeps all the objects in the air – the fast moving nuts and the heavy bell and the slow, looping ponderous hat – and his efforts to keep these four objects in the air become ever more frantic and ludicrous. Men begin to laugh. They nudge their neighbour at the sight of the idiot juggling with his hat and a handbell and a couple of big brass washers. Kasperl throws them a little higher, a little wider, and while he does so Brolin drags Friegang back up into the truck. But when Kasperl drops the nuts and they hit the ground with a ringing sound it seems to break the spell, and then Kasperl's bell clangs to the floor. It's Brock Spivey who steps forward at that point and grabs Kasperl and shakes him.

'Where're the boys?' he says. 'You say now, where're the boys?' and Brock Spivey has Kasperl lifted off the ground by the lapels of his coat.

Then suddenly above them all, rising out of the town square and up into the sky, the sound of a gunshot smacks, and then the echo shakes the air above them.

It is the constable, with the rifle. Alongside him is Stent. The small crowd look round. They see the constable, and Stent standing there too. A hush falls on them. They are children, it seems, caught in the act, waiting to be scolded.

'That's enough,' Stent says.

People look at him. The noise of the crowd has suddenly dropped away.

'Let them through,' Stent says. 'They are here to be asked questions, that's all. No one's made any charges.'

The crowd back off, enough to allow Friegang to stand up. Peretta, jumping down from the truck, pulls Kasperl up off the floor and retrieves Friegang's spectacles and Kasperl's bell. Friegang is bleeding from the nose and the lip. He is covered in dirt. He is shaking. Finally, when they are all down from the truck, the two policemen lead the internees towards the police station.

'They are animals,' Friegang says to Stent as the internees pass him. His voice has a tightness to it – anger crushed and smothered by fear. 'They should not be doing this. You should see to it.'

But Stent does not acknowledge Friegang. He stands still, watching the Laing men break up. The men begin to go back to their day's tasks. The internees are led into the police station. The men despatched from the mine continue to unload the sleepers for the Laing bonfire.

Rolf Stent begins to talk that night. He says that they were out playing in the woods above the houses on the Heights of Abraham. He says that they were cornered in one of the caves by the man who everyone laughs at: the one with the clanking boots and the girl's blond hair; the one who stands up like a question mark – Kasperl.

Rolf Stent says that Kasperl threatened them with a big knife and tied them together with rope. He says that they were told by Kasperl that they'd have their throats cut if they resisted or ran off. He said that they were being taken because it would teach the boys a lesson for stealing his juggling balls and for keeping them and not giving them back to him.

William is asked about all this by Stent in the third-class hotel in a corner of the cavernous ballroom where chairs have been set out for Stent to talk to him. He sits silent when he is asked by Stent to confirm the sequence of events. William's head stays bowed, neither affirming nor denying when asked 'Is this so, boy? Is this what happened?' And Stent leaves it there for the night, because of the state both boys were in when they had made it back to Laing, how they were bruised and cut, as if they had been dragged, their trousers ripped and muddy. Everyone knows the state they were in when they made it back. Perhaps it is no wonder the Emerson boy won't talk just yet. Perhaps he's not as strong as young Rolf. And so Stent leaves him, not talking – leaves him to Walt who has stood watching the scene from the entrance to the dark ballroom, not party to the questioning of his son but standing there and seeing it.

The next day the two boys are brought together. They are seated side by side. Rolf Stent describes the cellar under the gamekeeper's lodge on the edge of Salem Turn to which the boys were taken and held for three days with no food and little water. He says they heard rats in the cellar. He says that there was no light. After two days Kasperl had unlocked the cellar hatch from above and come down and taken Morton Filbin out and locked the cellar door behind him again. Later, Billy Tillotson was taken up. That night, when it was cold, Billy's younger brother Joseph was taken.

Rolf Stent, growing a little in confidence as his story spills out little by little, says that the two boys who remained were left in the cellar overnight. And so the two of them had finally elected to risk all – to risk their throats being cut – and to try and break out from the cellar if half a chance offered itself to

221

them, to make a run for it before they were taken away too.

On the next day, Rolf Stent said, with the house empty above them and the internees out somewhere on the beach probably cutting more coal from the outcrop, he and William Emerson had finally managed to work themselves free of the rope that had held them. They had succeeded in breaking the lock by using a brick as a hammer against it and had escaped from the cellar, snatching Friegang's sheath knife from where they found it in the kitchen in case they were met by the internees on their journey back to Laing.

Rolf Stent had handed over the knife when they made it back to Laing. His father has it now. It is the proof of their captivity, of their kidnap. When he'd handed it over, there had been blood on the knife.

The news that the internees are to be moved from Laing to face a tribunal rides through the town. Because the men are aliens, because their lives are governed by the Defence of the Realm Act, because the war is still being fought (even though D-Day and the slow winter advance by the Allies through Europe signals that the end of the war cannot now be far away) the case cannot be heard by a circuit judge as it would be for anybody else. The internees must be moved from Laing. There must be a tribunal set up by the regional Commissioner to hear the evidence of the kidnap. The tribunal will be held in Manchester. The internees will be given lawyers. They'll stay in a hotel. The evidence of the two boys who made it back will be ineligible because they are minors. The internees will not be required under the Geneva Convention to say what they've done with the three missing boys who will be left to starve chained up in one of the slate caves above the Heights of Abraham, or worse. The tribunal will send the men on a ship to Canada. They'll join the thousands of others who've been boated away to a safe life; they'll sail away to safety and to Canada like all the other prisoners, and they'll laugh at Laing and they'll laugh at what they've done and what they've got away with.

All the while, Rolf Stent's story becomes more detailed as he remembers things that the trauma of the event had initially blocked out. William will still not talk about it, but small remembered incidents keep coming back to Rolf Stent. He remembers, for example, that it was Kasperl who came down into the cellar and never any of the others. He remembers sometimes hearing other voices, though – voices in a foreign language, in words he couldn't understand. He remembers that just once, tied as they were below ground, they were given water to drink in an enamel cup. He remembers that the man who gave it to him carried a smell he didn't recognize. It was a strong smell – maybe mustard or old cheese. It didn't smell, he says, like Laing.

And still William is silent, too marked by what has happened to say anything. He mopes around the hotel. He stays clear of Joannie Kilner. He stays close to Gabriel. With Gabriel, there is no need for words. He says to Gabriel, 'Let's go to Cathedral Gill.'

To Gabriel's surprise, when they get there William kneels under the arch of the cave, hands clutched together, and prays while Gabriel sits back on the winter turf outside.

'Who are you praying for, Bubba?' Gabriel asks him.

'For me,' Bubba says.

'You're praying to God?'

'To Jesus, yes.'

'What do you want him to do?'

Bubba, white-faced, wonders. 'To bring Mama back. I want Mama. I want her to take me away.'

Joe Filbin leads a delegation to see Stent.

'Folk are saying the foreigners will get sent away by the tribunal.'

'Oh, yes?' Stent says.

'Folk say they'll be sent abroad. Canada. Like the others. And be given farms.'

'The others?' Stent says.

'From the camp. The internees.'

'Ah yes, the internees.'

'The tribunal won't be local men?'

'No,' Stent says.

'They mightn't feel as strongly as we do about what's been done. They might feel with all the killing that's going on for the war that things here don't matter. That with the war nearly done, with France being won back and everything, it doesn't matter in the scale of things. Folk say the tribunal might just put them on a boat to Canada and let them have farms.'

'And you believe this?'

'I don't know what to believe, Mr Stent. We thought that maybe as town clerk, you'd have a say in letting them go or not. To Manchester, I mean.'

'You make too many presumptions on me.'

'We just want you to make sure there's justice, Mr Stent,' Joe Filbin says. 'That's all the people want – just for you to make sure there's justice for what's been done.'

Rolf Stent remembers how at one point Kasperl – Kasperl

with the sour smell – fondled the boy's private parts whilst he, Rolf, was blindfolded. Rolf remembers Kasperl's hot breath and the softish bristles on his face. He remembers how urgently he broke the knot binding his wrists, how – heart beating – he chivvied William Emerson out of the game-keeper's lodge, how they fled to Laing with the knife.

'We did nothing,' Brolin says, tired, his palms rubbing gently at his eyelids. 'We know nothing. None of us, the boy, no one. We *saw* nothing. What do you take us for, that one of us could do this thing?'

'The boys who were taken have identified Kasperl,' Stent says. 'They have identified the gamekeeper's lodge at Salem Turn as the place that they were taken to against their will. They heard foreign voices. German voices.'

'It is not possible. There is something wrong here. Who are these boys? You will let me talk to them.'

'There are procedures,' Stent says. 'Such things are not possible.'

'We have not been charged. Should we not be charged or released?'

'You are to be moved from Laing.'

'When do you charge us then?'

'When the tribunal decides.'

'So why do we not have some lawyer to represent us at this tribunal? We are just four men charged without anyone to answer for us.'

'There is a war on,' Stent says. 'The law as it stands does not allow for you to be given representation. Nor does it demand that you must be charged now. The tribunal will hear the evidence.'

'And you?' Brolin asks. 'Do you think Kasperl did this

thing? He knows nothing else about the world. How could he? He is a boy.'

'In the eyes of the law he is old enough to commit murder,' Stent says.

'What of the evidence? What evidence is there that we have done this terrible thing? Or Kasperl alone?'

'The evidence is circumstantial. It is for the tribunal to decide if it is sufficient. There is the testimony of the boys, there is the knife, there is the gamekeeper's lodge, the animosity you bore the town, the way the idiot youth went chasing boys around the street screaming death to them.'

'I told you,' Brolin says, weary as if he has said it fifty times already, 'there is no cellar at the house. The knife I cannot say. The knife was stolen from the house two days ago when we were at the beach. About the blood on the knife I cannot say. It is not the boy's. For sure, it is not the boy's. You have to believe what I say to you or they will maybe imprison us for this thing. I know. I have seen this before where men are hung for things that did not happen.'

Stent makes no acknowledgement of this. He stands up.

'We should have someone to represent us,' Brolin says. 'Things should not be like this. You are a lawyer, are you not? You should know right and wrong.'

'I know the law,' Stent says. 'My job is the law. I have told you what will happen.'

17

The archive

I stayed at a distance from the Great Hall for a while after having followed them. After all, I already knew what there was for Gabriel's small party to find. I knew it would take them a little while to take it in – a little contemplation.

I can imagine the scene, the hush as they walked in. I know it was Gabriel who opened the big door. Without saying much, Gabriel would have taken charge. Gabriel would have led them into the hall – all of them sheepish, as if the presence of Henry Kyle still lurked up there on the stage, still looked down on them, the way it was imagined long after he was dead that the ghost of Henry Kyle still stalked the colony's buildings and was sometimes glimpsed at windows in the dead of night.

Of course, I knew what they would find in there. I had seen it all before. I knew all about Henry Kyle's archive. And I knew all about Kyle. How did I know? About the Great Hall? About its contents? About Henry Kyle? His life?

Simple. I am a thief.

From being a boy, I was a thief. Before my accident I was fast and lithe, too. Well coordinated. As a boy, my profession led me to be a thief – for the best of possible motives. In

Laing, too, I stole. It is a habit which is hard to lose. No sooner had I begun my time in the colony than I had lifted a pass key, a master copy, from Henry Kyle's superintendent who had been detailed to supervise the arrival of a small group of us. The poor man was so frightened of Henry Kyle's reaction, of Kyle's wrath – of *God's* wrath – that I believe he never dared to report the loss. As for me, I didn't dare use the key for several months. I hid it and waited. And I suppose to the superintendent's relief as well as my own, nothing happened. There were no obvious break-ins, no damage, no tearing asunder of the veil of the temple. And so, since then, I have been free to gain access to whichever buildings I choose around the colony, since the pass key gave me access to virtually every building on the site. It has made me somewhat nocturnal in my habits, since using my pass key has meant doing so at night. To use it in daylight would have been too great a risk for a coward like me. It has added to my isolation within the colony. But it always seemed a price worth paying. I could wander at will, claim entire buildings as my own, find the big open spaces which, even as a boy, I craved. To have lived cramped up like the other residents would have been too much for me to bear. Since being a child, I had lived an outdoor life, been free to do as I pleased, not been contained. Within the colony, my stolen pass key brought me a kind of freedom. No wonder I so feared the sideroom. No wonder I so cautiously kept my exploration of the colony to the night-time when the chances of being caught were minimal. No wonder I never mentioned to anyone else the fact that I was in possession of the key I had stolen in the blink of an eye in my first few weeks here from the unsuspecting superintendent who was himself too frightened of Henry Kyle to report the theft.

One final repercussion of the success of my nightly vigils was this – after Henry Kyle died, and I became a little less cautious in my wanderings around the colony's buildings at night, a little more careless about covering my tracks, my shadow was sometimes glimpsed at a window or passing a room, or a light I had left on framed my silhouette. And what could be more natural than for people to imagine that this was the ghost of Henry Kyle, unwilling to leave the colony – his kingdom – even after his death. People's fear kept them at a distance. No one wanted to go to inspect a redundant building in the colony for the presumed presence of Henry Kyle. The authorities came to accept that the colony was haunted by its founder, which allowed me as free a reign as I wished in my wanderings at night and which I took advantage of. If people passing across the colony at night ever heard an occasional noise or a bang, they certainly kept well clear of whichever building it came from, having no wish to confront the ghost of Henry Kyle. It is only now, as I spend my nights huddled in the eaves of the Icehouse, that I am less the wanderer across the compound. It is only now that the ghost of Henry Kyle is less frequently glimpsed walking around inside its redundant buildings.

Despite having access to all of the colony's buildings for so long, I believe it was my very first discovery which was the most remarkable. Within the administration block in which the offices of Henry Kyle himself had originally been sited, the director had stored a small number of files relating to the time that he himself had spent in Vienna between 1919 and 1920. The files were kept in his own private suite in an ancillary room, the key for which was kept separately in a cabinet which could be opened only by Henry Kyle himself or by the kind of master key I held.

Why did Henry Kyle keep such files within the colony? Why did he keep them at all? I don't know. My only thought on this, having read the files, and having had forty years to ponder the question, is that it was a kind of bargain he had struck with God. The files represented a contract. Outside of Vienna, only he and God knew of their existence (what did Henry Kyle know of poor Lukic and his light fingers and his pass key?). To have destroyed the files would, in his mind, have risked breaking that contract. And so he kept them, locked securely away (or so he thought), until his death at which time they were, on his instructions, finally burned in the colony's incinerator. He believed his secrets were safe. He believed he had taken them back with him to God. He had not reckoned on the idiot Lukic. He had not reckoned on me becoming the sole inheritor of his own story.

Over the years, since that first accidental discovery, I've tried to make the best possible use of the pass key I stole. I used it to give myself an education. I would go stalking the colony's offices at night, looking for books that I could read, to make up for lost time, to help me find out about the world that lay beyond my reach. I've managed to build up a small collection of books within the colony which I now call my own. Some of them – the ones I thought would interest him – I gave to Gabriel. Having a pass key to every building on the site was a big help in procuring them. My only problem was finding a good home for them, somewhere safe and warm and light so that I could read them at my leisure without Henry Kyle's men finding me, or them, and giving me two days in the sideroom as punishment – as correction – which they surely would have done. Henry Kyle's belief was that books, other than the Bible, were bad for us and would unsettle us.

So they were outlawed. Bread and bricks. All the world was bread and bricks.

I used to move my books around, from safe place to safe place, to reduce the chance of being caught, or of having someone like Roland snooping round and running off to tell the attendants. But it wasn't until recently that the ideal place to store my books presented itself.

Now my library has its own home. They are housed in the former caretaker's office within the Great Hall. The Great Hall isn't used any more by the residents. It hasn't been used since the falling roll of the colony made it too big to set down the dwindling huddle of remaining residents there for meals. The hall became too big; the cost of heating the place for so few of us began to seem too much. So we were moved to the smaller canteen which had formerly been for staff and which was nearer to our own dormitory.

My books are laid out in rows on the shelves along one wall of the former caretaker's room. The room was never really much more than a store cupboard. It was never really an office. The caretaker had organized a chair and a table into the room but he had clearly struggled to do so. They were sandwiched into a corner between mops and buckets and cleaning fluids and paints and paint thinners and detergents and methylated spirits. I have moved all of this cleaning stock down from the shelves where I found them in order to create room for my books, in order that my Dante and Goethe and the others may have space to breathe along the shelves in my new-found study. All the former caretaker's equipment, all the fluids and cannisters and mop heads, have been heaped upon the floor in the corners of the room. I have no need of them. No one has need of them. Not now that the caretaker has gone. The fact that he has gone is further proof that time is really passing. All these items were the stuff of Roland's trade as caretaker cum odd-job man, and now Roland has gone.

Roland was a poor caretaker. It was Rose who gave him the job. After he gave up trying to escape, after he grew reconciled to stopping here, Roland spent his years trying to ingratiate himself with the attendants. I know this for sure. I saw his file – I saw *everybody's* file. Roland spent his time feeding information about his fellow residents to the attendants. You could never trust Roland. He was always hanging around. He always seemed to be looking for something and you never knew what it was. It was because of this that Rose gave him a kind of semi-official job. Roland became a caretaker. He was given a small allowance and strutted around the colony like some *kapo* with a chip on his shoulder. Rose gave him some small tasks to do. Since he could hang around the residents without attracting much attention to himself, he was able to keep up a steady supply of information to Rose to help her in the struggle to rehabilitate those of us who were still left. He wasn't so quick or so clean as I was in his subterfuge, sneaking about the place in his efforts to uncover our secrets, but he was effective, for a while at least, and it was enough to persuade Rose that all would be well – that she would find the key to all of us and turn it with a little patience and a little work. In return, Sallis was persuaded to allocate the 'office' next to the Great Hall for Roland to use.

Of course, in the end Roland wasn't careful enough. Not as careful as I was. Not careful enough to prevent Peary from catching him in the dormitory pawing over some of Peary's notes about the colony, hidden from the attendants under the floorboards. That was the end of Roland. It annoyed Rose, I know, that she had lost such a vital source of information in the battle to improve us, but there was nothing she or Sallis could do. Roland recovered from the beating Athol gave him, but he never spied for Rose again. And before too long they shipped him out in the green transit minibus, past the infirmary and out for good. Puff! and he was gone. Such magic!

Roland's former unofficial office, the one which he had begged Rose to have fitted with a desk and a chair so that he could feel like a proper staff member, was left untouched. Probably no one could even remember that he had an office – it was that kind of arrangement. It was a sop to a stupid man. The room was abandoned as Roland had last left it. Only I knew of it – still exploring on my nightly forays with my faithful pass key.

In the tiny storeroom Gabriel, Evelyn and the others would have spied Roland's former treasure trove by now. Perhaps Ingerman would have spotted his sack first. It was one of the bulkier items stolen by Roland. It stood out. I know for sure that Ingerman won't have opened the tie cord at the neck and looked into it. In all the time I have been in the colony, I never once saw Ingerman actually go in his sack for his big something – look in it or pull anything out other than his abacus or his Rubik cube that he had to fish for down at the bottom. He only ever carried the sack around with him, slung over his shoulder. It was as if the weight of it was all Ingerman wanted, as if he didn't need to use whatever it was that made up the bulk of the weight or took up the bulk of the space in the sack, or even to look at it – as if it was enough for him to know that it was there.

When I first found the sack hidden away in Roland's hidey-hole, I remember being so torn. I wanted to steal it back for

Ingerman. I wanted to rescue it, because I knew how much it meant to him, and how hard life was for him without the reassuring weight of the sack as he moved around the colony. But if I'd done that, it would have been obvious to Roland that someone had got access to his room. It would have been obvious to the attendants that the sack hadn't been lost but stolen. As it was, they contented themselves with the fiction that Ingerman had simply lost the sack, just as Rose thought that all of us were always haphazardly losing things. If I'd returned the sack, a big investigation would have taken place and it was likely they would have changed the locks or, worse, found my pass key in some big organized search for the culprit. And so I stayed quiet. I said nothing, either to Roland or to Ingerman about the sack. I did nothing.

No, Ingerman will not have looked inside the sack. He will merely have picked it up and weighed the familiar weight in his hand and slung the sack over his shoulder and carried it again contentedly, weak as he is after the big winter. And maybe after that – as they are mooching around and Gabriel is giving orders for the rows of photographs and pathetic keepsakes to be gathered up so as to be returned to any of the residents who are still here whom Roland had stolen from – maybe, then, Athol would have found the lamp Roland had stolen from him.

It was Athol's Davy lamp. Athol and his brother had been drafted from the orphanage into the mines and were placed in a house near the harbour. They were given rooms with the Parish School teacher, Mrs Ingol, and her mother who couldn't walk and who minded the flower stall while Mrs Ingol taught. They ate their evening meal with the teacher and her mother who bickered throughout while Athol and

Artemis ate in silence. Mrs Ingol believed that her life was over now and she said so, both to her mother and to her two lodgers. She suffered different ailments – headaches, flus, abdominal pains – which the doctor could never pin down.

'I am like Jesus,' she told the boys. 'Put on this earth only to suffer and to serve others. That's why I have given you two a roof, because my lot is to suffer and to serve.' And her mother would sigh loudly at this and click her teeth together.

The Bevan boys in general were not liked or trusted by the regular miners in Laing. They were thought of as *nowt but kids*, as liabilities, and training them up was an inconvenience. The two boys themselves disliked the work. They did it because they had been conscripted and so had no option but to do it. Athol's mining lasted less than a year. His final act as a miner was to try to dig his brother out of a pit collapse caused by an explosion that brought the pit roof down. Athol knew that Artemis was in trouble even before the alarm was raised. And so, as the other miners were counted out of the pit away from the explosion, Athol was frantically making his way to his brother at the far end of the bottom gallery where Artemis had been with the pit ponies.

Athol never went down the mine again. He wouldn't go out of the house. His landlady told people afterwards that he used to talk to his dead brother in his room. Her mother said it gave her the creeps. The two of them agreed it wasn't natural. They both said it should be stopped.

When I do peer around the big door, I see that Evelyn has turned her attention to the crates of documents set out along the long tables. She is reading something from out of one of the boxes. It looks from here as if it is one of the punishment books. It's a green book, and the punishment books were green. Gabriel is close by.

'What does it say?' Gabriel asks her.

She shakes her head gently. 'They are for this place . . . this is here?'

Gabriel shrugs. The shrug means yes.

She reads. '. . . sullen and disrespectful at prayers, two days in sideroom.'

She flicks through the pages to another and another. '. . . very insolent, refused to work in laundry, put to bed for two days . . . argumentative, one day in sideroom . . . escape attempted, injected sedative administered, three days in sideroom.'

The others wander around the Great Hall, still cowed a little, I think, by Henry Kyle's ghost in this place, whilst Evelyn moves from chest to chest, from file to file. Eventually, she comes to a series of tea chests directly below the stage. She wanders along them. A wad of files lie on the table next to the final chest. She reaches them and spreads them across the table. From within the top concertina file a bundle of photographs, loosely ribboned together, falls out. She sifts through the photographs. They are black and white. They are old. They are obviously part of a series and each of them is indexed to a set of measurements and calculations. The photographs are of individual naked men, and women. Some of them are in profile, some are frontal. I know what they are because I left them there for her to see. She goes back to the previous chest, and then the one after that, and the one after that – all the way along the line are more and more. There are thousands of photographs. Men, naked, shameful, not looking at the camera. I know that there are prints of every resident in the colony from 1922 until after Henry Kyle's death. I know that I am in there, and Ingerman, and Peary, and Gabriel. And Roland. And the others. And those dead, and those gone. Some photographs are of full torsos, some of heads, tilted this way and that, held still in a pose for the camera. Some others are of ears or noses or genitalia – penises both flaccid and erect. Some are of deceased residents at some form of post-mortem, with brain profiles and cross-sections of internal organs and tissues set out on tables being measured to be classified.

It is Gabriel who brings her the photograph of Peary. I found it one night as I sifted through a wad of the photographic files Sallis was having indexed. I left it out for them to find. He gives it to her. In the photograph, Peary is standing in a small lecture theatre that Evelyn does not recognize and which is clearly somewhere beyond the colony. The rows of benches, which are occupied, run steeply down to a platform at the bottom, like a pit, like a circus ring. The photograph is taken from the top of the theatre looking down. The *subject* of the photograph is not Peary. The subject is the man who is lecturing to the group of people sitting on the rows of seats. It is the lecturer who is at the centre of the stage, talking to the audience, holding out his arms, expressing something, some idea, some theory. Peary, stood to one side of him, is naked. He appears to be covered in boils or scabs. The suited figure – Henry Kyle – is explaining something.

Peary was always susceptible to boils. His father cured them by forcing a vacuum in an old milk bottle – lighting a candle over the top and burning out the oxygen – and then pressing the bottle to the flesh to force the boil out, root and all. Peary never made a sound. Each time, he never made a sound. The boils kept coming. His father thought it was some sort of sign. From God. Some indication of deviancy. He thought it was a test to see if he could cleanse the boy.

Gabriel wanders off back into Roland's former tiny office. He is gone a while.

'I didn't know such things were possible,' Evelyn says. But I could have told her. I could have said that pretty much anything is possible with God on your side. I could have told her about the history of the world. I could have told her about Brolin's cathedral. I could have told her about the granite statue of Gabriel Emerson facing out from Laing. But, standing there in the doorway to the Great Hall, knowing Gabriel would not acknowledge who I really was even if he looked right at me, I say nothing. I leave Gabriel's angel to her own thoughts, to read and look around a little more. I say nothing.

The Mental Deficiency Act was repealed in 1959, but Henry Kyle continued unabashed until his death some years later. Nothing really changed. Even after his death, the colony continued to run on the very momentum which Henry Kyle had seemed to charge it with, in the same way in which it was believed that the charged ghost of Henry Kyle himself had still pursued his guardianship of the colony and grounds at night long after he was gone.

As for us residents, no one seemed to know what to do with us. Like Henry Kyle himself, we had not expected his great liner to dock in port. We had expected – we were conditioned to believe – that we would be at sea forever, separate from the world which Henry Kyle had cleansed beyond the colony walls.

A few families claimed their lost members back, but for

most of us it was too late. Like Ingerman's, their families had long since disappeared or, like Roland's, had forgotten them. Like Gabriel, the colony had become their home. As for me, I suppose I could have left. My isolation – the private world that I lived in at night – and the education I had pursued through my borrowed library of books had kept my sense of self alive and beating. When Sallis and Rose finally arrived with their remit to close the colony down, I suppose I must initially have seemed a promising candidate for release, but I was never persuaded that the cause was urgent enough. I was never persuaded by them of the need to try and build a new life. And besides, I had no wish to get better *for them*.

I remember that of all Henry Kyle's replacements, all the way through to Sallis, none of them ever seemed to wonder how we had come to this. None of them ever asked how it had *felt*. I suppose I could have made the effort. I suppose I could have been a Little Jesus for Rose. But I had long since resigned myself to staying on here. Ever since Gabriel had first arrived, I had resigned myself to staying. I knew even then that there would be little chance of Gabriel ever leaving this place in an organized sense, and so I knew I had to stay. Watching over Gabriel had become my mission in life. So I watched him and looked out for him and held the likes of Roland and Rose at bay from him. I kept his seafaring books safe for him and I let him dream his dream under the deep sea like some single narwhal. I became his guardian angel, and like all the best guardian angels I was invisible to my charge, although I was as much flesh and blood as he was. Pinch me and I would have cried out; cut me and I would surely have bled. And all the time I stood guard over him. So minutes passed, and years. All that time, and Gabriel has never seen me for who I am. Sometimes I think no one sees me. That's why I stopped here. I had no life left outside the colony. I lost that life. Sometimes now I think no one sees me at all. I am an angel that Gabriel cannot see. I am a juggler with one good arm. I am a dog with no bark.

I was christened Lukic, but I knew from an early age that I would need a performing name, a stage name. I had seen pictures of the great Berlin State Circus which performed at the PalaceStrasse to emperors and kings and in which every performer was a star himself – each performer a king of his own endeavour. So, at the age of ten, I left to find a circus of my own, remembering that our village had been so small that the only circus which I had ever seen had passed straight through without stopping on its way to Gdynia.

In running away, I took the name of a famous puppet character that all the children in Germany would know. It was Heimy who said that if I was serious in wanting to join the Berlin State Circus, I would have to be a juggler and yet so much more than this. I would need to be the King of Jugglers. And so I hit upon the idea of *Kasperl*. I would be a juggler and an acrobat – but a funny one, with big, heavy iron-soled boots that would make my demeanour seem awkward, clumsy, and would appear incongruous alongside my fast hands and clever tricks. I would use all of my boy's life to work to realize my dream alongside Heimy the midget clown who was my boss, and the horseback rider who always had the flu and whose nose streamed constantly, and the Turkish rubber man who spoke three languages but none that anyone else in the circus shared, and the Siamese twins, and the female strongman who could lift a donkey, and the animal trainer who was deaf but who heard music inside his head from when an elephant had kicked him.

Circus Prenzlau was never a great circus. It was just a making-a-living kind of circus for a group of men whose only way of fitting in was to stand out and be ridiculous. Sometimes I had to steal a chicken or a purse to buy us food, to help keep our ridiculous circus on the road.

'Send Kasperl into town,' Heimy would say, and everyone knew what was meant when we arrived outside a new place before we had the chance to sell tickets or hold a raffle and make any money. And so I went and stole whatever it was necessary to steal. I thought of it as part of my apprenticeship – though when we moved our base to England, to the hop fields of Kent, we did much better and I had less need to steal because people there liked circuses and paid to come and see us.

As a reward for my efforts, and because I was so popular, and because I was the smallest performer – apart from Heimy himself who was often too drunk or too hung over – I was allowed to lead the Circus Prenzlau into each new town. I had a bell to ring to announce our arrival to drum up support – to get the circus noticed. It was a handbell and I would ring the bell all the way into town in front of the rest of the circus in the six carts we occupied in total. (Circus Prenzlau was such a small circus, though I always thought of it as a small-circus stepping stone to the Berlin State Circus for which I was destined.)

When the Nazis came to power, Heimy still went on about the morons who were running the country but even more loudly. He seemed to grow more angry about things even as his height refused resolutely to increase, and only the Mozart

241

that he listened to each night seemed to calm him. And after he was let out of the work camp, he moved the circus to England. Of course, when war came we were all eventually interned as aliens. The only thing I was able to take with me was my bell, and the juggling balls. As for Heimy, he managed somehow to keep hold of his gramophone, but everything else, even the dog, was taken. At least in the camp Heimy could listen to his music. He would play it in the evenings, his face transfixed as he hung from a bar still trying to compel himself to grow, still going on about the Nazi morons running his country.

In the interment camp, everyone knew Kasperl and his circus bell, though it's true it rang less often than it had before. When, near the end of the war, we were allowed to volunteer for the work party in the small harbour town of Laing, I sometimes led the internees through the town with my bell, and sometimes brought up the rear practising my routine with the juggling balls given me by Heimy who had recognized my talent even as he despaired of his own. Always I was practising, for the Berlin State Circus, or for Circus Prenzlau to return for me one day over the hill with its caravan of six carts. But of course, Circus Prenzlau could never return, not after Heimy hanged himself in the camp. Heimy had been told that his name was down to travel on one of the first ships that was due to take internees away from England and he reasoned, since no one said otherwise, that they were sending him back to Germany. He said he knew what the Germans could do with recidivist dwarfs. His hanging body was still straining for length even in death when they found it and cut it down. That was when his few belongings were taken and Brock Spivey laid claim to the gramophone that had been Heimy's.

No one had the heart to complain about the oaf stealing the dead Heimy's gramophone. Not even Brolin. Perhaps they hoped that a little Mozart would work its way into his soul. Perhaps they thought that Heimy's music would improve Brock Spivey.

After the camp, Kasperl's bell seldom rang, especially after my juggling balls were stolen by the boys in Laing. Instead, Brolin began to teach me to read and write, and pass on to me his love of books and quiet words, and I became only Kasperl the idiot – the dog with no bark.

And sometimes in the Great Hall in the years that followed I would practise on the darkened stage when I had sneaked in at night with my pass key. After all, this was the only thing I'd loved. This was my purpose. And even if I had just one good arm and could never perform again in public, it was still the only thing I could do and so I liked to carry on practising. I liked to dream, just as Heimy must have dreamed. I would rig up the single pencil spotlight upon me which Henry Kyle used when he was addressing us, and I would practise juggling with my one good arm, but in truth it was the end of Kasperl. I was truly a dog with no bark.

And now? Now the Kasperl I once was seems as foreign to me as an unknown land. His contours, the extent and breadth of him, mean nothing. Looking at Kasperl, I have to look in from the outside and guess and measure him. I am Lukic now.

Of course, I could not help but to compare Roland's sub-terfuge around the colony when I discovered it with mine. His thieving, I told myself, was for gain, for profit – however per-sonal and perverse that profit was. Mine had been driven by different motives. But I knew that, in the end, the world would inevitably remember us as being both the same. To know that we both sneaked around surreptitiously was all right. I could accept that. I could live with that. But then to find that we were both thieves was a kind of final blow to the cocoon I had woven for myself in which I could justify my inaction. My cowardice. My silence. Roland's damning was mine also. It was then, of course, that I realized that I had nothing to lose any more. It was then that I found the courage to act – to surrender my pass key to Gabriel, to tell him in an anonymous note about the archive that Sallis was continuing to work on in the Great Hall. So small an act of courage. So long in coming.

And so it was that I, Kasperl (now Lukic, lifelong inmate in a former colony for the feeble-minded), knew all about Henry Kyle, knew everything there was to know about our founder. I'd seen his own files – the ones he brought back with him, the ones written by the psychiatrist Szas during two years of treatment and confession and catharsis and, I am sure, forgiveness. I knew about his war, about Joannie Kilner, about the alibi for the rape, about his treatment in Vienna. But what was that to me? To Kasperl? To the dog with no bark?

What could I do, faced with that knowledge? Escape? Run away? Run back to Laing? Run and tell the citizens of Laing that Henry Kyle's finery was nothing of the sort? Tell them that the golden threads which stitched his clothes were imaginary? Tell them that the king was naked?

The archive burns.

They have patiently carried out every tea chest from the Great Hall through the night and piled them across the former allotment ground. Then Gabriel has poured out bottle after bottle of flammable liquids, of solvents and cleaning fluids he found in Roland's former caretaker's office, over all of the tea chests and their contents. In their place, in the now almost empty Great Hall, left on a table at the very front beneath Henry Kyle's stage, (it is a smaller archive but a truer history of lives and hopes for the university in America), they have left Peary's writings.

'Everything they did to me,' Peary says. 'Everything that should be remembered. Everything and how it *felt*.'

It is Evelyn who strikes the match and throws it. The flame catches hold of the main pile of filled boxes. And the fire, licking its lips, burns, warming us and throwing smoke and an occasional draft of black ash high into the night air.

Now I know that they can leave the ship and risk the walk across the ice. Tomorrow, Sallis will kick his way, white-faced, amongst the ashes of Henry Kyle's archive, the smile folded out of his face. Rose will watch on from a window. She will be of no help. The residents responsible will have vanished into nothing. There will be no search organized for them, either within the colony or beyond. They will not be thought of as lost or in danger, merely as having run guiltily after the outrage of their arson, and after their substitution of Henry Kyle's record of their lives with that of Peary's.

As I leave the scene, I hear behind me Gabriel's long cry into the night – for all the pain of men, for all the souls who perished in this place, who took a kind of a refuge against the long winter in crevices and dreams.

18

Confession, absolution

Joannie Kilner cleans in the big kitchen. It is Sunday but there is no dance today. There will be no more dancing, she tells herself, in the third-class hotel with no name which goes about its business in the world as anonymously, as unprepossessingly, as she. Trade goes on – the hotel trade – but it is sluggish. There's flu about. Pale women still seen occasionally about the place are drawn with lack of sleep. Whores snap at each other, listless. Joannie Kilner can't sleep. At night she cleans. In the silence of the sudden early Sunday, Joannie Kilner's hard breaths people the room, in and out, in and out, she sucks and blows as she forces carbonized fat from the crevices of the black stove with a wirewool scrub and with a rhythm that sings. Strange to see the kitchen quiet. Usually it is the heart of the place. Usually people are passing by, spilling by. But now, this Sunday, danceless, the only sound and movement comes from Joannie Kilner herself and the rhythm of her cleaning until, in an unsuspecting moment, when she goes looking for a fresh cloth in the big pantry, she comes across William crouching on the floor with a tin of biscuits trapped between his knees. He has been eating biscuits, one by one, slowly – William who eats when he thinks but who hadn't eaten since he and Rolf Stent were returned to Laing. He looks up, happy enough, it seems, to see her, as though a decision has been taken from him.

'Are you all right?'

He nods.

'You're eating. That's good.'

William nods. 'I had breakfast.'

'Is Gabriel out?' she asks.

'He's gone to the woods.'

Gabriel had risen early, anxious to meet the new day. He had talked with his Dada who was falling to earth even as Gabriel was rising, then went out behind the hotel, up through the houses on the Heights of Abraham, into the woods at the top above the town, whilst William still slept and dreamed, perhaps of biscuits, or his Mama.

Joannie Kilner smiles for William in the big, quiet kitchen in the hotel. She asks him, 'Are you looking forward to being guest of honour tomorrow? At the bonfire?'

William and Rolf Stent will be the guests of honour at the Laing Fair. Each year, the Women's Protection League choose who will get to start the bonfire. This year, William and Rolf Stent have been chosen. Rolf Stent will throw the first torch, then William. Everyone will be there. After that, everyone will throw their torches one by one. The two boys have been chosen because of their bravery; because of their surviving. Laing folk are nothing if not survivors. The boys' story seems to be Laing's story. Maybe it's hoped that their selection – their being favoured – will be an omen for finding the other boys who are still missing.

William thinks about the question. He shrugs, then nods a little.

'Cat got your tongue?'

'No,' he says.

Joannie Kilner goes back to cleaning the stove in the kitchen.

'Do things always work out?' William is standing in the pantry doorway.

She stops her scrubbing of the stove. 'What kind of things?' she says.

He finishes the biscuit. 'If Jesus is around,' he says. 'If Jesus is always around, looking out for us, and he carved a cathedral with angels from the rock above Laing, will he always answer prayers? Will he always work things out – because he's here? Because he's always here?'

She wonders how to answer him. She must be patient, she knows. She must reel him in slowly or she will lose him. She stops and rests, then sits down on the immaculate kitchen floor with her back against the big oven. Her legs are tucked under her chin. She used to sit like this as a girl. She wonders.

'When I was a girl,' she says eventually, 'I thought that when I danced, if I danced well enough, I could make the world stop turning, because the angels would want to stop to watch me. I thought that because the world seemed to stop for me in the excitement of dancing so well, that it stopped for everyone. When I was older, I sometimes danced, though not as much. But the world didn't stop turning. It went on and on.'

'What can you do if you can't stop things?' William asks her.

It must seem such a simple question. It is a question every child must face at some point in seeing the unfolding narrative around them. It is a question every child must *think*, and the thinking it is a kind of Rubicon – a crossing. And the jist of Joannie Kilner's answer, as William will remember it to Gabriel, as Gabriel will tell it to Kasperl, as Kasperl – a dog with no bark – will remember it over some long life, is – we can survive; we must survive. That is what we can do. The only thing.

William doesn't answer. Joannie Kilner resumes her scrubbing of the stove. She is working so hard, William thinks.

'What does Gabriel say?' she asks him, thinking about it.

'He says I should tell you. He says you won't bend or break like Dada.'

'You can tell me what happened, William. You can tell me if you want.'

He nods. He isn't looking at her.

She scrubs and scrubs. He will tell her soon. If she is patient, he will tell her. Some mornings when she wakes, Joannie Kilner cannot bring to mind Peretta's face. It is a small and terrible treason. In two days the men will be taken away to Manchester for their tribunal, because people believe they took the boys. Around her, the kitchen gleams. The smells of ginger and cinnamon and the light, sugary, burned air of baking have been harried away, flushed out and suffocated and cleanness set down in its place.

'He said this?' Stent says the following morning.

'Yes,' Joannie Kilner says. 'It's like I told you on the phone yesterday. Till now, he's said nothing, but now he's spoken about it. You have to tell the tribunal.'

Stent rises from his chair and walks to the window. He pauses, weighing things in his lawyer's head.

'He is traumatized, of course,' Stent says to her. 'You can see that.'

'I see a boy who is finally admitting what happened.'

'It is understandable that he would want to repress the memory of what happened. Especially thinking he would soon be facing the ordeal of being a witness at the tribunal.

'You'd stop him from saying what really happened?'

'I would not let him make a fool of himself.'

'If you did that, I'd testify,' Joannie Kilner says. 'I'd go and tell the tribunal what William told me. And if not to the tribunal, to someone else. You cheated me once before. But not again. I'd *say*.'

'Yes,' says Stent, 'I believe you would.'

'I would,' Joannie Kilner says.

'You see, we must do what is best,' Stent says. 'People think that it is easy for men in authority in war – that what is best is the easiest path to take.'

'There is a Commissioner I could see,' she says. 'Someone who is over you. Someone in charge of things like this. I read it. A Commissioner the Parliament has put in charge of each region. I could see him.'

'I think that your doing such a thing might be too late now.'

'Why? Where are the internees now?'

'You don't know yet about last night's development? About their escape?'

'When did they go?'

'They were being moved to Manchester.'

'I was told they weren't due to be moved for another two days.'

'A change of plan. They were sent earlier than anticipated.'

'After I rang you to tell you about what William had said?'

'It may have been after that. I am not at liberty to say exactly when.'

'You had them moved early,' she says. 'You moved them because William changed his story. Because you were frightened your son would be shown to have made his story up.'

'Now, Mrs Kilner, you should know not to go saying things in public that cannot be substantiated. I am, however, sensitive to your, er, predicament. When the van that was taking the foreigners broke down, the four of them were able to make their escape. It seems that one of the boats is missing from the harbour. It seems possible that they made their way back to Laing in the night and used the boat for their escape. I have reported this to the Commissioner. He is understanding about it.'

'If you won't tell the Commissioner about William then I will,' Joannie Kilner says.

Stent studies her face. Finally he says, 'Very well. You can tell him now if you insist. If you are adamant. He is here.'

Stent rises and beckons Joannie Kilner to follow him. She frowns. They pass through two doors and along a corridor and through another door. It is a sitting room. The room is small. The curtains are drawn. A desk under the window has Stent's papers spread about. A fire burns in the hearth. A weighty man in an impeccable tweed suit sits facing the fire. Charles Kyle, the eldest of the three Kyles, puts his drink down slowly as they enter the room and rises from his chair.

He makes a little courteous nodding movement towards her. 'We meet again,' he says to Joannie Kilner, 'after all this time. And under no less perturbing circumstances, alas.'

He sits back in his chair and takes up his drink again. 'Please, sit,' he says.

She doesn't move.

'You are the Commissioner?'

He offers a little ghosted smile, a little nod for her. He looks her over.

'You seem to be a woman who makes a habit of getting yourself into scrapes,' he says. 'Tell me. Is it true – they say that you seduced one of these foreigners – a young man – whilst he was placed under your roof; and now you would be keen to find some way of having him back – yes? Whatever it took? A young man knowing just enough about life to make ice-cream wafers for a living before you took him.'

He inspects the amber liquid in his glass. 'You run a brothel, I believe,' he says. 'This is where you seduced the foreigner placed with you under a duty of care. Grounds, one might believe, for a town clerk like Stent to consider closing such an establishment down. You have a view on that, perhaps? You think the town clerk would be wise to close your hotel down?'

Joannie Kilner doesn't respond.

'The thing about sex, you have surely found over the years,' he says finally, 'is that it can be so indiscreet.'

Men have led them from the police station in the night.

They are told that they are being driven to Manchester to wait in detention there for the tribunal. They climb in. The van smells of dogs and tarpaulin and oil.

Three men sit in the front cab. Three more, armed, sit with the internees in the dog- and paraffin-stained van.

After twenty minutes, driving up on the tops away from Laing, the van stops. The men indicate for the internees to get out of the truck. The internees are led across a field and into a barn which is then barred from the outside. They hear Joe Filbin's voice shouting to Brock Spivey (who must have been sitting in the cab on the way up), checking that there is no way the internees can escape from his barn, no possible way out at the back.

'No way, no way,' Brock Spivey shouts back, almost clapping out the news. 'No way unless they jump like fleas. No way unless they're tired of living. Unless they're fools. Unless they're supermen.'

'The others can get something to eat while they're here?' Joe Filbin asks.

'If they don't mind the dogs,' Brock Spivey sings, loving the *belonging* of it all. '*She'll* make you breakfast up at the house, but don't mind the dogs.'

Inside the barn, their breaths at first are fast and quick. They wait and breathe and wait. And wait. But nothing happens. The night is damp and big and windy.

'What do they want?' Peretta asks.

Brolin shakes his head.

'It's outrageous,' Friegang says. 'You should say so. I will say so.'

But Brolin will not take him on.

'Maybe they ran out of petrol like the union man told us,' Peretta says.

'They are very organized for people who ran out of petrol,' Brolin says.

'They are madmen,' Friegang says. 'I will report them to the authorities when we get to Manchester.'

'They seemed to know the barn could hold us,' Peretta says. 'They seemed to know it was here when they stopped in the dark.'

The barn is built on two levels. There is a hayrack raised twenty feet above the floorspace, but the dilapidated wooden ladder is rotting away and needs attention. Kasperl has gone shimmying up the wooden scaffold post to have a look and is walking gingerly across the wooden slats towards the back of the barn, peering out to see what lies beyond. At the back, below the bailing doors, twenty feet below, is rusting machinery – old engines, carts, parts of a thresher and seed-drilling attachments for horse-pulled farming which Brock Spivey had inherited and never bothered trying to use in the poor fields and never got round to throwing away. His policy had seemed simply to be to dump the equipment behind the bottom barn. Out of sight, out of mind had seemed to be Brock Spivey's motto.

'So what do we do?' Friegang said. 'We should work out what to do. We are not all monkeys. We cannot all go climbing on the furniture.'

He means Kasperl.

'Is it too far?' Brolin asks Kasperl, ignoring Friegang's remark. 'Can you see in the dark?'

'Too far to jump,' Kasperl tells him.

'For everyone? Even for you?'

'Too far.'

'What about the other baling door over there? Is the drop just as far?'

Kasperl steps further along the hayrack. There is a creaking sound. The wood snaps beneath his leading foot. He grabs for the beam above his head while the dry-rotted timber crumbles and falls away to the floor below him.

'Shitfuckshitfuck,' Kasperl yells. His momentum leaves him swinging from the rafter beam he had leapt at. He hangs still, his heart thumping, recovering his wits. Bit by bit, using his hands, he levers himself back across to the safety of the intact portion of the hayrack further along and then slides down the wooden scaffold pole in the corner, panting, smiling boyishly at Brolin.

'I guess we have no way out that way,' Peretta says.

'So what now?' Friegang says.

Brolin looks around him. 'I don't know,' he says. 'We wait.' And so they wait for the light.

During the night, half dozing but with the cold waking him up intermittently, Brolin imagines that he hears music. It's far away but familiar. It's the cold, he tells himself, but it continues. He wakes Kasperl.

'Listen,' he tells Kasperl. 'You hear anything? Music?'

Kasperl, sleepy, ignorant of discomfort as only the young can be, listens, nods, closes his eyes again. 'Mozart,' he says, yawning.

When dawn comes, they send Kasperl up again to see more clearly whether there is any chance of getting free from the barn. He is up there when Friegang, watching out through the slats in the barn door at the front, announces that Brock Spivey is coming. Brock Spivey is walking down to the barn from the house with apples and a loaf of bread and a pot jug of something with a marble stopper in the neck.

'You best come down,' Brolin tells Kasperl. 'You see any way to get out now it's light?'

Kasperl shakes his head. Above the barn, Kasperl can see that the land rises high, like a shoulder, to Beacon Fell where the trek to the snow line begins. The land they are on is part of Brock Spivey's dilapidated smallholding. It is easily recognized. Brock Spivey's land is too rough to plough and in places too boggy for sheep. It isn't farmed in any organized way; it is simply tenanted – and Brock Spivey is walking across it towards them with a loaf of bread and a bag of apples and a pot pitcher for them.

He pushes the food through a small hole in the barn door where the wood had been snapped away, leaving a gap at floor level big enough for a dish to pass under.

'What is this?' Friegang says.

'It's your breakfast,' Brock Spivey tells him. 'We should look after you. You are our guests.'

'Do you know what will happen to us?' Peretta says through the door.

'Sure I do,' Brock Spivey says happily. 'I'm in charge. Joe Filbin said I could be.'

'We are going to Manchester?' Peretta asks.

'Not Manchester. Here.'

'Why here?'

'We have to keep you here near Laing till after the fair. That's what Joe Filbin says. The tribunal was going to send you to Canada, Joe Filbin says. Mr Stent told him when he called him in the other night. Said he'd found out. That's why he let Joe and the others bring you up here for safe keeping, out of the way. The tribunal people aren't bothered about finding the missing boys. If you'd been allowed to leave Laing and go to Manchester like you were meant, you'd have got farms in Canada and the boys would never have been found. And that's wrong.'

'What's this about farms,' Friegang says. 'He's a crazy man. They're all crazy men.'

'Shut up,' Peretta whispers at Friegang. Peretta puts his head back to the door. 'Do you know what's going to happen?'

'Course I do,' Brock Spivey says.

'Ah, Jesus God,' Friegang says.

'I say shush, you!' Peretta hisses. Then he asks Brock Spivey, 'What? What will happen?'

'It's after the fair,' Brock Spivey tells him.

'What is? What is after the fair?'

'It's after the fair,' Brock Spivey repeats. 'First we have the fair in Laing. The bonfire and the costumes. Everyone is in it. Me too. Everybody in Laing. Then tomorrow when everyone thinks you've gone and the tribunal has forgotten about you, you have to help us find the missing boys.'

'Oh God,' Friegang says, 'we said about that a hundred times.'

Peretta ignores him. 'Tomorrow? Tomorrow they'll ask us again about the boys. And that's it? And then they send us to Manchester. They just say they found us again if we help look for the boys?'

'I guess so,' Brock Spivey says.

'Fucksake,' Friegang says.

'We can help them look for their missing boys, can't we? That is the least we can do,' Peretta says.

'Now you can have breakfast. I have to go up to the house to feed the dogs. I have to get on.'

'Excuse me,' Brolin says. 'I want to ask about the music. I thought I heard music in the night. Maybe I am going crazy but I thought I heard music that I recognized.'

'I remember about you in the camp,' Brock Spivey says. 'You listened to music with the dwarf in the camp.'

'With Heimy. Yes. The music.'

'You like music? Heimy's music?' Brock Spivey asks him.

'Yes. Yes, I do.'

'That's good. You want me to play you some music? To pass the time? I have to feed the dogs now, but I'll play you some music. Is the bread all right for you? You have enough? I have whiskey at the house. Home-made. I'll bring you some.'

'What is this stuff in the jar?' Friegang asks him through the barn door.

'Sarsparilla.'

'To drink?'

'Of course to drink.' Brock Spivey sounds puzzled.

Friegang takes a drink. He coughs, and spits it out.

'Tastes like shit. You try to poison us?'

Brock Spivey shrugs. 'I got to feed the dogs now.'

He walks back up the field past where the truck is parked and towards the house. A little while later he reappears carrying a box. He sets it on the tailgate of the truck. From out of the box he lifts a gramophone in one hand and the big brass ear which attaches to it in the other. It is recognizable by the crest on the side of the wooden box it sits in. It is the wind-up gramophone that Brock Spivey took from the possessions Heimy left in the colony. He rests it carefully on the tailgate. He cranks up the handle and lays the heavy, bulbous arm on to the record he has set down on the turntable. Music rises out of the machine. Brock Spivey turns up the volume to full on the machine so that Brolin and the rest of them can hear it from the barn at the bottom of the field. It is Mozart. It is the *Requiem* that Heimy loved. It is the *Benedictus*.

Erland Kyle had seen the original Celtic settlers in Laing staging their bonfire. He'd watched them gather on the beach that first December he was there, burning their mock boat in their Cumberland Uphala, firing up the midwinter and beseeching spring to come again, and he hijacked the festival for his own troupe.

The next year, instead of setting fire to a Celtic boat, Erland Kyle's Lancastrian community built a more formal bonfire of pit props and driftwood on the beach at evening low tide. Everyone gathered to hear Erland Kyle say prayers and give thanks. They had a pig roasting on a spit and shared slices of pork and potatoes after the prayers and watched the sea bit by bit come in towards the town. Then, late in the evening, on a given signal, with the encroaching sea a hundred yards away, they lit the bonfire and threw into it tokens of the old world they had left behind.

It grew over the years into a full winter fair. People took to dressing in the manner of Erland Kyle's time. They moved across the beach carrying torches to light their way in the night, since dusk in December fell at five in the afternoon; children eating roasted potatoes and chestnuts from brown bags; men striking balls off their shies planted in the sand; everyone waiting for the beer barrel to be opened and the bonfire to begin to warm them all against the wind that every year came scudding in off the flat open sea beside them.

Boys and girls, giggling, came dressed as the Sheriff of Lancaster's men. Grown-ups came masquerading as demons and dragons, disguised in the masks they held before their faces, the stilled and stilted faces of sloth and avarice, all the seven sins of man; they came wearing masks of moons and suns, of cats and crows, came as the Devil's minions, and came finally as Death himself to show that even this – even Death – could be defeated if people had faith enough in God. People came down to the winter beach – families, husbands, wives, groups – enjoying the festival of their community, wearing the masks which they had made, smiling at how their friends and neighbours looked, at the foolishness and glamour of this one night of the year and waiting, excited, for the fire that would be lit. Then, when everyone had arrived from the town down on to the sands, when braziers had been lit to guide people across the dark beach and the bonfire had been lit and had taken hold, then it was time for the decorated masks, one by one, to be thrown on to the fire. After that they sang hymns in the open air and a sermon was read and, as people edged back to the shore, the tide came in and bit by bit swept the hissing ashes of the bonfire out to sea for one more year.

The Laing Fair had run each year since Erland Kyle's arrival in 1582. The sequence of years had only finally been broken by the blackout regulations of the war in 1939 which had been issued to prevent the German bombers from having a target to aim at as they flew in the skies overhead. For five years the Laing Fair had not been held as the war had run its course. But with the war in mainland Europe closing in on Germany itself, the town had been given permission for the fair to run and for a bonfire to be held on the low tide sands.

And so they come, down from their houses rising on the plateaus of the Heights of Abraham, down past the third-class hotel and Sam Wormold's surgery and the Parish School, down past the Crescent Hotel on the sweep of the harbour front towards the smell of the kelp and the sea and the bitter tang of fog on their tongues.

Most of the town seems to be down on the sands. Just a few people are away – just the harbourmaster waiting for one final boat to come in; just Walt Emerson standing guard in the third-class hotel; Joannie Kilner in her rooms high up in the hotel; Gabriel keeping his distance somewhere from all those masks that so unnerve him; the Parish School teacher and her mother sitting across from each other in their high-roofed sitting room listening to their fire cracking in the hearth and their hearts beating. But all the rest seem to be here. They smile at the sight of one another. They drink home-made beer and the women drink mulled wine served from wooden bowls. They eat roasted potatoes and cooked apples provided by the Kyles, and chestnuts in greaseproof paper bags that are hot to the touch, and they talk of the end of the war and when sons might be expected to be home, and the kind of world there'll be afterwards, and whether the three missing boys will be home soon.

Friegang says, 'We should tell them it was Kasperl.'

'What?'

'We should tell them. We should say it was Kasperl who took the boys. If they have my knife that was stolen, we should say this. If we say it's him, then they will let the rest of us go. We should shout to who is out there and say so. What do you say?'

'You tell that to them,' Peretta says, not bothering to look up, not turning round, lying quite still, 'and I will cut your throat.'

'You are only one. You don't say. You are too young to know the value of living. What about you, Brolin? What do you say? Now it comes to the crunch, I say the idiot for the three of us is a good deal. I say the tribunal would say that too. I say we're better men than some circus fool carrying his blasted bell around with him everywhere he goes. Jesus! I say we deserve to get out of this.'

Brolin says nothing.

'Brolin. I am talking to you. What do you say?'

Finally Brolin stirs.

'They won't.'

'Won't what?'

'They won't. I have seen it before.'

'They won't what? What won't they?'

'They won't listen to what you say.'

'You think? Why not?'

'Because they are so sure they know already. They don't want to hear different.'

'How could you see it before? You have second sight all of a sudden?'

'In Germany, I saw men hunt my father and my brother down in the streets when Blackshirts ran through the town. They thought they knew already, those men. They did not want to hear anything. They could not hear anything. To some men there is no point speaking.'

'Why did they take your father? Your brother?'

'Why do you think, Friegang?'

'You are Jewish?'

'Jewish, communist,' Brolin says slowly. 'What is the difference sometimes to men who have power in a place?'

'So you say what we should do? What the fucking hell we do? You say?'

Brolin looks up for the first time from where he sits. Perhaps he has been crying, though no one has heard him.

'We should drink now,' Brolin says. He sounds tired. Not like the Brolin who had sat with Heimy full of life while they had listened to Anna Mutter singing on Heimy's records in the camp. 'There is whiskey somewhere that the farm man brought,' he says. 'Who will take a drink with me?'

The bodies of three boys are discovered washed up on the rocks close to the mouth of the estuary. The flow tide has carried them in. They are glimpsed by fishermen from a boat approaching the harbour. The boat is arriving back from three days of fishing for Shetland cod. The skipper had aimed to arrive back in Laing before nightfall but they had been delayed by fog banks along the coast. There is still fog lying on the water near to Laing and the boat's foghorn sounds as they bring her in. Then her searchlight picks out what seems to the men on board to be the shapes of bodies, or maybe of fallen trees, as they approach the harbour.

They unload their catch by the light of the harbour shed lamps, then they go back on foot down the estuary path with hurricane lamps. They find the bodies lying face down, half hung over the rocks where the sea has deposited them. They are the bodies of Billy and Joseph Tillotson and Morton Filbin. The bodies are cold and hardening. Death, a mysterious kind of witchcraft, was several days ago.

The men make no noise as they emerge out of the Laing fog – six figures bowed with the weight of the dead boys hung between them. People on the beach turn as they sense the motion, and see. The men carry on walking through the crowd which grows more dense as they near the site of the readied bonfire. Everyone has gathered to see the bonfire lit, waiting expectantly for the first of the torches to be thrown on to the pile. The six men from the boat walk wordlessly through to the front of the crowd. Then they lay the bodies down on the sand between the bonfire pile and the Laing crowd. The illumination cast by the torches drops a pool of light on the sand around the bodies, and on the young, un-finished faces of the boys, grey and translucent, the colour of fish scales. The bodies lie like fish on slabs – three of them in a row on the grey sand, dead for maybe a week and smelling of the sea and only half draped with the coats of the fishermen who have carried them up from the estuary. A current passes through the crowd. The sob of a woman pulls at the silence. Someone whispers. A man cries out in vain. The sea, beyond the light of all their head-high torches and of the fog, drives in at them.

Sometimes, the thread can break. It is the thread that holds the narrative of lives together in a place like Laing, where dreams are cramped and small, and people live the same lives, each other's lives, over and over. These lives hang on silver threads, and all these threads are tied to a single thread which itself hangs down from the glass roof which arches over the town. This single thread hangs on a tension so that no one pulls too much or strays too far, so that everyone, living their same lives for the same reasons, is held. Always, though, there is the threat that one day the thread that binds and orders all of these lives together might fail, might be weakened by an act of God - a plague or a sea storm or a pit fall – and then have cause to snap, and the tension that holds and orders all things together may break them all apart.

'What do you dream about?' Brolin says.
   'I dream about Italy.'
   'Do you remember it?'

Peretta shakes his head. 'Some. A little. I'd like to see Sicily. My Papa talks all the time of Sicily. I'd like to make a little money. A lot of money. I'd like to *do* things. Different. You understand? You know what my mother dreams of? My wedding. Only that. Uncles, aunts, half of Sicily come to see me married and settled to a life.'

Brolin smiles. 'But not you?'

'Listen. Believe me. My girl, she's a good girl. Nice girl. Good legs.' He exhales the smoke from the cigarette he has in a long, wondering blow up into the air. 'But I don't know about marrying. Maybe my mother should marry her. As for me, I'd like to have a little fun. A little life, eh?'

'Kasperl? What do you say? What do you dream about?'

'Circus Prenzlau,' Kasperl says. 'Heimy leading in the first caravan. Then the others. Moving to the next place.'

'But Heimy's dead. What do you wish for now? For after the war?'

'Only that. That's all I wish for. Circus Prenzlau. One thing.'

Friegang is moping over by the barn door. Suddenly he says, 'There's someone coming.'

'Who? Who's coming.'

'I don't know. It's hard to see. Someone. Someone's coming. And . . .'

Friegang tails off. They look round at him.

They walk in procession up through the winter field. The men have walked up from Laing – the children sent home with the women, and the tall, dry bonfire left to fall into the sea – and they carry torches and hurricane lamps. At first there seems to be maybe twenty of them, then thirty, then fifty. And still they keep coming, walking steadily across the wet field of Brock Spivey's smallholding above the town. They carry the torches that they were given for the Laing Fair down on the sands and they are dressed in the costumes and the masquerades of the Laing Fair – as the Sheriff's soldiers and the Bishop's inquisitors, as imps and demons, as Pestilence and Plague, as the Devil and his Demons. There are a hundred of them now and more behind, and at the front – the torches of everyone around him reflected in the chalk white mask covering his face – they are led by *Death*, who is Brock Spivey.

And *Death* runs up the field, searching. He finds what he is looking for in the back of the truck which is still parked on the edge of the field. *Death* fumbles with the gramophone on the tailgate. He lays down the record he has found flat on the turntable and lifts the needle on to the turning platter.

The *Requiem's Sanctus* begins to rise from the gramophone. The volume is turned up full so that it seems to flood the dark field. And *Death*, leaping down from the truck back on to the grass, begins to conduct the music with his arms out wide in front of the crowd he has led, a grin like bliss across his big face, the soprano voice of Anna Mutter floating across the night as the procession with torches approaches the barn at the far end of the field. And *Death*, not carrying a light himself, takes a burning torch from the nearest Demon and throws it through the air. It falls and strikes the barn high up in the eaves, the pitch-dipped flame compelling a blue flash and then a ball of intense orange flame in a small rush of noise. Birds rise from the trees. And one by one the masked procession follow *Death* and throw their burning torches up into the rafters of the barn. The chords of the *Requiem* ring and rise, filling the field, and *Death*, drunk and happy and part of Laing, beams, and, close by, the flames catch the hay and the dry wood in the roofspace of the locked barn and take hold.

In the end, there will be quiet.

In the end there will be little more than the light of a whitish dawn, and the smouldering of the ashes of Brock Spivey's barn, and the crack of spent wood, and birdsong. Then it will be done. Then it will be over. Then no one will ever know. It will be a secret that the world won't get to know. It will be Laing's secret. Because no one else will have seen them. They'll just be people who'll have a tiredness on them like men vague after sex or battle – a lacklustre mood, a forgetfulness. A need to sleep. No one else will have seen the foreigners or heard them. No one else will have seen what was done when the fire had burned fast and hard and lighted the air clean across the field and crackled and smarted, gnawing at the once-fat beams of the barn.

No one.

No one, except for Gabriel Emerson. The men from the town all look up and see the boy as he finally dares to move and cracks a twig under his shoe forty feet away above them, almost hidden by the trees. Still the barn burns and music from Brock Spivey's gramophone – the *Requiem's Communio* – climbs into the hills towards the snowline, and beyond them all.

Sometimes, in the long nights of the colony, Gabriel still dreams the same grey dream he's had forever. He dreams of one man pulling, pulling through the snow and the ash-coloured sky. Sometimes it's dreamed, sometimes it's as if he's carried there to see it, as if Gabriel is part of it; as if he's there, as if it's him, or nearly him – this single man whose head is low against the wind in a plain of flat ice that doesn't end, and who is pushing on with some vague, unrealized destination in mind. He seems to have so far to go. And he seems to have come this far alone.

Gabriel wonders how this man will ever make it. Sometimes Gabriel has stood by the window when it's been winter, when snow's fallen and it's lying, imagining the man walking, wondering how far there is to go and when he'll stop.

The long, grey lands lie flat about the ship. Fog lifts, hangs, evaporates. The northern lights, in utter silence, sing of the end of the polar night. The lights vault upwards, changing colour and tone as they are projected on to the roof of the sky. They run like waves a thousand miles away across the sky, contrasting with the dull ice sea all about the ship. The *Endeavour* stays gripped in the ice, sits perfectly still. The crew watch the lights firing the sky at dusk, and wait. And wait.

Enough food has been packed for six weeks. Enough food, Gabriel envisages, for a journey to the edge of the Anian Strait and back – to confirm its existence – before the ice begins to break in June and sets free the *Endeavour*. Some salted pork, some biscuits, codfish, dried peas, cheese and butter are packed on to the sledge, along with some tools, the astrolabe, and the hide tent which had been bartered from the eskimos on Greenland for bags of nails, some tin pots and some ropes. The sledge has been constructed by Peary and Athol, using wood from the lower bunks and deck boards and set on runners. The four of them will harness themselves to the sledge each day with guy ropes to pull the supplies they will need. They practise pulling the sledge on the sea ice around the ship where the sharp blue corners of ice have risen as high as the decks. It works. They grin foolishly at each other when they find that they can manage the load that they have packed, when they feel the weight of the sledge sliding across the ice behind them. They open the last of Athol's beer to celebrate the possibility of success.

Alone, Gabriel tears pages from books he wants to take to read on the journey. He makes calculations about the Passage, based on what he could understand from the eskimos. He will take two muskets as defence against the bears who have so terrorized them through the polar night. The plans are for those who are staying behind to wait two months. After that, if the expedition hasn't returned, those on the ship are ordered to sail back when the ice cracks.

The days grow longer. At dusk each night, electric reds and greens and blues ripple on the sky. At night, the ice still moans, as if some invisible and distant animals even greater than the huge, white, silent bears are all about them somewhere. Gabriel hears them. And still they wait.

Sometimes the horizon vanishes – the land into sky and sky into land, everything belonging to a single pewter sheen – and it is hard to know where the man is walking.

Gabriel wants to ask him, 'Where are you walking? Have you far to go?' But the man doesn't answer him. He keeps on walking. His head is down. He cannot hear. Or maybe he can hear Gabriel asking him and it is only that he has no destination to say, no answer to give; it is simply that he must keep walking, or he will die there in the snow that he is trying to cross.

They grow less and less distinct.

From the ship, the four men walking away across the ice seem more fictions than real men now, weighed down in a silence that stretches in a skin across the landscape. The day is clear. The land is flat and long. The ice is everywhere. The sun is pale – weak and watered down. Far away the wind seems to blow, but here the day is still. Slowed. The four men each carry a pack which is heavy with supplies. Between them they pull a sledge which carries additional supplies as well as the tent. None of them, it seems, turn back. None of them turns to look at the ship. They walk steadily across the ice pulling the awkward sledge behind them, sea-boots snapping on the frozen land with each simple stride they take. The remaining crew stand watching them from the deck rail of the *Endeavour* which is beached in the risen ice.

No one wants to go back down below whilst Gabriel Emerson and the three men with him are still visible to them, but the cold gnaws at their bare heads and their ears sing. They wait and wait, and the figures out on the ice, moving away from the ship, become smaller and less real until the crew left behind leaning on the deck rail have to guess whether they can still see the figures out there at all in the long, still, white day all about them. In the end, there are no footsteps on the hard ice to be heard. In the end the men on deck go down one by one to warm themselves by the furnace. In the end they go back down to their jobs maintaining the ship and repairing the winter's damage. In the end there is only the ice outside, and the blow of the faraway wind, and the recollection of four men walking steadily away from the ship in sea-boots, pulling the sledge and weighed with packs, the skin of their faces pulled tight against the pressure of the cold and breathing warm men's breaths out like hope in the air above them.

19

Hearts and bones

It is cold in the room they have put him in. Gabriel can feel it, restless on his skin. The cold is so acquisitive, so eager to find a way through. So insistent. Down the corridor, the boy can hear voices. He can't hear what they are saying; he hears them only as a rhythm of sound beyond his four quiet walls. The voices seem a long way away. He knows he's been brought here, he knows he is waiting, but he isn't sure for what. He knows he has to wait. He doesn't know what is meant to happen next. The voices down the corridor rise and fall like music.

They have left him a chair, but he sits on the floor with his back against the wall. He pulls at his fingers, plays at the skin gathered and tucked at the knuckles. Gabriel's boy's thoughts are not registered on his face. Rather, they occupy a different, inner space. They are so large and so easily conjured. They are not memories, they are magic: set pieces not requiring judgement; scenes to be tumbled through at pace with a logic of their own. Hills, faces, geese flying over Laing; geese rising strong like pure white smoke, beating out in lines over the estuary – right over Laing. He can see from up there where Erland Kyle had walked across the water of Morecambe Bay, carrying the cross that bit deep into his stern flesh, and back all the way to Laing and to the woods above the town. He can see the small harbour boats, Laing's slapping sea, the people, the fells for miles beyond. But he cannot see his Dada. As high as he glides, as far as he looks, he cannot see Walt. Then the door opens.

It is minus thirty-two degrees. There is a cloudless blue sky which is made pale by the reflecting ice of the land. The walking keeps their circulation running. The breath from their mouths rises up around their heads, condenses, and settles on their faces then freezes into tiny shards of ice like needles on their beards. They strain against the weight of the sledge, against the pressure of the harness on their backs and legs. Every now and then they look up towards the horizon.

Even so early in the new season, they have fifteen hours of light each day in which to make progress. Gabriel has divided the day into three walking parts. After the first, they rest and drink as much water as they can, because their thirst is insatiable. After the second, they eat their one main meal together and make what repairs are needed to the sledge or deal with injuries from falls on the ice sustained on the day's walk while the light is still clear enough to allow it. After the third, they set down the hide tent, driving pegs into the snow to hold it down – then they sleep.

They are walking over the hard-frozen shore ice. The surface is formed of plates of ice which have been buckled by the force of the sea and lifted on to one another. As they walk further away from the ship, away from the jutting criss-crossed shore ice, the surface becomes flatter, smooth and white with symmetrical six-inch ridges every so often over which the sledge can be pulled more easily by the four of them. The only indication in this white and open land that they are making any progress, that they are *gaining*, is the sight of an iceberg far ahead of them which had been calved into a previous summer sea, then captured by it and frozen fast. It gives them something to measure against. It offers them imagined progress. The berg has smooth sides, rising abruptly out of the flat sea ice. When they pass it after several days of slowly, slowly gaining on this, their one landmark, the land becomes suddenly featureless again. It will be another four days before there's something else to aim for. Then, low on the infinite horizon, a purple line of hills shuffles out into view.

'They look like lines of elephants,' Peary says. They will fall asleep this night dreaming together of elephant hills.

There are no bear trails today. Most days they come across at least one set of tracks, criss-crossed over the naked land by some following white fox waiting to scavenge. The cold is kept at bay if they keep walking. It's when they stop that their feet and limbs start freezing. It's when they stop that the dry air cuts at them, at Ingerman in particular. And all the time ahead of them the purple shadow of the hills grows in their imagination into towers of basalt, into fractured towers of ice.

A softness suggesting evening grows on them. The day gives way, as each one does, to a grey, cold, subdued light. To stillness. It has been thus for centuries, Gabriel suggests in his notes. It is a place that remembers the beginning of time. The mountains in the distance fade, and are lost to their sight – as if they were only dreamed after all. Almost absently, Gabriel notices the reddening blisters on his hands from the ropes. He

finishes writing. Close by him the others are asleep. The wind
is rising.

Gabriel had been taken back to Laing. They had asked the
boy what he had seen, but he had not answered them. They
have told Walt that Gabriel has been found trespassing, and
that he should keep a closer eye on the boy. They have
reported to Stent where he had been found. Gabriel has said
nothing. He disappears for long periods each day, but no one
bothers so long as he continues to say nothing. Of course, all
the time he stays silent they wonder what he has seen.
Whether he'd heard the voices of the internees in the barn.
Whether he'd seen the people of Laing coming up from the
town still decked in the costumes and masks they wore to celebrate Laing's founding, and *Death* in the form of Brock
Spivey leading them. And whether he'd seen the fire being set
and taking hold and burning hard just before they saw him up
on the rise through the winter bushes.

He had.

He'd seen it all, though he continues to say nothing. But
he'd seen something else that they hadn't suspected, something which keeps him busy and distracted now. He'd seen
Kasperl jump.

It had been Brolin who had lifted Kasperl up to the hayloft
as the fire on the far side of the barn was taking hold.

'You can do it,' he had yelled. 'Aim for the cart. Leap for
the cart.'

Kasperl had tried to pull Brolin up after him. He truly had.
But the unstable hayrack in Brock Spivey's barn had creaked
and groaned and threatened to give way.

'Come, come,' Kasperl had shouted, pleaded. But Brolin

kept telling him: 'Jump, you idiot, jump.' The hayrack platform had rocked beneath Kasperl's feet. As the heat grew stronger and the black smoke thickened, he had stumbled, clutched the rafter beam to steady himself, then regained his balance. When he looked back, Brolin was lost in the smoke.

And then he jumped.

Kasperl had dragged himself down the gully and was hiding out in one of the slate-mined caves in the woods. His precious handbell was next to him. He'd jumped with it. Kasperl had jumped from the baling doors at the back when the fire in the barn was at its height. He had jumped thirty feet, leaping clear of the barn, flailing and righting himself as he fell through the air, over and beyond the old threshing machinery, striking his arm on a length of stove piping and tipping forwards out on to the downslope of the gully. Only his training – the circus skills, the acrobatics Heimy had worked him so hard to perfect as part of the apprenticeship for the life he had imagined – had enabled him to survive the jump, albeit with injuries that skewered him on the pain and dragged him in and out of consciousness. As Brock Spivey had said, only a fool would have made such a jump.

He had fallen unconscious again when Gabriel had come across him in one of the small slate caves in the wood. Gabriel had been looking for him for over a day in the land that ran adjacent to Brock Spivey's smallholding.

Despite his injuries from the jump, Kasperl had somehow dragged himself away down the gully before Joe Filbin's men came round inspecting the charred remains of the barn at first light. He knew he couldn't walk; the pain in his legs was bad and there was no movement or feeling in the arm he'd fallen on. He knew, left alone out there, that he must die. He knew that if he was to be rescued from this, then he would owe his life – whatever pieces of it were left intact – to his rescuer.

Gabriel had tended to him for eight days. They spoke few words to each other at first. What would there be to say? Kasperl's English was still poor at this stage of his life. Gabriel told no one. Not Walt. Not Joannie Kilner. No one followed him. No one seemed to notice. Gabriel came up from Laing each day to the cave. He brought food and water from Joannie Kilner's hotel, and aspirin. He wrapped Kasperl in blankets as Kasperl moved from fever to withering cold and back to fever. Gabriel found bandages for a splint to support the leg that was broken and the crushed arm that had struck the stove pipes as he fell and had no feeling. Pain rose and folded and dimmed and rose again in Kasperl as he lay in the belly of the cave, all the world except for Gabriel imagining him dead.

'Now to talk, boy,' he pleaded, knowing that to drift away into a deep unconsciousness now would be to surrender the slim thread that kept him hung to life, 'I want to live. Now to talk.'

He dreamed the Circus Prenzlau was passing by. He dreamed the caravans were silhouetted on the hill. He dreamed that Heimy was waiting for him. And so Gabriel, who was silent all this while in Laing, talked to Kasperl to keep him alive through the eight days. He talked to him about Laing. He talked about Bubba. About his Dada, the night badger, snuffling through the third-class hotel from dusk to each next day's light. He talked about the mariner who shared Gabriel's name and sailed from Laing to find the thing he most longed for in all the world, and how one day he himself would sail from Laing. And he told him what

William had said – what had happened to the boys who went missing from Laing.

Billy Tillotson says there are tunnels coming off the bottom galleries of the Wellington Pit. He says the tunnels are used by spies. Rolf Stent is sceptical but he won't give up the chance to look down the pits which his father won't let him near. His father says the boy won't need to dig coal; he tells Rolf he'll have a profession, he'll be a lawyer or an architect

'My father would know about anything like this,' Rolf Stent says.

'You saying you scared to come and look?' Billy Tillotson says.

'Course not,' Rolf Stent says. 'I'm not afraid. I'm saying you're making it up. My father would know about German tunnels and he's never said, he's never given anything away about them.'

'My Da says your father wouldn't give his shit away for free if he could charge for it,' Billy Tillotson says. Billy Tillotson says the tunnels go all the way back to Germany. Billy Tillotson is fourteen. He's started working in the pits now with his Da and his uncles and he's seen the tunnels that he's telling them about. And who are they to argue with him? He says the explosion in the Wellington Pit was the Germans trying to stop people from discovering them. He says they're big enough for tanks to come through from France while everyone's fighting the war over there. He says one shotgun in the police station won't do any good when the Panzers start rolling through the streets of Laing and take aim at the Meeting House.

They push past the boarded doors and the closure notices. They use the manual winch.

'Do as Billy tells you,' Joseph Tillotson says, enjoying not being last of all in the gang's pecking order because his brother Billy is here with him. Last of all in the pecking order now is William Emerson

*who tags along at the end, asking once or twice whether it is really
all right for them to go underground like this.*

*'Cissy,' Billy says as they cram into the cage. William watches
Billy Tillotson leering at him, then steps in last of all.*

'Keep your arms tight in,' Billy Tillotson says.

*'You the pit manager or what?' Rolf Stent says. The others laugh
as they ride down. In the confined space of the cage, Billy Tillotson
blushes angry red.*

*'You have to follow me,' Billy Tillotson says, 'or you're for it.
Remember that.'*

Rolf Stent blows a raspberry and the others laugh again.

*They go in search of the spy tunnels. It's dark down there. They
have one hurricane lamp that Billy Tillotson carries but there's no
lighting down the central corridor of the gallery. They follow Billy
Tillotson in single file, but it's hard for Billy to remember all the different turn-offs. They get lost. They double back but turn into the
wrong gallery. They spend an hour walking further and further,
trying to retrace their steps back to the central corridor they're on,
but the passages get narrower and wetter underfoot and the boys
grow more nervous and start to hurry more and lose their balance,
especially Joseph Tillotson who's the youngest, and now and then one
of them trips and falls and makes a cry as he tips in the wet mush of
cinders and mud and the others, barely able to see him in the dark,
have to help him up. They hear water. The walkway they are on gets
narrower. It slopes away to one side. They move across one by one,
gripping each other's hands as they shuffle on. Billy Tillotson leads
them. William Emerson is at the rear. Morton Filbin trips. He
loses his balance. He can't hang on. He slides away from them down
the slope, taking Joseph Tillotson with him into the flooded pit
twenty feet below the walkway. Billy Tillotson grabs for Joseph and
loses his footing and falls away too. Rolf Stent and William Emerson*

hang on, clutching at the floor that seems to be subsiding beneath their feet, scrambling back up the scree to a kind of safety above the water that suddenly seems closer now in the corridor that's dark as pitch. Their hearts are bursting. Fear, let loose, scrags at them both. Blood bangs behind their eyes and knocks at their throats so that they cannot swallow. They are sick with panic.

There are no shouts from Billy Tillotson – their guide – or his younger brother, or from Morton Filbin. There had only been the noise of their hitting the water, and then the blackness that seemed to swallow them whole, and then the echo of their own shouts chasing after the fallen boys, and then another, and then nothing more.

Rolf Stent and William hide in the gallery for two days. At one point, William begins to cry. Rolf Stent tells him to shut up. Rolf Stent says they'll be beaten. He says they'll be sent away to borstal. They'll become borstal boys and have their hair shaved. He says they'll be charged with murder.

'You want that?' he says. 'You want that?'

They wait for two days. They have a small, kept-alive hope that the three boys who fell into the bottom gallery might yet somehow emerge from the water. They have a sort of hope that Billy Tillotson, being a good swimmer, might have rescued the others further down the shaft. But no one comes; no one rises from the black water below them.

After two days, too hungry to speak about it, sick with a thirst for water that overrides even their fear of what will become of them, Rolf Stent leads William Emerson and they begin to search for a way back up through the galleries and out on to the surface, and down the hill into Laing.

When Gabriel ran out of things to say himself, he brought his Mama's notebooks – the ones bequeathed to him when she had died – and read from them. He read about the golden child she carried. He read about her need to keep him safe from the terragots.

After eight days, the fever and the pain grew worse again. Kasperl was feverish and drinking more and more. He passed out for hours at a time and at one point grew delirious. Gabriel wondered what to do because Kasperl had said they would surely kill him if the boy told people in Laing about him.

Until the sledge breaks, the need for them to think is minuscule. The need to think is secondary to the will that leads them on, to the dumb accrual of miles. They manoeuvre the sledge over the rough ground. They breathe hard through the noise and confusion of the wind. They bicker at each other. Athol, who leads at the front with Gabriel, complains that Peary and Ingerman are not taking their share of the weight in the harness. Ingerman in particular is struggling to keep up. They walk through a wall of falling snow, a tunnel of sound. Twice, Ingerman falls forward on to the heel of Athol's boot in front of him and howls at the pain.

'You keep slowing and making us stumble,' Peary screams.

'You should watch out if I have to slow, you oaf.'

They re-form and walk on. They're too afraid of standing still for long. They are afraid of the violence of the cold. It is a cold that holds their narrowing bellies tight, and sucks and claws at their limbs, and sets fire to their feet, and blights and blinds their thinking.

Powdertops of snow are blown into the air. The wind turns it into a mist that they bend their heads against as they pull the sledge forward yard by yard over the rutted ice. The cold seems to blow inside each man's head. The ice lies inside their skulls and drips, freezing, under their sorry skins, bleaching all hope. This land runs on forever. The cold leaks into the sockets of their eyes, their teeth. Gradually, it will overwhelm them as it has overwhelmed the land. The storm inside their heads blanks out everything except for the weariness that comes from pulling the sledge day after day; except for the pain. They stumble. They fall over things. They pick themselves up. They lift the sledge over obstacles when it becomes jammed in the ice. Then they take up the weight of the harness again and move off over the ice, yard by yard, inch by inch, and the cold – like the polar night before it – eats at them. And when Ingerman falls down a slope and the sledge is overturned, the sledge breaks apart and one of the runners is fractured, and the four of them sit crying on the ice, till Gabriel is first to rise and stubbornly begins to help the others one by one to their feet.

Their fingers freeze as Gabriel directs them in mending the sledge. They realize that the load on the sledge must be lightened or it will not survive the journey. They share the extra load between them. Only Ingerman among them is not given a share. They move off again. The wind cries. It fills them up with cold they cannot bear. It's a cold that begins somewhere in the tension of their high backs beneath the shoulder blades and burrows into them until it grips their kidneys and their spleens, until even their once-warm centres are rotted with the cold. They bend into the wind as they take the weight of the sledge again, this time with the weight of extra supplies on their backs. Their eyelids ice over. The stars shine brilliantly on clear nights, and centuries of silence lie on them, and prayers seem the only answer – except that they know now for sure in this last, desolate place that theirs is a godless universe of blind and simple elements. The only one to beseech now – the only one who'll hear their pleas – is the man harnessed beside them and pulling too.

The boy came down the track and into Laing wheeling the heavy wheelbarrow erratically into the town. His progress was slow. His face was white and blank with effort. He forced himself to keep the barrow level though his hands hurt and his arms burned. Some children saw him from a distance pushing the barrow down the track, and laughed and giggled at his unsteady progress. And it was only when he got closer that they saw that the weight in the wheelbarrow was Kasperl, laying still in the barrow, deadweight but breathing, and that was when they heard a bell sounding somewhere as if announcing the arrival.

When Gabriel grew closer still, they saw that the quiet 'ding' was the handbell in the wheelbarrow with Kasperl, ringing each time the wheelbarrow bumped on the street and the bell nudged Kasperl's unmoving arm as Kasperl lay, apparently sleeping. Gabriel, his eyes looking ahead of him, his arms straining to hold his final course, moved past them, and they backed off. One by one they backed off, and Gabriel walked past, his eyes looking straight ahead of him, the barrow scraping its contact with the road and the bell tapping Kasperl's side.

'Ding, ding, ding.'

Everybody saw Gabriel finally arrive at Sam Wormold's surgery after his slow and painful progress through the town. When they arrived outside Sam Wormold's place, the crowd of people – children pushing to the front, adults behind –

who had followed him stopped too. Gabriel laid the wheel-barrow at the door with everybody watching, and turned. He paused, then he leant over the wheelbarrow and took the bell away with him from where it lay on top of the unconscious Kasperl. He left him there, and Sam Wormold who had come out to see what all the fuss was about had no choice but to take Kasperl into his surgery and arrange for his arm to be set and treat his wounds.

There is nothing but to walk across the endless ice. Nothing changes, except the toll it wreaks upon them. They walk, and sleep, and walk. And walk. They have lost count of the days and of the distance they imagine is still to go. The ice freezes their puny bones, soddens their clothes. Ingerman is visibly decaying in front of them. He has been relieved of his harness duties. He carries just his food, a blanket, and one of the guns together with his own brown sack tied with cord which he will not relinquish. When he urinates on to the ice, it is dark and sometimes red. He coughs blood. It runs out of his nose instead of mucus and this blood freezes black on his face and on the whiteness of his beard. After their rests, Gabriel has to help him to his feet. He is too weak to stand up on his own.

They have to stop frequently now when the sledge catches and snags on ice humps. They lack the strength to pull it clear. Sometimes they have to unload everything from the sledge so that they can lift it over the obstacle in their way, and then repack it piece by piece with black hands and aching knuckle joints, though the tips of their fingers now have no feeling in them and are useless and difficult to manoeuvre. It can take half a day to make a mile's progress over the ice. The rests they take grow longer. They try only for shorter sessions now, walking just an hour at a time. When they are not walking they are asleep or lie resting in the hide tent, often lacking the energy even to sleep, just leant against each other. It's a small warming, a frugal love.

Gabriel's hands have grown large blood blisters down to the second joint, which caused him to wince handling the spade as they were burying Ingerman.

They took him out and buried him during the night – the three of them digging slowly, silently – one spade, then the next, then the last, in turn, lit by the moon, until the hole was dug. They buried Ingerman's brown sack with him. They had opened it before they buried him. Inside was a violin. It was the one which had been his mother's, the one she'd carried the sheet music for on the train to the Salem Turn school each week when Walt Emerson and Brock Spivey as boys had watched her reading it.

'You can *read* music?' Brock Spivey had asked incredulously one day on the train. It was a tale Walt would tell Evelyn. 'How can you read something when there's no words there?' The girl had just shrugged and not taken Brock Spivey on – just watching him for a moment above her glasses – and carried on reading and imagining the sounds of the music in her head, and now her son was being buried with the violin she'd owned and which no one had ever heard her play. She had left the violin with him on what proved to be the last time she came to see him, when Ingerman had been twenty-eight.

They laid the sack beside him and covered him with the colony's earth – and then when it was done they were swallowed again by the cold, blue-grey bowl of land.

Their boots are frozen hard. Their fingers are useless. Athol, who had increasingly taken the largest share of the sledge's weight before it was finally abandoned, has broken blisters on his fingers. The flesh beneath them is raw and runny and swollen. When they are not pulling the sledge, he nurses the fingers in his damp and insubstantial gloves.

They walk in single file now. It was too much effort to continue to drag the sledge over successive ice ridges; it was too much to clamber over each one and to haul the sledge on again. The tent, too heavy to carry without the sledge, has been cut up. Each man now carries a portion of it as a sheet to sleep under on the ground. They lie close to each other. They had started by building a snow pit each night after the day's walking and covering it with the tent sheets. Now they just curl on the ground against whatever shelter they can find, and lie together.

The ice is rutted. The snow drifts. Peary shits in his pants. He stands there like an infant when his conscious mind finally realizes, saying it, saying what he's done. Gabriel calls a halt. Athol and Gabriel clean him up and bind him with clean cloth. They move on.

Some nights they dream of how the ship left Laing. Some nights they dream of how the *Endeavour* slipped from harbour carrying Gabriel Emerson and Peary and Athol and poor Ingerman and the crew away from Laing. They dream of how they passed by near the shore to offer their farewells to the people of Laing who had gathered on the harbour to see them away. They had said farewell with the noise of trumpets and the artillery of the ships. Laing answered with a wheeling of high white birds and the waits on the shore and with shouts from the shore which could still be heard a mile out by the ship, bidding them fair voyage and good days ahead.

Peary comes up on Gabriel's shoulder. They walk together for a while, stumbling and bumping into each other. Gabriel finally reacts in anger.

'Walk in front or behind,' he says, 'but not like this.'

Peary drops behind. Gabriel hears his uneven steps and Peary's low grunts each time the pain comes.

'You must understand,' Stent had said to Walt, 'I wouldn't, myself, want to see the boy taken from you. It may be, though, that in the end there is no choice.'

Walt's only thought was that Evelyn would have known what to do.

'You see the problem I have,' Stent said, 'trying to be reasonable here?'

Walt acknowledged that he did.

'I can't allow this to continue indefinitely.'

Walt fidgeted on the chair Stent had given him.

'I can't allow your boy indefinite licence to go on ridiculing us, embarrassing you, the town. It needs to stop. You need to stop it. You agree?'

'I don't know how to stop it,' Walt said.

'We cannot,' Stent said, 'jeopardize a whole town who are busy digging coal for England's victory in this way. You can surely see what is the right thing to do for Laing.'

But Walt knew that he would be faced again by Gabriel's condemning eyes and by silence.

'You must see,' Stent said, 'where the greater good lies. You need to confront him yourself. It's you, Emerson, who must stop this nonsense for all of us.'

'I thought,' Walt said finally. ' . . . I thought . . . that love would be enough. I do love him you know. Them.'

'I cannot have that child behaving like this. It hangs on all of us like some wretched fog. I am sure you understand what is at stake here. I'm sure you understand what needs to be said, what must be done to stop him.'

It was snowing a big February fall in Laing and Gabriel was in the kitchen when he heard the latch lift on the front door. It was cold in the big kitchen where he sat. Through the window he had seen that the roofs were edged in white. He went through to the lobby. There shouldn't have been anyone up at that time in the morning, so he went to see.

He knew when he saw him at the door that Walt was leaving. There was a small bag hung on Walt's shoulder. He had not shaved. His tall, spartan shape was framed by the big lobby door of the hotel that opened out on to the steps and below them the street.

'Dada?' Gabriel said softly.

Walt heard. Gabriel said that Walt had heard. Walt paused at the door, but he did not turn around. He could not turn around. He paused, and a breath seemed to catch high in his throat, but he could not turn around, and the heavy, unmended door closed on the latch, and Walt was gone.

Kasperl mended in the end, of course, except for the arm that he'd fallen on which was all but useless.

For a while they left him be. He moved back to the game-keeper's lodge at Salem Turn. He dug coal on the beach. He didn't eat and looked more unkempt. Sometimes Gabriel came up and sat on the edge of the woods and Kasperl watched him from a window, but Gabriel never came closer and Kasperl never went out to him.

In Laing they said he was someone else. They said he had nothing to do with the internees who had come to work in Laing. They said he was just some poor soul who had been left behind when the internment camp across the fells was finally wound down, who had come to live in the lodge. They said he was some poor fellow who'd wandered down to Laing off his own bat and whom Gabriel Emerson found one day out in the slate caves living like a hermit – who'd fallen and broken a leg and dislocated a shoulder. He had a passing similarity, they said, to one of the men who had escaped from custody and who had fled Laing in a fishing boat that had been stolen from the harbour. For a while, the impending celebrations for the war's end seemed to be enough of a distraction for them to leave him be and Kasperl was left to wander in search of Circus Prenzlau.

In the end Kasperl disappeared. In his place Lukic arrived at Henry Kyle's colony out on the fells. Was there the remembered shadow of a black Ford? A screech of tyres? Perhaps. Perhaps there was. It's hard to say. It's hard to find anyone who can remember now that the last of them have gone, now that the last men left have sailed and only I am left behind.

My name is Lukic.

I am a juggler with one good arm.

I am a dog with no bark.

I tend a few vegetables in a small plot they have given me. The digging and the nurturing make me happy enough. It pleases me no end when things ripen in the soil and can be pulled.

They hanged Brock Spivey after the war. I found out from the woman I recognized when she came to the colony, the woman who had gone to live with Brock Spivey on his small-holding above Laing, the one with the thick brown glasses, the one who came to visit Ingerman because he was her son and on her final visit left a violin no one had ever heard her play. Brock Spivey was hanged for the murder of four foreigners. There had been rumours swirling about, which would not go away, about what had happened at Brock Spivey's barn. The newspapers further afield got hold of it and a little fuss was stirred. It was investigated, and then they hanged Brock Spivey, and that was that.

As for Gabriel, he had taken to ringing the bell. He had hidden it out in the woods so that it couldn't be found by anyone from the town. He would go into the woods above the town early in the morning or late in the day and he'd ring the bell, and they'd hear it down in Laing, and like Stent said, it hung like a fog over them. And in the end, because his Dada could neither stop him nor condemn him, Walt had left him in Joannie Kilner's care on a day when the snow was falling soft as gossamer from a dark sky on the houses.

'Sometimes,' Gabriel Emerson writes to his son, 'not going is the death. Sometimes, not setting off is the betrayal.'

It's hard to write. The words come slower now.

It's a letter from a father to his son. The son has been abandoned in Laing. The father, at the far end of the world, waits for death. It's not so far away now.

'Sometimes,' Gabriel writes, 'it is the thing which must be done to avoid a greater destruction.'

How to paint love? How to explain desertion? How to say

one man can leave another, can desert, or deny, or despair because of the forces pressed upon him and still feel love, still think and dream him, still picture him each day, every day, growing and moving out into the world, still see him pulling, pulling; still ripped asunder and bleeding love and never healing?

They are lying, covered by the sheets in a hollow in the frozen ground, in the half light of a dawn. They lie still. Athol's feet were so painful that Gabriel had cut his friend's boots off for him and wrapped them instead in pieces of hide from the tent and bound them with rope from a shirt-tail. When Athol moves, he coughs blood, and so they lie unmoving against each other. Peary's sight is all but gone now with the harsh glare of this white land. They are out of food. The last of the biscuits went five days ago. When the hunger becomes too much, when there is the energy and the will, they chew on the leather strips that are left of Athol's boots.

Beneath his beard, Gabriel's face is cracked by the frost. They are all so tired. So bone-deep tired. Gabriel wonders if he'll ever rise to his feet again. His limbs are hard to move. He has lost weight too quickly in the last week to be able to go on much longer. His gums are swollen; they bleed often. He feels a little movement beside him.

'Brother?' Athol says. Gabriel reaches for Athol and grips his hand.

It is a noise that rouses him from his thoughts. A rush like wind but harder, more precise. He wonders what it is. It is the end of night. A milk sun is rising. The land which is sulphurous about him is almost motionless and white and clean. The light is breathed upon the land. The world is all ice and the blue-grey sky of this farthest winter.

Lying, looking up at the last stars, he hears the noise again, like wind. He hears their distant, high-pitched barking, their cries, their steady line of flight. The snow geese returning to their homeland fill the simple sky above him. Their wings slap at the air. They keep coming, and their sound becomes a hammering and a flash of wings in the big sky, more and more descending on the cold flats a mile out beyond the tent, arriving back. They drop immaculate, miraculous, slowing in articulate mathematics. They fall like perfect leaves, genuflecting to the ground, rolling down inches apart from each other. They settle, white even against the water-washed white land and the white sky. Above them, another wave, another mile away, beats the air, returning to their ten-thousand-year-old nesting grounds. They are the first snow geese of the short summer and they have come home and they are all about him.

They have taken Kasperl's bell from Gabriel now. He would not stop ringing it, no matter what anyone said, no matter how Joannie Kilner pleaded or Stent petitioned. Gabriel only rang the bell more from the woods above the town so that the music of it sang in the morning as people's eyes met each other's and in the evenings when they gathered their day's thoughts about them. And though Gabriel wouldn't speak, the bell spoke for him, and everyone in the town knew what the bell said.

Stent is with Gabriel in the high room with the beamed ceiling. There are other men. Gabriel doesn't know who. They have asked him questions again. Stent is saying that there's been a complaint about the burning of another barn. The farmer wants to prosecute Gabriel for the burning of his barn. But he has been dissuaded by Stent. We can hush it up but you must help us, Stent is saying. He can understand that Gabriel is struggling. That's why he is going to have Gabriel moved to the orphanage at Broughton. It isn't right that he has been left by his father to be brought up in a brothel. It isn't right that he's been left like this in Joannie Kilner's care. All this has affected him adversely, as it would any child. Mrs Kilner has been informed. She understands the necessity of moving him. She understands that she is in no position to protest. Does Gabriel want to say goodbye to her? Stent can arrange it if he wants. But Gabriel makes no move.

To help, he would become 'Gabriel the evacuee'. To help, he would be given a new start. Stent will give him a new start. He will become a Gabriel whose parents had been lost in the bombing of Manchester. William will go elsewhere. He will be allowed to write to Gabriel. Then Stent is saying that the man Gabriel had rescued was not Kasperl the youth at all. He was some other poor wretch. The internees had left Laing the night before the Laing Fair and drowned in a boat. To believe that he could have seen Kasperl or the others – to think he might have seen Kasperl after that, or that he might one day see Kasperl again – would be for the boy to be tricked by his own imagination. To think that it was Kasperl he'd looked after in the woods – even to indicate that Kasperl was still alive – would be proof that Gabriel was losing his senses. It would show that being made to live in a brothel – to be exposed to the kind of corrupting obscenity he had been exposed to in Joannie Kilner's so-called third-class hotel – had irrevocably disturbed him. To claim that he could ever see Kasperl again after they had drowned in a boat escaping from Laing was for Gabriel to risk being designated mad and being locked away. And if Gabriel was proven to be mad, then the man responsible would be seen to be Walt, and then Walt would need to be hunted down wherever he had fled and locked up too. Walt would be held responsible for Gabriel's madness because of the way he had brought the boy up, because of what he'd allowed the boy to live through and to witness at Joannie Kilner's place. And he would be hunted down. Stent could promise him that. Walt would be hunted down. Did the boy understand? If Gabriel was shown to be mad, then Walt would have to be hunted down and locked away, too, for the sin of making him so.

And then Stent smiles. Now is the time, he says, to begin again. We have won the war. Be happy that we have won the war, Gabriel. Rejoice. But Gabriel makes no sound.

I used to watch Gabriel walking blankly past me in the colony, not seeing me. I had been here almost ten years when I saw Gabriel arrive. I could tell it was him even though he was grown. I could tell in the first moment I saw him. I thought at first it was just that he hadn't recognized me. I thought it was simply I who must have changed so much in the intervening years. At first I used to go chasing after him when I saw him.

'It's me, it's me,' I would say. 'It's Kasperl. You rescued me. You saved me. Don't let this Lukic name of mine fool you. Lukic is just the name I was born with.'

But he never saw me. Except for once, when he was moved to say, 'Kasperl is dead,' and something in the way he said it, something in the finality of it, the simplicity, the very plainness and lack of protestation in his words, made me stop, and I did not chase him any more after that.

I almost came to believe him. In a way, Kasperl was dead. In a way, Gabriel was right. There was only a juggler with one arm; a dog with no bark. And I knew then what I had to do. I knew that the one thing left was for me to watch over him. And so I became his guardian angel, the one he could not see, and I found a kind of purpose as Lukic that had, in the end, eluded me as Kasperl.

And sometimes he dreamed of one man pulling, pulling, head down, moving through the snow that seemed to fall around him, though whether the man he dreamed of was Emerson the mariner, or whether it was Walt, I was never sure.

And now he's led against the great unmoving bulk of Athol, and writes the last sentences he will complete. There's a dullness about him now. There's a distance between what his heart sings and what his flesh is capable of. And the distance drifts and drifts.

Outside their cover, the tundra is shadowed with a fabulous sky of returning Banks Island geese. They join the land. They settle. The light breathes its benediction. The land is silent and complete and swallows these last three men.

'Men will find our bones here and will see a story and imagine that this is all there is of it,' Emerson writes. 'Bones become the stories of poor and insubstantial men who have nothing else to bequeath to the world. But we were men who, like most poor men, fought and fought, and scrapped for life – for pieces of the stuff in crevices and dreams. Our story is not in the leftover bones of our lives to be found bleached here in a heap on some shelf of ice, but our hearts that brought us here, and the dreams that drew us on.

'My epitaph is this: I did no harm. I went in search of dreams. I failed. Forgive me.'

*

The three of them were found together, clutched to each other for warmth against the bitterness of the place they had died in. No one seemed to know who they were or why they should have died in such a way. Someone said that once there had been a colony for the feeble-minded on the site. There were some notes scribbled out, held to the chest of one of the men who had been found, but they were perished and unreadable, and there was no one left to say how things had come about.